OF
MACHINES
&
MAGICS

ADELE ABBOT

BARKING RAIN PRESS

Of Machines & Magics

Copyright © 2012 Adele Abbot (www.adeleabbot.info)

Edited by Ti Locke

Cover artwork by Michael Leadingham (www.michaelleadingham.com)

Barking Rain Press
PO Box 822674
Vancouver, WA 98682 USA
www.barkingrainpress.org

ISBN Trade Paperback: 1-935460-30-7
ISBN eBook: 1-935460-31-5
ISBN Hardcover: 1-935460-37-4

Library of Congress Control Number: 2012930036

First Edition: January 2012

Printed in the United States of America

978-1-935460-30-5

ACKNOWLEDGEMENTS

Special thanks to the Barking Rain Press team, especially
Ti Locke for her editing skills,
Michael Leadingham for his atmospheric and intriguing cover,
and Sheri Gormley for her efforts in publishing this book.

DEDICATION

To family and absent friends.

COMING SOON FROM ADELE ABBOT

Postponing Armegeddon

WWW.ADELEABBOT.INFO

CONTENTS

CHAPTER 1

The Concourse separated the City from the Lake. It was a broad swath of transparent and diamond-hard Lucite stretching for seven furlongs along the water's edge providing its boulevardiers with astounding views of the denizens of Lake Mal-a-Merrion. Cafes and restaurants abounded along its length; shops, bazaars, emporia lined its city-side flank. A light breeze, a zephyr, flickered the flames in the table lamps, here and there a tendril of smoke curled away as though recoiling from the salty odors of the water. The so-called *noon* chime had sounded from Barto's tower and the cafes were filled with patrons eating alfresco. Calistrope the Mage sat at one of the many tables, seemingly relaxed; but through hooded, knowing eyes watched the activities of a thief.

"Look," said Calistrope, pointing. Ponderos turned and looked where Calistrope pointed. A young fellow, dressed in a tattered yellow shirt and too-small breeches, dipped his fingers in to the pocket of a passer-by. A moment after, the hand reappeared, a glint of bright copper was visible for an instant and the boy had disappeared into the crowd.

"A child and already a petty thief," Calistrope sighed.

"And a thief of some skill," Ponderos observed and turned back to his wine. "Though I would keep my voice low if I were you."

"What do you mean?"

"He might consider *petty* thief to be derogatory."

"Sachavesku allows too many criminals to flourish."

"Too many," Ponderos nodded, his expression grave. "It would be more agreeable if just a few were allowed, just the more picaresque of course. Um, a cultural activity."

Calistrope looked at his friend, trying to decide between indignation and drollery. Humor won the day. He chuckled. "Crime..." he began and stopped as he felt furtive fingers searching for a way into the purse at his belt.

Ponderos looked up at the pause but warned by Calistrope's expression, looked away again. It took a few seconds for Calistrope to remember the cant he needed but then...

To the young cutpurse who had chosen to thieve from the Mage, it seemed that the little bag—no bigger than a pair of fists—opened itself. Two rows of pointed teeth lined the opening; the bag had eyes as well... little red ones. When the teeth snapped shut on the boy's hand, the eyes looked up at him and one of them winked. The illusion was entirely visual but Roli could not imagine teeth sinking into his flesh without hurt, thus, he felt pain which was no less real for being imaginary. Men and women sitting at tables round about turned and looked at him but since what the thief saw was visible only to himself, they frowned and returned to their refreshment with shrugs.

Calistrope turned in his chair and grinned, a great wolfish grin. To Ponderos, he said "Crime is far too prevalent here on the concourse." The Mage looked down at the boy in the grip of those illusory teeth. He tut-tutted. "I'm afraid it's the Justiciary for you my boy. We'll take you along presently, as soon as we're finished here, then the Deemster can think up an unpleasant punishment for you."

"But Sir..." wailed Roli looking from Calistrope to the vengeful bag of teeth and back again. " I..." and paused.

"You?" Calistrope prompted.

"I only..."

"Mm?"

The two men could see Roli's mind working: thinking as he spoke and considering how his own interests might best be served by the truth—not all of the truth, of course. "My family is very poor. There is often no food to put on the table."

Calistrope's expression softened. "In that case, we must attend the Public Works office. We shall find work suited to your skills, my friend and I will recommend you."

"Work?" Roli's expression was one of horror. "Employment? But that will take up all my time, when shall I find time to enjoy myself?"

"You don't find the idea appealing?"

Roli did not answer.

"Very well. I myself shall find something for you to do. I need a serv... an assistant." A little shocked at his sudden whim, Calistrope paused to reconsider, then... "Yes, yes," he stood up and snapped his fingers. The bag, which still held very fast—so it seemed—to Roli's hand, pulled on the lad's arm. "Well, what do you think Ponderos?"

"Excellent idea," he got to his feet. "If you're sure about this?"

"Oh, I think so, I think so," he looked down at the boy again. "Apprentice."

The two sorcerers walked off and the bag trailed after, like a woolly balloon. Roli, still in thrall to the delusion stumbled along in their wake with arm outstretched and fist covered in a small and unremarkable bag.

"Sirs," he called. "Please."

Calistrope stopped. "Wouldn't you like to be a sorcerer's apprentice? It's a chance that is not given to many."

"Sorcerer?" Roli took a step back. "Sorcerer! Now that's the way the cricket jumps!" A blinding light seemed to suddenly ignite behind his eyes, his expression turned to one of horror. "Sorcerer? I tried to pick the purse of a sorcerer?" he fell silent.

"Quite right. You tried."

Roli looked up at the tall spare figure with the dark blue eyes and face as thin as a hatchet blade then to the other with his gleaming bronze skin and muscled like a genie. Ponderos seemed a force of nature.

"You are a Sorcerer, too?"

Ponderos nodded. "Of the fourth grade."

The boy could think of nothing to say. The circumstances were so bizarre that he could not grasp the situation, even when the magic bag let go of his hand and returned to Calistrope's belt, he was hardly aware of his freedom. "A *sorcerer's* apprentice?"

"Give it half an old year; we'll see how we get on. We should go to see your parents of course, we should obtain their permission."

"My parents forbade me to return home the third time the Constables came for me."

"So you have been to see the Deemster already?"

"No. Oh no, they couldn't catch me."

⌧

High above the valley floor, the Bumanda tree lifted gnarled and massive branches to the sky. Its trunk, as wide at its base as three men were tall, sprang from a tangle of twisted roots anchored in the lower slopes of the massif. Higher, the trunk swelled to even greater proportions and the sun's orange light glittered from the colored glass of widows set into the trunk and the more substantial limbs. Matt black leaves cast trembling shadows across the enclosed walkways and staircases which sprang from branch to branch. Calistrope the Mage had hollowed his manse into the Bumanda tree when it was but a fraction of its present age, when the ether was still rich and the sun still marked out days.

⌧

Roli had lived with Calistrope now for several months. The boy's working life was split between domestic duties and starting the long path of learning. Calistrope had taken pains to explain the nature of the apprenticeship. He pointed out that there was but a single initial goal: to learn to live long enough to learn the arts of wizardry. Progression from novitiate to master was a task spanning several generations of ephemeral humankind.

They had walked the deserted shores of Mal-a-Merrion with Calistrope introducing Roli to nuts and roots, plums and apples. Foods which grew wild and ready for the gathering was a concept both new and novel to one whose short life had been spent on the infertile streets of Sachavescu and in its manicured pleasure parks.

They sat now in a small glen where a cold breeze had frosted the trees and grasses. Roli listened; his expression that of a skeptic while Calistrope explained the nature of magic.

"There is no such thing," he said and Roli smiled lopsidedly as the Mage denied his profession. "Magic is the name given to effects we no longer understand."

"In that case," replied Roli, "of what use are seven hundred and thirty two Magicians who sit in the College Tower debating the efficacy of magic?"

"You may well ask. I have also wondered at this, but then I am an eccentric and often a thorn in the sides of my fellows. Still, I tell you there is no such thing. The old arts of science and engineering were used in ages past to create and change the world about us; these skills were of many different kinds. But if I was asked to comment I'd say steam power was the most ubiquitous of these."

An ocular dangled from a twig, its single great eye rotating within the transparent globe of fluid until it could watch as Calistrope held up a fist and extended a finger: "Mechanics." Another: "Mentation." One by one, he extended fingers. "Galvanism. Numerics. Nanotics." Coming to the end of his fingers and what he could conveniently remember, he finished off, "and many more."

Roli was bored and watched the progress of a wanderlust beetle as it trundled from one patch of gravel to another. "All ancient sciences, all long forgotten even though they were practiced for hundreds of millennia. We but enjoy the results of long ago labors. Magic is those few bright shadows left behind by the forgotten dazzle of science."

"Why are insects very small or very large?" asked Roli, watching the iridescent beetle bigger than a man's head which left a trail of singed and burnt grasses behind it.

Calistrope paused to assess the *non sequitur*. "The wanderlust beetle," he said, "Searches out particles of radium and other unstable elements among the rocks. The creature's alimentary processes pack each iota away in a stomach sac lined with lead where their decay has been designed to generate a great deal of heat. The heat accelerates the beetle's metabolism."

Calistrope had taken care not to answer the direct question yet a clue had been given to his apprentice.

"Why are insects very small or very large?" Roli repeated. "The water skater stands half as high as you do and is twice as long. It makes a loud buzzing noise which often breaks into screeches and clicks. The parlor fireflies that ladies keep in cages in their bedrooms are quite silent."

"And when were you in the bed chamber of a lady?"

Roli pressed his lips together and ignored the question.

"The water skater's tracheal bellows are not very efficient. The firefly breathes by absorption only."

The Mage climbed to his feet and the ocular, alarmed by the sudden movement, assimilated its suspension thread, climbing speedily back to its branch.

Roli was silent for the twenty minutes it took to return to the Manse. Then, outside, he stopped, a frown of concentration on his brow. "Large insects grow large because they breathe more efficiently?"

"That is the case with waterskaters though not with wanderlust beetles," he looked up at the Gargoyle which guarded the doorway. "Have there been any visitors?"

"Visitors? I saw no visitors."

"Still, the waterskater—its forebears I mean—did not always breathe in this way nor did the wanderlust beetle always snuffle up hot dust?"

"No. In an earlier epoch, a mage saw how to improve the ways in which insects functioned. He experimented over the millennia and *bioengineered* his designs into several species of insects. The insects grew larger, and some became intelligent; others, just more efficient. What did the Gargoyle say?"

"It said, 'No visitors.' None." Roli continued his questions, "Intelligent like the ants?"

"Just so."

They entered, climbed the stairs. Roli took the basket of fruit and vegetables to the kitchen, Calistrope continued on to his study.

A moment later he stopped and stood, rooted to the spot, aghast at what he saw. For many minutes he stood silently.

The house waited.

"Roli," he whispered at length, staring at the empty cases and the open doors. "Roli." Even his whispers stirred long blue and purple sparks from the air. Quivering phantasms hung about him and winced with each new imprecation; outside, above the front door, the Gargoyle thrust stony fingers into its ears and cowered.

Roli heard the whispers and came running.

"Master?"

"Larceny," he hissed, his voice low and hard. "Roli, you are the authority in these matters. Tell me, *who* would rob the manse of a Master Sorcerer?"

"Master! Who would dare? Surely no one but another sorcerer." The air carried the odor of lightning, Roli sneezed.

"Of course," Calistrope nodded slowly, "who else?" he paced his study and dust wheelers scattered before his feet, scurried for safety in the wainscoting. "None but another," he repeated. "Look there," he grasped Roli's shoulder and pointed at a bare expanse of wall. "There was a tapestry there. Each stitch was a microscopic knot tied by manikins from my vats, an old century in the weaving and not done yet. Oh, I shall have revenge for this! Bring me food—food to stoke my wrath."

Calistrope looked from one empty place to another. *My marionettes,* he bemoaned and wrung his hands, *each with its own personality and volition. My liqueurs, a thousand years in the amassing.* He flicked his fingers. *Gone in an eye blink.*

"Roli, food. I grow faint with hunger."

"Here Master, right here."

"What's this?" Calistrope poked at the dish, sniffed at the carafe. "Pickled fish? Green wine?" Calistrope shook his head and then paused, his mind going on to other matters. "Roli. What *did* the Gargoyle say? Exactly?"

"It said..." Roli screwed up his face in concentration, "Near as I can remember, 'Visitors? I saw no visitors.'"

"Well now, that's near enough. The Gargoyle has been interfered with, compromised. The thing prevaricated. Hmm. I'll have anchovies on a bed of samphire. Leave the wine."

Hardly had Roli gone when there came an insistent tapping at the window. Outside, a silver sphere with iridescent highlights bobbed and floated, a bubble of quicksilver. Calistrope was not in the mood to listen to messages; in high dudgeon he crossed to the casement and opened it, the sphere drifted in, rising and falling in the air currents left by the Sorcerer's recent rantings. It came to rest, or nearly so, in front of Calistrope; he reached out and touched a fingertip to its cool surface. The film coruscated, broke, vaporized.

"This," spoke a sibilant voice, "is Voss."

"Who else would it be?" Calistrope muttered. "The Despondent One. Still, he is one who *has* grown in wisdom since he suckled at his mother's breast."

"A meeting is called for the twelfth hour. I have selected *you*, Calistrope, to be honored in a quite extraordinary way."

The message sphere reproduced the words, the precise timbre of Voss' voice. Calistrope's imagination supplied the gloomy features, the compelling eyes, the thin lips and narrow nose.

"I look forward to your attending." And the silence drifted slowly back as Calistrope connected thefts and invitation.

"Your meal master," Roli stood in the doorway, bearing a wooden tray.

Calistrope looked at the food and shook his head. "My appetite has gone, I'm afraid." And his mind turned over the injustices done him. *Who had been paramount in advocating those experiments that he had castigated?*

Voss the Mirthless.

Who had watched as each boulder was ignited to burn with an eternal flame or to glow with a self perpetuating heat?

Voss the Somber.

And who had been the most irritated at Calistrope's remarks?

Calistrope nodded.

Voss of the Thin Smile.

"Voss," Roli. It was Voss who came here while we were away. Voss the Despondent. Who else would dare to enter the manse of a fellow mage?"

Calistrope had been right in his criticism of course. No man-made fire could replace the sun's waning energy, not a thousand, not a million. But the Mage was guilty of being tactless, worse—of expressing his doubts in front of others and worse of all, Calistrope had been right. Voss, he had no doubt at all, was taking his revenge.

The Mage left the room and took the winding staircase within the north branch; he crossed an aerial walkway to his sleeping chamber and passed through to the dressing room. Here he glanced from the window, the weather—as almost always—was calm and chill.

He chose garments from his wardrobe: a pair of grey leather breeches tooled with convoluted patterns, a pair of boots of similar color with blue inlay and a matching tunic with blue enameled plates of insect chitin on the epaulettes.

He glanced in the mirror. The effects of his choice of garment were as he expected. They signified aloofness, reserved judgment, dignity.

The College had been constructed with the successful intention of making it the most impressive building in the City. It was a single slender shining column of fused basalt rising over a thousand spans in height which to the citizenry *was* Sachavesku: the City without its spire, the College without its jewel-like setting could not be imagined. The interior of the column was separated into two hundred and seventy seven lecture theatres and laboratories and in its heyday—when the sun still blazed a golden orange, every level was occupied. The lower floors thronged with students, while the middle and upper floors became steadily less crowded until only savants, mages and archmages were left from the lengthy climb to knowledge.

Calistrope entered the ground floor, a vast circular space with floors decorated with tiled tessellation; tall windows behind each dark wood lectern illuminated the manuscripts from which masters once lectured the novitiates in the elements of their selected profession. Entrants were few in these latter days, few enough for instruction to be carried out on an individual basis so that vast areas of the College were empty, dark and dusty places visited only by echoes.

There were ten portals spaced evenly around the walls, stairs led from floor to floor as far as the seventh level, beyond that, there were only smooth bare shafts. It was considered that anyone aspiring to rise beyond the seventh level must be able to do so by their own efforts entirely.

Calistrope entered the nearest portal and exerting a minor effort, levitated himself to the highest floor. Here, the meager rays of the latter-day sun shone through sloping casements decorated with richly colored designs and pictures of ancient events.

The Great Hall of Assembly exerted a curious influence on many who gathered there. Most were content to contribute nothing more than an occasional *Hear, hear* or an *Aha* to the debate, to utter a discrete cough or a telling shake of the head. However, those who addressed their fellow Mages were often afflicted with an excess of gravity. Gestures grew slow and ponderous, words were burdened with portent, speech became pompous and grandiloquent.

The Mage was aware of this bizarre effect. When called upon to speak, he acceded with reluctance; he took pains to be brief, eschewed sarcasm, avoided malice. Though each of his fellows professed the same self-control, Calistrope considered himself to be the only true master of the terse remark, the concise exposition.

Calistrope took his seat precisely as the tall pendulum clock struck the twelfth hour on its thick glass bell. Voss the Despondent, who had been at the head of the table for some minutes, struck the small iron gong and called the meeting to order. His long lugubrious face was occasionally known to smile briefly but there was no trace of such an expression now.

"I and two of my fellow Archmages have completed a new task. As a result, I have decided on a new undertaking," he told them somberly, without preamble. "This is the only possibility we have found which may ensure the survival of the human race."

A murmur ran the length of the immense table, Voss waited patiently for the sound to subside. "Our present power is insufficient to rejuvenate the sun or to find alternatives to its heat and light which dwindle as we talk."

Calistrope considered clearing his throat but decided that silence was the more pointed comment.

Voss raised his eyebrows a fraction, surprised that Calistrope should waste the opportunity of making a remark.

"We have made a new search of the archives; we have a new course of action," Voss sat back and flicked dust from his sleeve. "Since arcane powers are no longer enough, we must restart the engines at the heart of the world. As the sun shrinks, the Earth must be made to follow it."

A shocked silence followed his words, a silence which stretched on and on before being gradually filled with the sounds of breathing, of murmured comments, scraps of conversation.

"Move the world?" said someone, disbelief writ large in the tone.

Voss lifted his voice somewhat. "Accordingly, we have conferred with those who have a more exact record of history. The Ants."

Pandemonium broke out. Arguments, comments, oaths, counter arguments... all of which dwindled to a most unusual silence. In ones and twos, in groups, the gathering became aware of the new presence at the head of the table—polished chitin, spiky red whiskers, black faceted eyes, trembling antennae.

"May I introduce Micca, the Ant? I have requested engineer Micca join us and address us."

The magicians gazed at the ant. She stood as high as an average man, her chitin armor shining dully with ruddy highlights, there was a faint susurration—the sound of her tracheal bellows. She raised her antennae and a hum filled the air as they vibrated. After a few seconds, the tone became modulated and the insect essayed an imitation of human speech.

"Venerations," she greeted and tilted her head in a series of small jerks as her glittering black eyes were brought to bear on each of the sorcerers in turn. "At the request of the Archmage Voss, we have made an examination of the Nest's records; we have established several unquestionable facts." The insect moved two of its legs, they made a metallic scraping sound on the floor and as she shifted, the sunlight struck a series of green iridescences from her thorax. The ant's exhalations imparted a faint acid quality to the air in the chamber.

"The Earth's orbit was once inside that of the cinder world, Mars. Humans constructed engines which moved the Earth from there to its present position, beyond the reach of the sun which was expanding into its red giant stage."

Impassively, the ant waited as a new round of conversation swelled. A sorcerer at the table's far end signaled for silence, the murmurous dissonance diminished. Sarra Rivera looked along the stretch of ebony wood with its shell and scarab wing inlay; he held Micca's attention with his cold, silver gaze. "This notion is a myth, a story the *Ephemerals* tell each other for comfort. The movement of a whole world at the bidding of a human being is ludicrous."

"Yet it happened," said Micca. "I have seen the memories stored in our records. The journey had already been under way for half a million old years when my species recorded the helium flash."

"The possibility is discounted by the Sorceress Almatirra's *Principle of Equivalent Mass,*" Rivera continued, hardly listening to what the ant had said.

The ant nodded, a peculiarly human gesture which seemed at variance with the insect's anatomy. "Your objection is perfectly valid—according to the tenets of *your* science."

Voss nodded and spoke to Rivera. "The universe is stranger than you imagine, Sir, stranger than you *can* imagine."

"Quite so," added Micca. "The ancient science of physics places no such restrictions upon the possible—fortunately. The sun is now shrinking to its dwarf stage and the Nest agrees the Earth must be returned to a narrower orbit."

"And how," asked Issla the Inquisitive, "is this to be done?"

"The mechanisms which control the engines are in the eternal City of Schune," Voss interjected. "Oh yes," he said as he saw expressions of disbelief about him, the City exists."

Issla continued with her doubts. "The Ants have never been interested in helping the Human Race before, why should we believe what she says?" She gestured dismissively at Micca. "Can she persuade us of her goodwill?"

Voss was at a loss but Micca, to whom rancor was an alien concept answered without acrimony. "The Nest draws its power from the remnant heat of the world's core. It will last us many millions of years, far longer than either of your species. However, the sun will last us longer if we follow it."

"*Either* species?" Queried Calistrope.

"The *Ephemerals* and ourselves," Voss explained.

Calistrope raised an eyebrow and tapped a front tooth with a fingernail. "Why then," he asked, "why does the Nest not organize an expedition to Schune. Why come to us?"

"Higher castes cannot travel so far," Micca told him, "our intellect resides within the Nest."

"In the Nest?" Calistrope stroked his chin. "A communal intelligence?"

"That is the case."

"And naturally." The Mage stepped forward, nodding. "The intelligence fades with distance?"

"Over several of your leagues," Micca told him.

"Thus, our goals are yours."

"For the present," agreed the ant.

"In short," Voss broke in, "the Ants will teach a sorcerer to revitalize the engines."

"Oh come now, Voss."

"Calistrope, you try my patience."

"If this confederate is expressing doubts, Archmage, then it is correct."

"Correct?"

"There is no possibility of reclaiming skills lost as long as these, Archmage. No. Neither is it necessary. Whoever goes to Schune has merely to contact the guardians."

Voss' forehead wrinkled. "And these guardians will revitalize the engines? Will they still be there after such an age?"

Calistrope inspected a nail on his left hand. "Suppose there is a community at Schune, Voss and suppose we call them *engineers* rather than guardians and say *restart* rather than revitalize; the scheme begins to seem a little more practical," Calistrope caught a fleeting smile on Voss' face and cursed himself for a fool.

"Exactly. You show me the proper interpretation Calistrope and I am in your debt. Now, let us be practical by all means. The Nest can provide maps, an adventurous fellow will discover the way to Schune without … with only minor difficulty. Someone like your…"

"I received a message," Calistrope said, his tone a grim one. "It mentioned an honor. If this is the honor referred to, "he looked back at the fingernail which had caused him concern before, "my attitude to travel beyond the valley of Mal-a-Merrion is well known. My reluctance to tread upon unfamiliar pathways is proverbial."

His comments received a variety of responses both pro and con. Voss stretched his face into an unaccustomed smile. "All is taken into account, my friend. It is understandable that you are overcome by the honor but a moment's reflection will convince you that you are the natural, the best and only choice.

Calistrope was disconcerted. With hindsight, it became obvious how he had been manipulated, right from the moment his treasures had been pilfered from the manse.

"Naturally, a great deal of prestige attaches to the venture, the status of Archmage becomes a formality."

This is the carrot, thought Calistrope; *without doubt the whip will be the return of my possessions.* He inquired, "A posthumous formality?"

"Ha ha. Such wit, I am overwhelmed." Such was clearly not the case and Voss hastily turned to other matters before announcing arrangements for a celebratory banquet. He was visibly relieved as the delegates left the hall without Calistrope precipitating a confrontation. Nevertheless, as Calistrope rose to leave, Voss signaled that he wished to speak privately with him.

When all but Voss, Micca and Calistrope were left, the Mage went to the head of the table; he drew a chair out and seated himself. "Well?"

"Well? Well," Voss assumed a reasonable tone of voice, "I am certain that you now see things in different light."

"No," Calistrope replied.

"I am certain that you look forward to this excellent adventure."

"No," Calistrope shook his head. "The title of Archmage seems to me to be poor recompense for the discomforts and dangers of such a journey," he tapped a fingernail against a tooth. "Perhaps I lack a proper perspective but I must refuse this offer," Calistrope invoked the similitude of aged infirmity. "I am tired; I am victim to some disease which drains my vigor." His cheeks became sunken, creases furrowed his brow.

"Ha, ha," Voss countered with an injunction to eternal health. "I sympathize with your condition, my friend, you need to get out more, to see the world. Out there," he flung his arms out and Calistrope's face filled out with plump flesh, his eyes brightened; a smile came unwillingly to his lips. "Out there, you will find yourself. See? Just the thought has made you feel better. However, one moment."

Voss rummaged through the capacious pockets of his gown. "Aha!" A fat tube stoppered at both ends with wooden bungs. He placed it on the table and felt again in his pockets. "Ah," he said and placed a long flat case upon the table beside the cylinder. He opened the case. "Now. Here, stored for safety while you are off on your travels,"

"Bless me, my collection of miniature succubus," Calistrope brought out a pair of magnifying spectacles and peered closely. "It is. Each one fashioned after a notorious courtesan," he looked up. "I knew it was you, Voss. Voss the Vile, the Thief."

"No, no, no," Voss was not even ruffled by the epithets. "You misunderstand. At your manse, they are unprotected. When you are away, any vagabond might chance by and take what he fancied. Here they are secure," Voss leaned down and opened a chest at his feet. He took out a roll of fabric, held it up. "See; is this not your tapestry?" he let it fall open, a cloth of such fine weave it seemed like soft vellum, "the one you are so proud of?"

"Voss. This is pillage. No other word suffices unless ... unless it is blackmail. My manse is sealed against all except the most adept," Calistrope placed a finger on the artwork. "This tapestry you handle with such carelessness has been a thousand years in the making, a hundred tiny manikins have worked upon it diligently all that time and you filch it to serve your own selfish ends."

The Archmage seemed unrepentant. "Selfish? I think not, Calistrope but there is more," he went on. "Do you not want to know the whole of it? Here for example," he pulled a cedar wood casket from beneath the table; he laid back the lid, "your pandect on Hypnotism, your unrivalled collection of aphrodisiacal spells. Hmm? What do you say to that? We shall keep them all here safely against your return." His chuckle was dry and humorless.

Calistrope was silent for some considerable time. Although suspected, Voss' admitted duplicity had come as a shock. "How did you gain admittance to my home?" he enquired at last. "How did you pass the Guardian and what of the curse of *Overburdening Guilt*?

Voss smiled briefly. "Do not trouble yourself about my safety and health. I came and went without disturbing your excellent precautions against thievery. Now, it is time to speak of more practical matters, Calistrope," he became brisk, businesslike. "It is a long way to Schune and there is much to be done before you leave. Micca—" he paused abruptly and stared. "Calistrope, does something ail you?"

Calistrope had turned very pale, his eyes bulged, slowly he brought up his hand and extended a trembling finger, he pointed. "A memory vault."

All of the Sorcerers kept a memory vault. For those who lived so long, there was just too much to recall, too much for a single brain to organize and so every few centuries, older and less useful memories were removed and committed to the memory vaults.

Voss turned to look where the other pointed. A slim cylinder with a metallic hue, perhaps a span in length, rested upon the tray set in to the top of Voss' chest. "Why, so it is," he closed the lid. "So it is."

"It is mine, Voss. I recognize it; there is no other like it. Let me describe it to you. A silver ceramic container, there is a thumb print seal on one end and if I place my right thumb against it, a small spot illuminates to show the print is recognized," Calistrope held out his hand. "Let me have it and I can prove it is mine."

Voss' shoulders slumped. "There is no need, Sir," he mumbled guiltily, suddenly humbled. "I admit that it is your memory vault. It was taken…" he paused, searching for words," taken on a whim and it should not have been. Still," he looked up with a brighter expression, "it should still be stored here, where it will be safe. You owe this to the College; your memories are a valuable asset, not to be risked. You owe them to humankind."

"Well, I suppose so." With the complement, Calistrope's rigor eased somewhat and his complexion began to look more healthy. "The vault should be brought up to date, however."

"You are correct," Voss hurried to agree. "Oh, absolutely. Let it be done after this business with the Ants, though."

Calistrope raised his eyebrows, a silent inquiry.

Voss gestured toward the ant which had been standing motionless during the altercation. "Micca has made arrangements for you to go to the Nest to be instructed as to the matter of charts and maps, perhaps to hear details of these ingenious engines."

Anger suffused his features once more. "The Nest?" Calistrope brought his fist down on the table top with such a force that a million tiny fragments of inlay leapt into the air, a glittering cloud of greens and blues, of pinks and mauves hovering above the surface. "Do I have *no* say at all in my own destiny?"

"Beautiful," breathed Voss as he watched the haze of dust sink back to the table's surface again. "Enchanting. Calistrope, do that again."

⌒⨯⌒

Voss had, of course been quite certain of securing Calistrope's agreement or, at least, his capitulation. To some extent, his violation of a fellow sorcerer's manse troubled his conscience. *Still,* he told himself, *it had been necessary. All would become apparent to Calistrope should he prove successful. So much rested on the undertaking, it would not be untrue to say the future of mankind was in the balance.*

History would surely vindicate his actions.

A day or more later, when Calistrope's anger had cooled to a smolder, he took himself along the road to the south, a distance of several leagues where, among lumpy hills, the Nest was situated. Two of the ants' specially bred soldiers guarded the entrance. A little larger than Micca and protected by considerably thicker chitin, they were a darker color and conveyed a sense of menace.

Closer, he saw other differences between the breeds of soldier and thinker. The guards' eyes were protected by great horny plates, the joints of their limbs by overlapping scales. Their mouth parts too, were different to those of their nest mates. Careful breeding had extended the soldiers' mandibles into a double spike, visible within were ducts which led toxins from a multiplicity of poison glands at the base to the razor sharp tip.

How should I gain entrance? The soldiers ignored him, there was neither herald nor messenger. While he was still wondering what to do, Micca—or one closely resembling that ant—appeared behind the guards. An invisible signal from Micca instructed the guards to stand apart and Calistrope, at a twitch of the ant's antennae, walked under the roughly shaped archway of the Nest's main entrance. He followed the other downward and the tunnel sloped more and more steeply and seemed to wander at random from side to side as they proceeded.

They met ants and other insects traveling in both directions, many were grotesquely shaped and Calistrope guessed they had been bred to perform specialized tasks. Lower, they passed by terraces where green foliage was grown in the light from luminous beetles which crawled about the ceilings. A long, long millipede raced by on its way to the surface, a score of worker ants clung to the scales on its back.

Calistrope shivered. Everywhere were signs of altered form, nature bent to the will of the Nest—in Micca's fellow ants, in other insects and grubs. Even the shape and path of the tunnels were undeniably... organic. The environment was a disturbing one.

Micca took him to a long unevenly cut tunnel where ants came and went on incomprehensible errands. His guide signaled to a passing worker, a swift conversation of hums and clicks and touching of feelers took place. The little faded pink worker hurried off and returned very quickly with a roll of parchment clutched in the secondary claw of a forefoot, almost an opposable digit.

"These are charts," said Micca. "You are familiar with geographical representations?"

"Certainly," Calistrope replied.

The charts were unrolled on a flat but rough surface. "This is our present location." One of Micca's antennae drooped, bent, and touched the map. The worker—or perhaps, insect clerk—used a stylus to make a dark smudge at the indicated spot. Calistrope saw the edge of what he assumed to be the Lake; the mark represented Sachavesku, or perhaps the nearby Nest. "The water you call Mal-a-Merrion lies along the western edge of a high massif. It narrows here, do you see?"

Calistrope nodded. The ant was indicating a long peninsular which hung down past the equator from a broad continent. "From here, there is a rift which has been eroded into a wide valley. Even at its highest point, the air is thick enough to breathe and it cuts all the way through to the east side of the massif."

"Is this a river?" asked Calistrope. "It must be a thousand leagues long if I have grasped the scale properly."

"Men call it the Long River or the Golden River, depending on the vicinity. It runs to the Last Ocean where Schune is situated."

"Schune again. The stuff of legend."

"To the contrary," Micca told him. "As real as Sachavesku which in parts of the Earth is also believed to be no more than a myth. Schune is to be found on this mountain. Again, the clerk used its stylus to make an annotation. Note its shape, easily recognizable. Fumes are vented near the top, an almost permanent emission. It may be volcanic and what is seen is smoke. However, equally likely; it may be one of the old core-heated steam powered atmosphere plants which recirculate the water and measure out new air, and that which we see is steam."

"How far?"

"Forty of your old days. Longer if you experience difficulties."

"What difficulties? What sort of difficulties?"

How could the insect shrug? Nevertheless, Micca gave such an impression.

"The places you will be traveling have been visited only by human hunters, little is known. There will be wild insects, insular human communities; we will send an escort of soldier ants with you to protect you."

"And what will we do when we get there? How can we start engines and turn the Earth back towards the sun?"

"All that is necessary is for you to find those who are there. Inform them. I told you this at your convocation."

"Indeed you did but it sounds as fantastic now as it did then. People who know how to work the controls even after all this time?"

"That is so. It is fact. Beyond that, however and at this distance, we can tell you nothing more."

"It seems flimsy evidence."

"There is no flimsiness whatever."

Calistrope remained silent but unconvinced.

"Those you will find there may need waking."

"They are asleep?"

"So the records say," Micca took something from the worker ant which stood patiently by them. She handed it to Calistrope.

Calistrope felt his eyebrows climb upward. "How did you get this..." he applied his thumb to the end of it, nothing happened. "This isn't mine. It is identical but not mine."

"I did not say it was. It is a human memory vault though. Is that correct?"

"Yes," Calistrope turned the ceramo-metallic cylinder over and over. There were no identifying marks of any kind. "An old one, a very old one—like my own."

"It was owned by a human who came this way once, from the place you now seek; Schune."

CHAPTER 2

Ponderos picked up a half dozen canapés from the plate he had brought back with him from the buffet table and crammed them into his mouth. "I could do with something a little more solid than this stuff," he complained. A swallow of red wine from his goblet washed them down and he was able to speak once more. "Too airy-fairy. I don't know where he trawls for it but sorcerous food is all the same, too gassy. Voss' parties don't appeal to me," Ponderos belched.

Calistrope flinched. "I see what you mean. However, it salves Voss' conscience. He has blackmailed me into fulfilling a task for him. A dangerous task for which I am certainly not the right person. I mean, I am no explorer."

Ponderos was silent for a moment. They were on a balcony about halfway up the College Tower and the view over the Concourse and across the lake Mal-a-Merrion into the haze-shrouded north was quite breathtaking. "I think you underrate yourself my friend," he said at last. "You have many qualities which your fellows lack. Which I... I admit it, which I lack."

Calistrope made a derogatory noise.

"It is the truth. You are older than me, Calistrope. I know that is a trivial matter when none of us who are sorcerers can remember our formative years, but you are older than me by an order of magnitude."

Calistrope was silent. What Ponderos said was true... as far he knew without consulting his memories. But then, what difference did it make?

"Your point of view is different than ours; you see solutions to problems which we don't or different solutions than those we do see," Ponderos turned and leaned back against the wall of the Tower behind the balcony. "Who are the best engineers you know of?"

Calistrope did not even stop to think. "The Ants of course." Despite his antipathy to their works, there was still no doubt that the Ants were born builders and constructors.

Ponderos raised his goblet high, sloshing some of its contents over his jacket. "Exactly. And in some ways, you think in the same manner."

Is this so? Calistrope wondered. *Are my thought processes really so different to those of my fellow Sorcerers? And if so, will it give me an advantage?* He thought about it for some time. *No,* he decided. *It gives all of us an advantage.*

"Let's go back to the others," he said, and made a mental note: *must review my early memories before I leave on this journey.* It was a mental note he had made like every one of the Mages, a hundred, a thousand times before. And had he ever looked at those memories edited from his brain? Not as far as Calistrope could remember.

The event was drawing to its close. All those present were pleasantly overfilled with rich food; they had been lulled by too much wine into a mellow and comradely spirit. The windows to this chamber were tall and the sunlight was augmented by long vertical lamps which emitted restful lavender light.

Voss chose his moment carefully. He struck the iron gong and conversation died, all looked towards the Archmage. "We have a final matter to settle," he told them. Calistrope has agreed to set out upon this quest on our behalf. It is only proper that we help him where we can."

There were a number of puzzled expressions among those who merely wished Voss to finish pontificating.

"Calistrope goes in harm's way. We, between us, possess a number of artifacts which might be of great help to him. I have spoken to Calistrope and I have urged him to select a few items which might be of most use to him. Calistrope..." Voss gestured to the Mage, "the floor is yours."

A murmur greeted him, a murmur in which dissatisfaction sounded rather loud. Calistrope shrugged his shoulders.

Ponderos belched again. "Pardon. Magical food, all wind and no body to it."

The company laughed and tension eased, a situation which Voss leapt into before Calistrope could take up his invitation to speak. "I, myself give this freely. A miniature self-perpetuating model of the sun, an experiment which was made some little time ago when we were testing such things. It will shine in dark places. May it be of use to you, Calistrope," he placed the globe of pearly radiance on the table and again directed attention to Calistrope.

"I thank the Despondent One," he said. "If the sun should set, it will be of great value. As Voss suggests, I *do* have one or two requests which I would like to make." Some there were who seemed relieved that his wants were so few; others, with more to lose, were dismayed. "The first concerns a packet of dust which ... Issla has. The Dust which came from the Hall of Shandokar.

Issla sprang to her feet. "How do you know this?" She jumped up and down in exasperation.

Calistrope smiled.

"No."

"Issla!" Voss pitched his voice low but no-one failed to hear the authority in it.

"Oh, Take it then," she thumped the table with her tiny fists, "But take care; used recklessly, it will suck out every last iota of magic from your body."

"Thank you my dear. Is she not as generous as she is beautiful? And her beauty is great indeed."

Issla was not placated.

"Now. Something a little more mundane. I am a man of peace; I carry no weapon save a small poignard, hardly sharp enough to cut an apple. I shall need something to defend my person, a sword, something trustworthy. Sermis has such a one, I understand, a sword with an edge that cannot be dulled."

Sermis stood with a swirl of his cloak. It was sewn with overlapping silicate discs which chimed with any movement. "A poor thing, an heirloom, of sentimental value, of crude workmanship."

"I have heard you say," Calistrope averred, "that it will pierce an ell of bumanda wood at a single thrust."

"An idle boast. I am shamed."

"Yet I would have it."

Sermis glanced across at Voss and Voss looked away. Sermis drew the sword and laid it upon the table where it glittered in the lavender light and the red.

Calistrope took the sword up and examined the blade of faintly blue glass. It glowed slightly with an inner light and sent the faintest of tingles through his fingers. "Thank you my friend. Perhaps I might also have the loan of the scabbard; there seems little point in separating the two."

Resigned to the inevitable, Sermis unbuckled the baldric and passed the scabbard across to Calistrope

"I shall return them of course, when I return."

"*If*, Calistrope. *If*."

Calistrope nodded. "As you say, the *if* lays heavily on my mind," he looked along the table. "Now, finally. I crave a boon from my oldest friend. Ponderos, you have a sigil which you have sworn by for as long as I have known you."

Ponderos heaved himself to his feet. "And neither of us knows how long that is, eh?" He took the talisman from around his neck and crossed to his friend's side. He placed it around Calistrope's neck. "I fancy it has little power left in it now; it was once potent against any weapon of iron or glass, bone or stone. What little power is left, is yours. However, there is one more thing I can give you."

Ponderos stood back from his friend. "I have spent longer than I can remember dabbling in the arts, exploring this or that scroll or book, looking for something to keep me interested. I have grumbled at the meaninglessness of it all and now, suddenly I have a chance to join my friend in a worthwhile venture."

He turned back to Calistrope. "We go together, you and me."

Calistrope found himself quite overcome. His eyes filled with tears and he breathed deeply until his emotion was under control. "I don't know how long Ponderos and I have known one another, no doubt it is indexed in our memories but it does not matter greatly. What does matter is what Ponderos has done for me. Before Ponderos, I was introspective, I considered the company of others to be a waste of time, only my own experiments had value, only my own conclusions were valid."

"Aha," said someone. "And Ponderos—for all his size—has changed him not one iota."

Calistrope heard but made no direct comment. "Ponderos showed me a larger world than the one in which I lived. He showed me that not every thought which is different to mine is as inconsequential as a mayfly's." Here he glanced at Hadrice—the one who had made the interjection—and turned back to the larger audience again.

"I thank you all," the Mage looked around the gathering. "For your gifts, for your support," he moistened his lips from a goblet of wine. "These fine examples of the magician's art which I have asked for were not selected idly. And like Voss' globe of cold light, all have a certain rare aspect in common." Again he looked around.

"There are many places where the ether is thin, others where we have detected great vacuoles extending for leagues. Places where it is difficult or even impossible to perform wizardry and where magical entities cannot endure. These gifts all have their power locked within. They do not rely upon invocation; they don't need to be within a region of rich ether. Issla's gift in fact is so bereft of magic that it will soak up whatever it can find," Calistrope sat down. "Thank you," he said again then embarrassed at the length of his address he grew morose and silent.

Voss now stood. "And I thank you, too. Calistrope's words are of great interest. His thought processes are often a source of irritation to us; often he comes to disturbing conclusions via routes which are hidden from his fellows. He is even known to have a certain antipathy to sorcery and an inclination toward technology. He is, therefore, a natural choice for this quest."

Voss lifted his cup. "I give you—the Mage, Calistrope."

There were more speeches, their eloquence growing with the consumption of wine. As the subjects veered farther and farther from the matter in hand, Calistrope left the table and went out again onto the balcony. Out here, the air was clear and cold; frost glittered on the stonework. Beyond the nearer spires and minarets of Sachavesku, the smoothly heaving expanse of Mal-a-Merrion stretched and drew the eye to those enigmatic lavender mists which hid its more northerly reaches.

Sermis had indeed spoken the truth when he had said *"if."* The Mage by no means thought of himself as invincible. Even with the full panoply of sorcerous power as protection, he could meet his end upon that broad lake as easily as in some far off exotic region. Had anyone asked him, Calistrope would have admitted freely that he was afraid. Still, as Ponderos had expressed it, his life had been bounded for far too long by the mundane, by the known. He looked forward to the future not only with a frisson of fear but with a renewed interest. Maybe with Ponderos accompanying him there would be no point in consulting his early memories.

CHAPTER 3

Mornings... the last morning had dawned nearly two millennia ago—the day the world stopped turning, But even so, the bell rang the midnight chime from Cristoline's Tower, and every hour thereafter until the great bell at Barto's took over at midday and chimed the remaining hours.

"Mornings," Ponderos insisted, "are when all journeys should start." His face suddenly creased into a grin. "Following a really excellent breakfast, of course."

Mornings... No matter that every hour was just like every other hour, every arbitrary morning like every other morning. The bells gave shape to the activities of the citizens of Sachavesku, if one said "I'll meet you at the Bourse for tea at the sixteenth hour," then the parties would be sitting down when Barto sang his fourth baritone chime of the day.

In the same way, Calistrope met Ponderos just before the seventh hour as sounded by the Cristoline. A light mist hung over the water as they ate fried fish and crisp cabbage. By the time they called for another flask of piping hot Takshent to share between them, the mist was gone and Mal-a-Merrion gleamed blue as a slab of lapis. A tumble of clouds to the north showed yellows and pinks against the darker blue shading to black along the horizon. Mal-a-Merrion's waters were shallow at this end, islands lifted above the water, the nearer ones in tones of lavender, behind these came purples and farther off, a dozen subtle shades of indigo.

If there ever had been a Lord of all Creation, thought Calistrope, *he had been a surrealist.*

The travelers went aboard. The awesome soldier ants went to the stern, out of the way as preparations for departure were completed. The humans gathered amidships. The moorings were slipped, ropes coiled; people on the quay waved farewell.

Exactly on the ninth chime, the pilot tapped a code on the steering lines and the squid snorted water and blew it out behind. A gap opened 'twixt quay and raft. An eel jumped out of the water and slid back again; a chain's length from the shore, a waterskater ran across the surface on its great padded feet.

Mornings... Mornings were for the beginning of a journey and from a balcony at the top of the College; Voss watched the departure through magnifying spectacles. The Archmage's scrutiny might have been a physical pressure reminding Calistrope of the way in which he had been maneuvered into this journey.

He brooded on the injustice done to him. Ponderos and Roli were accompanying him, but it was he himself who had been given the responsibility, been coerced into undertaking the quest. It would be Calistrope the Mage who would succeed or fail—no one else.

He could remember the anger he had felt when the Archmage had shown him the treasures snatched from his manse, hot emotion rose in him once more. Those works of art had been the better part of two thousand years in the making and one still was unfinished. Calistrope remembered the scornful remarks he had made about the experiments which the High Council had embarked upon: spells and sorcery to magnify the sun's waning heat and light—as if anything so puny could effect a change in something so stupendous. Mere experiments with planet-bound phenomena, to augment the dwindling energy.

Now his contempt had been repaid. *My masterworks sequestered and I have been compelled to make a journey as dangerous as it is inconsequential.*

CHAPTER 4

The sun was an orange patch spreading across the south western horizon behind the overhead mist; the distant massif, a black silhouette against the brightness. Below the layer of cloud, the air was clear and still and smelled of life: of water-borne plants and fish, pollen from the reed beds along the shores, the myriad exhalations of animals and insects since the dawn of time.

Mal-a-Merrion's waters were restless, however. Monstrous bergs, calving from the high glaciers, crashed into the Lake's northern waters with monotonous regularity and sent vast and stately ripples down the length of the lake. Here, where the depth of water was unknowable, the undulations slid silently beneath the raft, rising gently and as gently, subsiding.

A soft touch upon his cheek drew Calistrope's attention from the squid which towed them along the Lake. Turning, he followed the insect's gaze and counted the distant specks. Black against the orange mist.

"Five, six, seven. Dragonflies?"

The ant's carapace tilted in agreement.

"Seven," Calistrope rubbed his prominent nose. Two or three perhaps, could be ignored; a pair coupling over the waters or males fighting for a female were not that unusual but seven ... Seven must be a foraging party, uncommon in such still weather when fish were so easily caught. "We had best prepare," he said but the insect was already gone and conferring with its fellows. "Ponderos," he called and both his fellow Mage and Roli looked up from whatever task they were attending to in the stern. Calistrope pointed to the marauding party. "Dragonflies."

Some minutes later the high pitched thrum of their wings thrilled the air, sunlight coruscated from the membranous wings in colors of fire opal. The dragonflies scouted the craft, darting back and forth to hover now over the stern, now above the bows

There was no warning of the sudden attack, no perceivable signal given. Two of the insects plunged towards the raft, their bodies arched to bring the blade-like stings to bear.

Calistrope's armament was already primed—the final word of a mantra and he hurled a tight ball of incandescence at the nearer of the two creatures. Simultaneously, the raft's pilot loosed a quarrel from his crossbow to strike the other in its side. The one insect erupted into smoky flame but the second ignored the glass quarrel lodged in its thorax and lanced an ant through its compound eye. Discommoded only and plainly immune to the effects of any poison, the ant retaliated, clamping razor sharp mandibles around the dragonfly's neck and squeezing. A third dragonfly plummeted towards them, attacking the ant which held its fellow. Calistrope's fireball and Ponderos' throwing club struck together. The fire consumed it from the inside and greasy smoke vented from the insect's joints and mouthparts, hiding the combat from view. A dragonfly's head rolled free, spinning in chance directions as its mandibles snapped spastically.

Behind him, the Mage discovered another duel just ending. Roli was belaboring a dragonfly with a pole while an ant chewed through its leg. The attacking insect sprang into the air as its upper joint parted and Calistrope drew upon his power to send more spheres of lightning as it rejoined its three companions.

Three. There should be another ...

An unnerving scream turned all heads. The fourth dragonfly had seized hold of the pilot and with a flurry of glittering wings pulled him from the pulpit. The man screamed again as he was borne off across the water, carried in a cradle of interlaced forelegs.

There was nothing the ants could do, they watched impassively as Calistrope flung fireball after fireball and Ponderos hurled whatever he could find. The insect with its piteous burden was quickly out of range and the remaining dragonflies hovered, waiting for further opportunities.

Suddenly, a strangely cold feeling overtook Calistrope, the energy field had weakened alarmingly and his weaponry was dwindling in both size and strength. "Oh, *corruption*," he whispered dismally, "of what use am I now?"

The dragonflies seemed to sense their lack of defenses and swooped as one. An ant was killed immediately in the onslaught, pierced between head and thorax. Ponderos knocked a dragonfly from the air to float, twitching, on the salty waters until some denizen of the Lake took it from beneath. Calistrope wielded a boat hook and was holding off the last insect until he took a cut in the left shoulder. The pain was unbelievably fierce; his arm began to stiffen almost at once.

"Boy," he called, teeth clenched against the pain of the spreading venom. "Roli, take this and help Ponderos."

As Roli ran to his master, the ether grew thick with power once more and the Mage was able to throw off the effects of the poison. "It's all right for now," he said, "the magic has returned," he flung another fireball and watched a moment as the dragonfly he had hit perished in flames.

The energy dwindled yet again and he stumbled, crippled by the return of the pain. Even as Roli tried to support him, Calistrope was knocked to the deck by a stunning blow and Roli was flung away to lie senseless in the scuppers. Distantly, Calistrope felt stiff limbs embrace him, felt himself lifted, saw the deck recede below him.

Calistrope felt disconnected from events. He watched as an ant reared up on its hind legs and brought its tail forward. A jet of clear liquid flashed briefly and the ant, spent by the effort, collapsed. The dragonfly which held him dissolved, parts and limbs falling away around him, the raft seemed to leap up at him to strike a final blow at his limp body.

When the Mage regained consciousness, there was intense pain in his shoulder and dull aches everywhere else. His eyes would not focus; his limbs were slack and refused to work. When his vision *did* clear at last, he saw two ants methodically cleaning the raft of bodies; the dragonfly carcasses had already been disposed of and now they were rolling their own dead companions to the side and over the edge.

The pain and the sharp smell of formic acid recalled those final moments to him, when he had been taken by the dragonfly and the ant had saved him, it had obviously been the creature's last resort. *Which one of them had saved his life?* He wondered.

A harsh sound grated upon the Mage's ears and put an end to conjecture. One of their remaining insect companions was shivering violently, producing the strident note from the joints between the bands of chitin at its throat.

Ponderos," he called, his voice weak and low. "Ponderos, the creature is injured; it has lost its antennae."

The other ant, partly blinded in one eye, touched feelers to the face mask of the trembling insect and the unnerving noise ceased. The two antennae had presumably, been torn off during the battle and now the creature was unable to communicate, it would be expelled by its nest sisters. Should he feel sorrow? Sorrow seemed as out of place as his earlier thoughts of gratitude, the ways of these insects were curious, even bizarre.

"Ponderos," he said again and realized he had been leaning against the huge man's chest all along; Ponderos' arms supported him,

"They don't feel pain as we do," said Ponderos. Life and death mean little to them. Machines, living machines."

But Calistrope still wondered as the world went out of focus again.

Calistrope's wound continued to trouble him, the ether grew no stronger and there was little he could do in the way of self-healing. Even so, he helped in whatever way he could to restore order to the raft and in doing so, belatedly discovered why the dragonflies had attacked them.

While clearing away debris left by the battle, he found that one of the huge sacs of honeydew—the soldier ants' only food—had been steadily leaking since they had left Sachavesku. A trail of the rich, aromatic liquid across the lake must have led the party after them; dragonflies had been known to scent honeydew from leagues away. Quickly, he sluiced all trace of the sweet, sticky stuff away and resealed two more of the bladders which had been damaged during the fighting.

One more thing he discovered: there was no way to steer the squid which had been swimming aimlessly for the past five or six hours, since the attack. The squid was controlled by long nerve fibers taken from an insect pupa and surgically inserted into the cephalopod's musculature. No sequence of taps or tweaks or pulls provoked the same response twice running and finally, they cut the squid free and thought about sails and makeshift oars.

If their attempts had been successful, Calistrope might well have considered turning back but there were no materials on the raft to work with. The ants, for whom the Nest's instructions were irrevocable, had other and very fixed ideas. They waited until the humans were clearly at a loss then, squatted, one to each side of the raft, and extended their three outer legs into the water. They began to paddle the ungainly craft onward.

Meanwhile, the powers of the two Mages waned steadily. Calistrope had detected such depleted regions in the ether before but why they should occur in the relatively undisturbed regions of Mal-a-Merrion's central waters was a mystery. Neither he nor Ponderos could offer a theory to explain it.

The mist began to clear soon after the fateful battle. It lifted and dispersed until the sky became its accustomed purple-black and the sun's bloated disc hung just above the south western horizon, giving them a sense of direction and purpose. Three more days passed before the ants, occasionally aided by one or more of their human companions, brought them to the farther shore, far up the Lake from Sachavesku. The insects sculled the craft slowly along the bank in search of a place to disembark.

Calistrope's wound was now giving him continual pain, the poison had spread and often, he was only semiconscious. In a more lucid moment he asked one of his companions to bring him his bag. The ant—the one with the injured eye—complied and neatly snipped the drawstring with its mandibles so that the bag fell open. Calistrope groped within, withdrew a glass medallion and with difficulty, set it spinning on its edge. It wobbled, straightened up again and continued to spin but so slowly that the detail on both faces was quite plain.

"Take us northward," he said and fixed a tiny part of his mind and remaining power upon maintaining the rotation. "If it speeds up, stop."

Calistrope slumped back, his eyes closed, his gaze turned inward.

The glass disc spun slowly and the water lapping alongside the raft was a soothing, somnolent sound in his ears. The Mage slept more peacefully in the dark sunlight.

Images swirled around his mind, memories.

☙

Sometimes, larger waves spread down the Lake from the north and would break viciously along the shingle, sending tongues of salty water up along the banks. The larger ones would flood into the many pools of supersaturated water, splashing salt crystals as high as the road.

The silvery glass medallion still spun slowly

Ponderos had fashioned a travois from branches and a piece of fabric from the abandoned raft. The ant which had lost its antennae dragged the conveyance behind it with Calistrope, unconscious still, tossing and turning on it. The two ants, one speechless, the other all but blind in one eye, pressed on resolutely or stood impassively when the humans needed to rest.

A day's length passed, another. There was little significance to the term except as a measure of time; the stars wheeled about; infinitesimally, the planets wandered among the stars, their evolutions just as minute, just as precise. Humankind kept to its own rhythms, resting when weary, eating when hungry, laboring when necessary.

However, there *was* one transition which went quite unnoticed for some time. Calistrope's spinning disc, perched on a corner of the travois like a gyroscope, gradually spun faster. No one noticed the phenomenon until the increasing speed became audible as a rising whine. It continued to accelerate, the whine becoming a shriek, the disc becoming a milky colored sphere. Still the rotation increased, the sound rising up beyond even the insects' hearing until it was gone, burst suddenly into a scatter of bright dust.

A minute or two later, Calistrope sat up. He rubbed his eyes and massaged his right shoulder. Peeling the bandages away, he found the flesh around the wound to be purple and swollen—his body battled against the poison. Now that the ether was stronger, he stroked the discolored skin and the angry colors began to fade, the puffiness diminished.

"Ah. That is better," he breathed. "Much better."

His face still looked drawn however and pinched; his hands were thin and corded, the fingers like dead twigs. He put his scabbarded sword to the ground and leaned on it as he eased himself from the travois; he managed to stand and to slowly straighten. "Another hour or two and..." he leaned, began to fall and only Ponderos' speed and strength saved him from measuring his length upon the ground. The Mage was a great deal weaker than he seemed.

"I think," said Ponderos, looking at the various bluffs and rocky outcrops, "I think there's an inn not far from here. The magic has come back but Calistrope needs food and rest while he mends," He made Calistrope comfortable once more on the conveyance and signaled to the ant to move off. It clicked its mandibles and the other hummed a double note, they moved off. "A league or so. Not far."

Roli groaned. What might be an invigorating ramble to Ponderos the Immovable, the boy saw as a considerable effort.

There was no further delay; they marched off along the high bank, following a game trail which skirted small clumps of brush and alder and the occasional earthy pillar of an insect domicile.

Ponderos considered the temperature as brisk—around the freezing point of water, it varied from place to place. Here, puddles were rimed with ice or frozen solid, there, a shallow sheet of water with long snapping larvae crawling over the black mud bottom. Flat rosettes of lime green leaves edged the beaten pathway; where it was warm enough;

thin black stems raised pale yellow flowers and even a few clear fruit like oversized drops of water.

Presently, the path led them to a narrow paved road which wound along what had become a low cliff and not far off the league which Ponderos had forecast, it turned around a sharp bluff and followed the line of a wide bay.

Across the water, at the far side of the bay, they could see a promontory on which stood a long, low rambling building.

Its landward end was constructed from stuccoed stone with mullioned windows, lights inside shone through the rich colors of the glass. Further out, the structure had been extended over the lake on a platform supported by a forest of thick stakes driven into the lake bed. Here, the walls were of timber with lath and plaster, the windows fashioned from the bottoms of glass bottles cemented together in the window frames.

The *Raftman's Ease* was an inn which catered not so much for the raft pilots as for the hunters who returned there every few months to trade skins and the exoskeletons of certain insects. These would later be sold on to the artisans in Sachavesku where the raw materials would be processed into garments, into body armor, jewelry and a host of other items.

They approached the inn. Benches made from old grey driftwood leaned against the walls; an iridescent beetle, harnessed to a sled mounded with skins, waited patiently for its owner to return. One of the double doors stood open and warm air, misted with condensation, swirled white against the outer chill bringing with it a burden of smells—cooked fish, alcoholic beverages, tobaccos and the smoke from a brazier of coals. Roli found the place inviting, even exciting, and failed to notice the dilapidation.

Ponderos bent and lifted Calistrope from the travois and set him unsteadily upright, he supported the injured Mage to the door and then stopped. "Unhitch Charylla," he said to Roli, having learned the names of the two ants only shortly before.

As Roli unclipped the harness, Faramiss, the other insect, helped to push the conveyance off the road and out of the way. The two ants then climbed slowly up the rocky inland side of the road, each of them with a pair of honeydew sacs slung across their narrow waists like ungainly balloons.

"Will you know when we leave the inn?" Roli asked.

"Go," hummed Faramiss. "We shall watch, we shall see you."

The place was much as Ponderos remembered it though perhaps another layer of dust had been added to the ledges and shelves along the walls. The main lounge had a low vaulted roof of stone supported upon slate pillars. Tapestries and carpets—dark with age hung between the old walls and the innermost rows of pillars to form a number of semi-private booths, each lit by an oil lamp and holding a round table with stools and benches. Untrimmed furs and woven mats littered the flagstone floor, they soaked up spilt beer and absorbed the trodden-in scraps of food and other detritus.

A score or so patrons quaffed beer and ate from bowls of bouillabaisse—a specialty of the Raftman's Ease.

Ponderos stood for a moment just inside the door, letting his eyes grow accustomed to the dimness. His bright clothing and huge physique set him apart from the gathering of hunter-traders who preferred to dress in dull greens and browns, the better to avoid becoming prey to those creatures they hunted. Almost without exception, they were tall and thin with lean and hungry looking features.

A quickly-spreading silence overtook the conversation as everyone looked up to examine the newcomer and watch as he guided Calistrope to a corner seat in a booth as close to the fire as possible. He went to the bar where mine host was pouring drinks and serving plates of fish stew, and apart from one or two women who were obviously somewhat struck by the big man's physique, the patrons returned to their drinking and discussion.

"Landlord Perspic?" Ponderos enquired.

"Dead these five months," grunted his replacement filling another bowl with soup, deftly catching a drip with his thumb and licking it lest it go to waste. "Old Perspic—we gave his body to the Lake last Lamagan's Day." The new landlord was a dark and saturnine individual with a complexion like lake-bottom mud and a paunch which hung over the front of his trousers. "I bought this dilapidated place from his heirs for an inflated price and will doubtless live to rue the day."

Ponderos chewed at his bottom lip. "The Raftman's Ease is a tavern with a long and honorable history."

"And history does not pay the fishermen who sell me their catch at far too a high a price. I shall end up a pauper and catch all manner of diseases and die with no one to mark my grave."

"That will be an end to your miseries then," replied Ponderos with finality. "Now, I require a room, a room with three beds, one bath and the usual conveniences."

The Landlord stopped in the middle of ladling out the stew. "A room is it?" he finished filling the bowl and passed it the serving girl. "Well Sir, require whatever you like. What you may have, at the cost of a copper flake—which is nowhere near its true worth, is a mattress in this common room after the lights are doused, the use of a bar of soap, a basin of cold water and the privy over the lake. As you see," he waved a greasy hand at the many hunters of both genders who filled the tavern, "the inn is near full. The traders are late and there are many who have been waiting here a week or more."

"You must be making a fair fortune then, if they have nothing to do but to drink you dry," Ponderos shrugged. "I shall have two flagons—no, make it three, of Merrion White and three no, make that four bowls of bouillabaisse," Ponderos took two thin discs of beaten copper from his purse and put them on the counter. "My friend is still very ill, he was stung by a dragonfly and his life has been hanging in the balance ever since. He needs warmth and rest."

He pressed his lips together, in an expression of unhappiness and went back to the booth to find Roli had arrived and was tucking Calistrope's cloak around his shivering form.

A minute later, the girl arrived with a tray bearing three flagons and as many leather cups. There was also a dish of salt and mixed herbs to flavor the fish stew.

"Sir," she said to Ponderos. "I heard what you said about your friend, my room is small but it is quite snug and warm. Let him rest there and I will sleep in the scullery for a night or two."

"You will do no such thing, daughter," said the Landlord who had come up behind her with the four bowls of stew.

The girl turned and scowled at her father. "What harm is there?" She asked "The poor man is in pain."

"Where would it end if people knew your room was for hire? Perhaps they would think that you were also available. Word would get around that Fashlig rents his daughter out by the night, by the hour. My trade would dwindle, my borrowings would not be repaid, I would be destitute."

"Or people would throng here, I would become a famous courtesan and your takings would multiply, you would buy a new and fashionable alehouse in Sachavescu and retire with a belly twice the size of this one," she poked him in the region of his navel. "One outcome is as likely as the other."

"You have your mother's tongue."

"I have my mother's sense and I have made up my mind. The poor man sleeps in my room and that's an end to it."

"Thank you," said Ponderos, grinning at the exchange.

Calistrope nodded his gratitude.

"I thank you for my Master, who is too ill to speak," said Roli expansively, assuming the status of squire rather than apprentice.

"This is less than the truth," Calistrope's voice was little more than a husky whisper. No one heard him.

"My name is Roli," Roli continued, "perhaps you will tell me, tell us, yours?"

"Perhaps I will," she replied, an impish spark in her eye. "Then again, perhaps I won't.

When the lamps were extinguished leaving red sunbeams stabbing through the dusty atmosphere of the common room, Fashlig's daughter came to them and took all three to her room, Ponderos supporting Calistrope up the narrow staircase. It was indeed a small space, tucked into the eaves above the main doorway with a small window overlooking the road outside.

Calistrope lay back on the bed. "Thank you, all of you," he croaked, looking at his companions then, to the girl, "and thank you to ... er..." he said to the girl.

"You had better say what your name is," Roli suggested. "It will be very awkward to discuss you behind your back if we don't know what you are called."

"Hmm," she said, folding her arms. "I think you and your huge friend here had better leave. The room is not large enough to hold you all."

"Oh no," said Roli. "I should stay, at least until my Master is asleep."

"Well then. I will leave you to it; I still have work to do before *I* can sleep."

"When my master is resting properly, I will come and help you."

"Now there would be a wonder. A man helping in the scullery." And she pulled the drapes across the window and left them.

Ponderos followed her down soon afterwards. In the common room, he found himself a straw filled mattress in a corner and within a handful of heartbeats he was snoring as relentlessly as any of the others.

Upstairs, Roli sat by Calistrope and wiped his brow with a sponge and cold water. It was the first time that he had paused long enough to consider their situation and realized how near they had come to being overwhelmed by the dragonflies. He held one of Calistrope's hands. "Don't die now, Master, will you?"

Calistrope, who had been 'twixt sleep and waking smiled, his teeth agleam in the gloom. "I'd not plan my wake just yet, Roli. I am getting better. It's just that with such weak magic, it takes a lot longer."

"No such thing as magic. You told me that. Made me believe it."

"A figure of speech, boy. Inside me," Calistrope tapped his chest and spoke on hoarsely, "there are millions of tiny machines which repair the damage that my body suffers every day."

"I know this," Roli sounded disgusted. "You have expounded on germs and diseases and how our bodies defend us."

"I'm pleased that you remember but this is different. What I speak of now is what makes the difference between you and me. You have to learn to make these tiny machines and to fill your veins with them, only then will you live long enough to be a magician. But they work exceeding slow when the ether is as devoid of strength as it is hereabouts."

Later, when Calistrope was sleeping properly Roli went down to the kitchen and guided by the noise, found the Landlord's daughter washing up crockery and cutlery. He helped a little, carrying piles of soiled dishes to the sink and piles of clean ones away but mostly, he lolled against the counter top and watched the girl at work.

"Do you like it here?" he asked after awhile.

"No. Would you?"

He shook his head and another long silence ensued.

"I wanted to be a hunter but Father wouldn't let me go. Mag Jorris was happy enough to take me and teach me the skills but father wanted someone to fetch and carry and wash up."

"Why not go anyway?"

"With Mag? Mag has to come here to trade. Father could easily put in a bad word for her and then what? No more trade. Couldn't do that to Mag or anyone else, could I?"

"No. No, I can see that."

Dishes went in to the soapy water, dishes came out. Roli carried them to a long trestle table and stacked them, then there was another barrel of Ordinary to broach and fish to be taken out of the salt boxes and left to steep in rain water.

"You want a drink?"

"Um. Yes please," Roli smiled. "What shall we have, a tot of your Dad's best kelp brandy?"

"Tea is what I had in mind. Good strong tea with a dash of pepper on top." And she made tea—tea with a dash of pepper for her and without a dash for Roli.

"Where are you three going?"

Roli took a long swallow from his glass before answering. "We're on an adventure," he told her solemnly. "Ponderos and Calistrope are two powerful magicians and I'm Calistrope's assistant and we have two ants with us to help defend us from attack. What's your name?"

Roli ducked as the big leather jug swung but not quickly enough. The dregs caught him in the face.

"You think I'm a child to believe such nonsense?"

Roli found a towel and wiped his face.

"What's your name?"

"Jiss."

Upstairs, in Jiss's bed, Calistrope dreamed and slowly mended.

Chapter 5

With three good meals inside him and a jug or two of the best wine the Raftman's Ease could provide, Calistrope was almost back to his usual self. Ponderos had scouted the way meanwhile and had discovered the steep and narrow lateral valley they must take.

"Unfortunately," he told his companions, "there has been a rock slide not far from the entrance. We shall have to climb it. It is not high but blocks the way completely. Do you feel able?" he asked, looking closely at Calistrope.

"Oh yes. I have no doubts," he leaned back in his chair. "Give me another old day..."

And so, a final meal of thick fish stew and black bread, a final flagon of Merrion White, a second of Merrion Green and they set out once again.

"Roli. Where's he got to now?" Calistrope looked back from the base of the rock fall. "He's been lagging behind ever since we started."

Ponderos shrugged. "He went late to his own bed. No doubt he'll be feeling a little sad now, since he's leaving the landlord's daughter behind. He'll be along—probably before those ants are back from reconnoitering, there's fog at the top of that rock climb."

"Oh they'll not lose their way. If we start now they'll find us as we climb," Calistrope turned once more and looked for Roli. "Is that the boy back there?"

Ponderos looked back at Roli's distant figure, he had just come into the light of a candlethorn tree, a second figure joined the first. "Oh, I see. All is clear. We had better wait," he replied with a sigh.

Calistrope frowned and looked again, seeing the two figures. "Hmm, well. We'll just sit down here, behind this rock and wait. Were you never young, Ponderos? Did you never feel the need to satisfy a little lust?"

Calistrope felt a certain sadness. Lovemaking was a pleasure that had faded long ago. While he remembered certain occasions when his passions had been aroused in the recent past, they came now all too seldom and to remember when love had been flavored by the freshness of youth was no longer even a possibility.

Ten minutes passed, five more. Roli turned the corner where they sat. "Well well, Roli," Calistrope smiled up at his erstwhile apprentice. "Where's your friend?"

"Friend?"

"She is just here," Jiss said, coming round the rock to stand beside Roli. Jiss wore a suit of hunting clothes like those of the hunters who patronized the inn, dull green jacket and trousers sewn from amphibian leather with thick soled boots protected by an outer layer of chitinous plates. A large knapsack on the girl's back was stuffed with kit and provisions.

It had become obvious that Jiss had been lured from her Father's employ.

The two Mages looked her up and down and climbed to their feet. "Hmm, well," said Calistrope, somewhat vexed at the situation. "The ants have gone ahead, to find the easiest route over the rock fall."

They walked along the stream which ran down the centre of the valley to where it percolated out of the tumbled stone blocking their way. Jiss and Roli followed them. All looked upward. The mist covering upper levels made it impossible to guess the height of the barrier.

"So, we'll start," said Calistrope. He and Ponderos started to climb, Roli and Jiss stood at the side of the stream.

"Well? Are you two coming or not?" Calistrope looked down and realized that a tender farewell was in progress. "Oh!"

"Us two?" asked Jiss. "Up there? Me? Oh no, I've had enough of the tavern, I'm off to find Mag and I don't think that Mag is foolish enough to hunt up there."

Calistrope did indeed feel foolish at his misunderstanding. "I see. So, goodbye then."

"Goodbye."

And Calistrope and Ponderos resumed their climb, leaving the youngsters to finish their good-byes in their own way.

The fallen rocks were mostly squares and stable enough to make the early part of the climb easy. As they ascended, however, the stone became wetter, fog condensed and ran in small trickles to join and form streamlets banked by brilliant green mosses.

They crawled across landscapes in miniature; swift rivulets and dashing waterfalls, soft green hills and rugged rock outcroppings. Odors of damp and decay filled their nostrils; rushing water was a constant clamor in their ears. As the mist closed around them, the gloom hid the diminutive realms and left each of them alone at the center of a pale sphere.

The mosses which covered the rocks were smooth and slippery. Footing was treacherous and handholds lay beneath the cushiony covering and had to be sought for.

The ants returned and conferred, Faramiss indicating that they should angle their climb to the right since a lake on the far side was easier to pass on its southern edge.

Descending on the farther and sunless side was, if anything, more difficult than the ascent. The ants could merely point themselves downhill and crawl; the humans had to climb down, feeling their way—a laborious business.

Roli suddenly found his foothold crumbling away and he was left swinging from two slick handholds from which his fingers were gradually slipping. "Calis..." he husked from a suddenly dry throat. "Calistrope, Ponderos... I'm going to fall..."

"Hold on," one of them called back.

Seconds ticked by, Roli's left hand came loose and frantically, he sought for another support. His efforts only loosened the grasp of his other hand. His grip failed and he fell... fell into the strong arms of Ponderos who had managed to climb to a point just below him.

Below Ponderos, the two ants stood, their front legs extended to catch the boy.

Calistrope came third, rummaging in his bag to find a small bottle. "Drink this," he advised. Roli, severely shaken and ashen faced, took a swallow and coughed as the strong spirit hit the back of his throat. When the coughing subsided, Roli was red in the face and whooping for breath. Ponderos massaged the boy's numb fingers. Eventually he regained his composure and they continued the descent.

Beneath the cap of mist, the valley with the still and silent pool against the rock-fall dam, was a somber and silent world, the air was dank and laced heavily with methane from the stagnant waters. Guided by the ants as they descended, they veered to the south where the valley side was less steep and the black water easier to pass. Finally, they reached the floor where a stream brawled down the center of the narrow valley—little more than a crack driving into the landmass which reared up from the old sea bottom trench occupied by Lake Mal-a-Merrion.

Crossing and re-crossing the stream whenever it swung against one vertiginous side or the other, the band followed the valley. As they left the edge behind, the rock walls towered higher and higher so they walked on into deeper and deeper gloom. Ponderos brought out Voss' radiant globe to light their steps. Even when the mist no longer shrouded them, the sunlight was confined to a narrow bar of orange reflecting from the upper reaches of the northern walls. Where the light penetrated the obscurity, it tinged the white water to the color of old gold and where it was refracted through the churning surface, the stream waters boiled with underwater life scurrying for the comforting shadows of crannies and rocky shelves.

They rested every so often, sometimes stopping as long as seven or eight hours when Roli felt the pressures of sleep. At such times the ants also relaxed into a watchful somnolence which was their nearest equivalent of sleep. Calistrope and Ponderos conversed in low tones or went hunting in the stream for soft shelled crustaceans or juicy insect larvae which they lured from crevices and cracks.

"Did you hear that?" asked Calistrope as they paused, waiting for a creature to crawl out of its hidey-hole.

Ponderos put his head to one side, cupped an ear. Finally, he shook his head. "Snow or ice falling from the heights? Was that it?"

Calistrope shook his head. "Something following us. Two or three somethings. Listen," he stopped and followed his own council. "Back there, I'm certain of it. Waiting for an opportunity."

"An opportunity to do what? Hmm? There aren't that many insects big enough to hunt us." But in the silence which followed, Ponderos too heard the click of a hard claw on the rocky surface, the scrape of chitin against an outcrop. "Yes. You're right. Let's go back."

Faramiss and Charylla were already standing, stiff with concentration, staring past them into the gloom.

"If only there was magic in these parts," Calistrope complained and then bent towards Roli. "Roli," he said, tapping the boy's shoulder. "Up and get your sword out."

Roli shook his head to clear the drowsiness and made ready, standing between the two Mages. Ponderos lifted the globe of light high and rested it atop an angular jut of rock. Three pairs of eyes reflected the light back at them, white from each leftward eye and the red of the fire from each right hand side.

"What are they?" asked Roli, his voice low, tense.

"I don't know. They have the look of pack insects, hunters. Probably not sure how to deal with us—mixed species like this."

Hunters and hunted stared at one another for several minutes, the pack of three moving in an intricate pattern which would have made it difficult to fire a bow or use a sling. The stand-off continued and just when the humans thought the insects were going to slope off, they darted in.

The lead creature swerved around Faramiss and underneath Charylla while the other two engaged the ants. Ponderos was ready for the leap and wielding his blade in a blur of blue glass, he cleaved one of the front legs away and half of the mandible. Roli took it on as another dashed away from the ants towards the softer looking targets.

Calistrope's and Ponderos' swords almost met in the insect's thorax while to the side, Roli decapitated the injured one. Meanwhile one or other of the ants had bitten through the third's waist and the two halves—dead but still deadly—twitched on the ground with a stinger emerging from one half and its jaws snapping from the other.

The engagement had lasted no more than four or five minutes but all three humans were breathing heavily as though exhausted. The affray with the dragonflies out on the lake had in no way prepared them for hand to hand combat, it was not yet an activity which they could react to with equanimity. Calistrope hoped sincerely that they might never become so accustomed.

Leaving the carnage behind them and with a heightened awareness of possible predators, they trudged onward, comparing landmarks with those marked upon their chart.

Ponderos pointed to a rough pillar of rock which must have been half a league high yet no more than thirty paces across at its base. "God's Finger. Do you think it's natural or artificial?"

"Natural," said Calistrope, not greatly interested in its provenance. "Though which God? Hmm? According to the notes in the margin, it stands close to the high point. How far do you think?" he thrust the map out towards Ponderos.

Ponderos squinted in the gloom. "Three leagues?" he shrugged. "About three leagues."

The chart showed the massif as a long narrow peninsular of highland trailing southward from a great continent more than a thousand leagues in width. On the western side it was bounded by Lake Mal-a-Merrion, on the east—the farther side—the Long River emptied through its vast delta into the Last Ocean.

Another three leagues and they did, indeed, reach the watershed. The ground underfoot had become soft and marshy, the stream they had followed became a series of stagnant pools where pale insect nymphs wriggled away from the light and other—more developed—larvae snapped wicked claws and mandibles as their shadows fell across the scummy surface.

The humans trod carefully through or around the noxious ponds and came at last to where the valley floor tilted imperceptibly towards the east and water drained sullenly from the bogs and sloughs. Bubbles rose sluggishly and burst on the surface tainting the air with the smell of things long dead.

Gradually, their footing became less spongy; the water collected into a sizeable river which coursed downhill carrying with it a murky burden of silt and mud. In past epochs, this side of the landmass had undergone greater erosion; ahead, the valley widened considerably and the sides sloped away from the vertical.

In the final narrow throat of the ravine, the ants insisted upon a halt. This, Faramiss told them in its buzzing tones was as far as they would go.

"But your instructions," Calistrope frowned, "you are to go with us to Schune." This arbitrary decision quite bewildered Calistrope, it was a truism that the lower orders of ants—the workers and the soldiers—obeyed the Nest to the letter, acquiescence to Nest orders was cemented into their genes.

"Our food is almost exhausted," Faramiss explained. "Only so much was salvaged from the raft after the attack. We will stay here for as long as we live and protect you from the pursuers."

"Pursuers?" asked Ponderos. "What pursuers?"

Faramiss waved her antennae expressively. "Creatures of the marsh. Eight have followed us. A fire will halt them for a time, after that we will kill them until we die."

The humans looked back the way they had come. Was there a suggestion of shapes and stick-like limbs lurking in the shadows? Perhaps.

"Surely you can forage for food?" Roli asked, outraged at what he had heard.

Calistrope shook his head. "Their mouth parts can cope only with the honeydew in those bladders," he explained. "Even broth, their gut cannot digest it," Calistrope bit his lip. "This is something that had not occurred to me, I must admit."

While Charylla and Faramiss watched the prowlers, the humans collected great piles of brush and dead wood. They heaped it up in mounds across the open ground, effectively sealing off the way they had come. Ponderos set it alight at several places and as it began to burn, slowly at first and then more furiously, they backed away from the heat.

How are good-byes made in such circumstances? The two ants continued to stare into the gloom beyond the flames and ignored them. Eventually, Calistrope just said a simple emotionless goodbye and when there was still no response, they turned about and glumly resumed their journey.

Calistrope and both his companions had come to regard the two insects as friends simply because they had shared so many leagues of their trek with each other and had fought first the dragonflies and more recently the pack insects together. The comradeship they had felt was a false relationship, Calistrope saw that now. The ants were so far removed from humans that there was not the merest chance of social understanding.

Calistrope remembered the remark he had made to Formicca: "our goals are yours." The high caste ant had agreed. The air was not cold but Calistrope shivered and drew his cloak protectively about himself. There really was no comprehension between the two species. Even so, he felt depressed that the two ants were not the brave comrades he had briefly supposed them to be.

He trudged after his companions.

A well-defined game trail ran along the riverside, meandering around bushes and copses or outcrops and rejoining further on. Often, there were signs of past flooding and the trail branched from lower to higher levels.

They moved at a good pace on the downhill grade until the river—now a sizeable watercourse—crowded them closer and closer to the southern side of the valley. There were still trails to follow but they became narrower, worn into the mosses and clay by more sure-footed creatures than humans. While the far side of the river was flat and home to small swarms of grazing insects, the paths to which they were confined were often narrow ledges or passages between fallen boulders.

They came to the end of one such trail which had taken them fifty or sixty ells above the water's edge, the trail turned a corner and opened out onto a series of wide terraces. "There's a light ahead," Ponderos observed as he rounded the corner. "A glow."

The gorge opened out before them into a wide valley with a well-worn, dry flood plain on either side of the river which curled through the valley in a succession of curves and discarded ox-bow lakes. To one side was a small settlement—a dozen or so houses and other buildings clustered around an open space with a larger meeting hall on one side. A few outlying structures bordered a rude track way running the length of the open part of the valley. A faint suggestion of smoke came to them on the air. They could discern no activity however, no people, no animals.

After some discussion, they decide to skirt the village by remaining close to the steeper slopes until they were well beyond the farthest house. The companions crossed the end of a small gorge where a busy stream tumbled down to join the river below them. Beyond, they continued again and a league onward, perhaps a little more, came to a point where the valley once more closed up and the river funneled between almost vertical cliffs. They found a way well above water level which, from its well-trodden appearance they judged would take them all the way though the narrows.

They marched single file along a ledge little wider than a pair of feet, their new familiarity with such walkways lending them some skill. Calistrope, leading the group, stopped abruptly after stepping around a cracked column of rock; he move forward a pace or two to give the others space to stand on and pointed.

All three of them could hear a constant hum, just audible above the sound of the rushing waters below them.

"What is it?" Roli asked.

"A nest?" Suggested Ponderos.

"A wasp nest," Calistrope shook his head. "I don't care to get any closer than this. If only Valdemar had been a little more circumspect with his improvements."

"Valdemar?" asked Roli.

"Valdemar?" Repeated Ponderos in the same tone.

"Valdemar the Entomophile."

"Entomo... Insect lover? The improver? Ah! I thought that was Nimilick?"

"Nimilick favored crustaceans."

"I never heard of intelligent lobsters."

"Just so."

They stood and gazed at the gigantic pear shaped nest which hung over the water and at its largest girth almost filled the gap between the cliffs. It was suspended from the trunk of a tree which had fallen—or had been felled—and lodged between the two cliff faces. There was an entrance near the bottom where great black and yellow furred insects came and went. Guards were posted at strategic positions around the nest, on ledges, on tenaciously clinging shrubs, in cracks in the rock walls, wherever possible.

"It's bigger than the Inn," Roli ventured.

"The Raftsman's Ease? By the Lake?" Ponderos rubbed his chin. "Perhaps you're right."

"Bigger. Much bigger." Calistrope was firm. 'There is room for several man-sized stories in there. Nine perhaps, or ten. There will be thousands and thousands of insects inside."

"So what shall we do?"

"That settlement. Surely people need to leave the valley now and again. Perhaps they know of another way out."

"It may not be all that old an obstruction," Ponderos observed. "It does not take long to build something like that. A swarm could construct it in, what, forty, fifty hours? Perhaps they aren't aware of it yet."

Calistrope shook his head. "It is quite mature, I'm certain. Look at the stains on the rocks to either side, observe the rubbish which has accumulated on the banks underneath."

"I'll wager there will be someone who would take us down river in a boat," said Roli, his eyes shining with excitement. "I'd wager someone will shoot these rapids just for the fun of it."

Calistrope looked at the white foam swirling between jagged limestone teeth and the great standing waves of water leaping high into the air. "Perhaps a boat is not the best way out of here. Perhaps we could climb the cliffs, walk past that way."

Ponderos looked up at the edges of the high cliff tops against the dark sky, as sharp as newly broken glass. "I fancy that we would find it difficult to breathe up there, my friend and it is a very long way to climb. Under or around, that is the only way."

"Let's consult with the villagers first."

Chapter 6

They turned back and retraced their steps, leaving behind the humming nest and its dangerous occupants. They approached the village once more and began to descend the terraces. As they came nearer, a pall of smoke became visible—first as a thin layer, then as an overhead stain in the air which shrouded them and the village in an artificial twilight. A few minutes later, Ponderos threw out his arms to stop them.

"A strange thing," he said. "Strange," Ponderos frowned for a moment. "Go back a few paces then watch the village as you come back."

Calistrope and Roli backed up as Ponderos had suggested. From a few hundred paces away, the village was a ramshackle collection of structures built from logs and unpainted planks with often unglazed windows gaping at them. As they walked forward, between one step and the next, the dilapidated houses were metamorphosed.

The buildings stretched and twisted, changed color; overhead, the stars became softer, the sun brighter but smaller—now just peering over the south western end of the valley. Dressed stone replaced rough-hewn logs, colored glass and delicately carved mullions shone with the quivering light of candles.

They walked on, into the village. Most of the changed buildings were low: one and two stories with high pitched roofs of red terra-cotta tiles. There were several taller structures though, tall and narrow, towers with many stories and tiny windows, masts rose from the tops with long gauzy pennons flapping and wriggling in a make-believe breeze.

At the center was a small plaza bordered with low box hedges. The open area was paved with smooth mosaics depicting knights mounted on unlikely looking animals and engaged in some sort of dual with long curved swords. Coy maidens looked on from the side lines.

"I am tempted," Calistrope said, "to believe I have reached some kind of latter day heaven, that I have left Old Earth entirely."

Ponderos was already touching finger tips to the stonework around them, rubbing them and feeling the dust between his fingers, tasting it. "This is all marble," he said.

"That's what it looks like," Calistrope agreed.

"But it's real," he said. "Real. Not an illusion, glamour."

Calistrope looked about him at the many different colors of marble: red and green, pink and blue and white with here and there black or silver tracery weaving its way like lace through the mottled colors of the stone. Windows and doors were tall and narrow with high-arched lintels, they were lined with glazed tiles showing leaves and flowers and abstract designs. Roof lines were bordered with tessellated patterns garnished with colored stones and glasses.

A scene from a story book, a fantasy.

"Magic?" asked Calistrope.

"Magic?" Ponderos wrinkled his brow. "We have detected no magic since departing the Raftman's Ease," he drew a long breath through his nose, repeated the exercise and raised his eyebrows. "A trace maybe. Just a trace."

Calistrope followed suit and nodded. "A trace."

Roli, ignoring the interchange, put his own point. "I want to know where everybody is. No sounds, no cooking smells, no people. Where are they?"

Calistrope shrugged. "It looks well kept, someone must sweep the paths and clear away weeds." Three pathways converged upon the square, the one which they had followed back from the wasps' nest, one on the northern side and a third on the western side. Calistrope nodded to the north side where the alley led between a saddlery and a baker's shop—the latter with still-warm ovens and fresh bread on the shelves. Both contributed a redolence to the air, one pungent, the other piquant. "The village is empty. Shall we try down there? It must lead down to the river."

The lane took them to the rear of the shops which fronted the square. Behind these were high blank walls enclosing silent courtyards where fruit trees lifted boughs over the walls, boughs laden with apricots and apples and dark rich plums.

"It seems darker," said Roli, turning a full circle as he walked. "Look at the sun, it's almost gone and the stars are brighter."

"That's remarkable," Calistrope stopped and looked at the last fragment of the yellow sun shining between jagged escarpments. "Does the world turn again?"

"Has the world returned to its old orbit?" Ponderos added. "If so, it saves us going any farther on our journey," he sighed. "However, I suspect after all, that magic is responsible."

"Perhaps but it is a spell that I have never come across before."

The lane wound between two of the secretive dwellings and out on to the level ground beside the river and here was a vast tent pitched upon the grassy expanse. Scores of animal pelts had been stitched together to make the canopy which was supported on a multitude of poles and drawn taught with hundreds of guy ropes pegged into the ground.

The side nearest to them was raised so they could see inside where people—the villagers, they assumed—were reclining on silk cushions and thick carpets. Tall golden jugs stood everywhere and from them the villagers poured the liquid into enameled goblets. They drank from their cups and ate fruits and sweetmeats from beaten gold plates. Men gazed at dark-eyed women and smiled, the dark eyed women smiled back and licked their red lips in anticipation.

So engrossed in each other were they, that no one seemed to notice the travelers until they stood between the sun and the nearer of the village folk.

"A good day to you all," Calistrope greeted them. Some nodded, a few replied with murmured words, most turned their gaze in other directions and ignored the newcomers. The sun vanished but even so, darkness did not come at once as was the case with eclipses or storm clouds.

"Perhaps I should bid you a good evening, for that is what it seems to be." And even less interest was shown.

Roli asked, "Why don't we just join them? There seems to be plenty of food and drink here. Enough and to spare."

"There is the philosophy of a street thief," Calistrope said to Ponderos. "Taking without asking."

"In this case, I think Roli has the right of it. No one here seems capable of caring one way or the other."

Roli had found a tray of cups and passed three of them to his comrades. He took up a jug and filled them with an effervescing liquor which smelled of apricots and lemons.

They drank. It was the most refreshing draught any of them had ever tasted. As they drank, a moon rose in the darkened sky—a silver boat against a velvet sea sparkling with individual snow crystals. They became drowsy. They sat, overcome by a delicious languor which could only be dispelled by more of the delicious liquid.

Those who reclined closest to them began to notice them and to complement them on their choice of garments. Calistrope was dressed in a blue silk gown belted at the waist with a jeweled tie which supported a curled sheath holding a dagger. Ponderos was similarly clothed though the color was peach and a vast round turban covered his bald head with a chrome yellow feather raised to one side. Calistrope touched his own head to find that he was also wearing a turban. He took it off to look at it—blue to match his coat though smaller and less enthusiastic than Ponderos'. A tuft of crimson bristles sprang from a diamond clasp which held the folds together. Calistrope replaced it and looked to see how Roli was accoutered but Roli was nowhere to be seen.

Calistrope shrugged. What did it matter? He poured another cup of sherbet and investigated a plate heaped with sweet pastries.

"They are good? You like them?" asked someone, a female someone whose lips were so close to his ear that her breath stirred his hair.

He leaned back a little and turned. "Oh yes. Yes thank you," he said. The woman was beautiful, her pale features set off by a cap of hair as black as the night above. Her skin was as white as alabaster almost everywhere, he noted, for she wore a few wisps of gauze and save for a cluster of gold rings on either hand, little else.

His pastry broke in half and crumbs fell all over his new companion's knees. Calistrope brushed rather ineffectually at the debris. "I'm terribly sorry."

She looked steadily into his eyes and took his hand. "That's quite all right. Please, do it again." And she brushed his fingertips across her knees again. She asked temptingly, "Should we find somewhere alone?"

Calistrope considered her suggestion carefully, for several moments—long enough to swallow nervously, just a little nervously; well—hardly nervous at all, really; he decided. "An excellent suggestion."

He got to his feet and helped the woman up. Calistrope would have told Ponderos he intended to be back soon but like Roli, Ponderos was no longer there either.

The hours of the sorcerous evening passed in delights that Calistrope had thought himself too old to enjoy. But the woman was unbearably enchanting and when they finally fell asleep, they were entwined together, his nose filled with the soft fragrance she wore. The counterfeit moon spanned the heavens, dew-drops formed on grass blades and spider webs, the warming rays of an imitation yellow sun shone from the replica of a long-ago sky. High clouds were turned to golden wisps, morning mists to saffron.

Calistrope awoke, astonished to have slept and still more astonished to find the beguiling woman still breathing slowly at his side, a secret smile curving her red lips.

She was real and not a dream. He touched her face and kissed her lips, he kissed the rosy nipples, touched the warm smoothness of her breasts, ran fingers over her belly, unable to take his eyes away from the loveliness.

Minutes passed slowly and slowly, she came awake, smiling up at him from the pillows.

The mouth opened, rouged lips grinned lasciviously to reveal broken yellowed teeth. Hard fingers with dirty nails reached up to draw him down against the fat belly and flaccid breasts of the old crone who lay on the grimy rags and sacking. A louse ran out of her lank hair and sought refuge among the broken pillows of what had seemed a sumptuous bed.

With a cry of horror, Calistrope drew back. Pulling his travel worn cloak in front of himself protectively.

She looked up and laughed, cackled. "Never mind lover, you're not the pretty boy you seemed to be either. Wait until the glamour is come again. Soon..."

Calistrope pressed his lips together and looked down at the bundle of clothes he was clutching and at his own body. There were rents in his coat and breeches, his knees were skinned, his fingernails were cracked and broken, wounds had left scars...

"Sadly Madam, you are in the right. Neither the boy I once was nor the man, yet my standards are fixed and will not be changed. I prefer to see things as they are and not as the make-believe world of these past hours would make me.

Calistrope pulled on his clothes haphazardly, he saluted the less-than-perfect maiden. "Goodbye, enjoy your dreams." His erstwhile lover pouted her lips at him, Calistrope left her and went outside the hovel they had found for their trysting. Almost at once Ponderos met him and minutes after came Roli, hopping on one foot as he tried to fit the other into his breeches.

Each of them opened his mouth to say something but all remained silent. What they had taken part in was best not talked about, was best put behind and forgotten—if that were possible.

Calistrope took out Issla's purse of silver powder and tossed a pinch into the air. Ponderos and Calistrope felt a weird tug inside them as the dust tried to pull at their own magical qualities then like smoke, the insubstantial stuff puffed indecisively hither and yon before divining a direction and snaking off towards the center of the village— now a huddle of log buildings again with gaps stuffed with moss and windows covered with sacking.

The companions followed it to the square where the streamer darted down and into a dark workshop, less broken down than some with smoke rising from its chimney.

A distant chuckle sounded. Words: "You enjoyed your night of abandon then, I'd dare to wager on that."

The door was ajar and they pushed their way inside. A wizened old man sat by the hearth with a pipe in his mouth, a tray of rusted tools on the table beside him.

"Enjoyed yourselves, did you?"

"In a manner of speaking," answered Calistrope. "Are you responsible for this wizardry?"

"In a manner of speaking." The old man managed a fair imitation of Calistrope's tart words. "A little conjuration and this," he patted a machine built from brass and leather and glass. It was perhaps, the only dust-free thing in the place, at one end was a cluster of lenses like the compound eye of an insect; at the other, an oil lamp with a polished reflector to channel the light into the box like body. "My magic lantern." And he patted it again.

"And you live your lives under the spell of this—this contraption."

"As much as possible. It's a poor enough existence here since the wasps came, there's been no trading down the river since I was a youth."

"As long as that?" asked Ponderos.

"Aye, indeed. We grow parbalows in the fields and trap shulies in the river, neither are very tasty until we transmogrify them with the aid of this," he patted his shining machine.

"What a way to live."

"And what's wrong with that. Hmm? Soon the river will dry up and the very air will freeze solid. Why should we not enjoy what is left of existence before our time comes? Eh?"

Calistrope was silent. Neither of his companions had anything to add. "I don't know," he said at last. "I can offer no argument against it. All I will say is that I'd not choose such a life for myself."

The other nodded. "That is all that matters then. Choose this or choose some other way. Choose what we know or what is unfamiliar."

"We will leave now. Goodbye."

Again the other nodded and as Roli—last in line—was about to leave, he asked: "Is there no other way past the wasps' nest?"

"The wasps' nest? Hmm." The magic lantern operator thought for a while as he scanned through a portfolio of pictures—a valley on the far-off world of Caldeburn, a city of immense towers from ancient Earth, a hillside of rich vineyards and golden cornfields. He selected this last and took an image of a primitive Moorish town from his projector. "Farming, you see? This will get them harvesting for a season then we'll have a bit more merriment.

"Now, past the wasps. Hmm. There's a side valley to the south. Half a league along there is a cave, it has a perfectly round entrance. It's of no use to haul produce through and I can tell you some of our young people went that way to leave the valley when it became too cold to grow anything but parbalows."

"In spite of your make believe, they left here for good?"

The other shrugged. "None returned to tell us how much better it was beyond."

CHAPTER 7

They stood on a ledge below the cave mouth. As they had been told, it was perfectly round; too round to be anything but artificial—a reassuring realization.

Calistrope looked studious, "Do we go then?" he asked. The other two nodded. "Very well. Now, a moment," Calistrope felt around in his bag and came out with a ball of thread. He wound the end around the stem of a convenient shrub and knotted it. "I think we have enough residual magic up here to make it stretch as far as we need it. Ponderos, the light if you please."

One by one they clambered up to the cave and stood inside the opening. It was perfectly circular inside as well and almost perfectly smooth, regular undulations in the tunnel's surface made it easier to climb the incline which they faced just inside. Eager to be on their way, they pressed ahead, the tunnel bored onward in long straight stretches with short curved sections where it changed direction. The changes in direction and slope were minor though, the tunnel always tending to the heading they desired. This was the case for more than a league at which point it swung around in a vast curve and split into four different routes.

"A pity that whoever bored this did not post signs," Ponderos grumbled. "That way seems to curve around again, perhaps towards the main valley."

They ventured along the new tunnel and eventually came to a dead end, the *cul-de-sac* being a perfect hemisphere bulging into the circular tunnel and closing it off, as if a large dull stone globe had been rolled into the tunnel.

"Now where?"

"Back again, oh!" Calistrope pointed upwards. "What about there?"

In the ceiling was an oval hole, the product of a second, higher, circular tunnel intersecting the one they occupied.

"Here," said Ponderos to Roli, "I'll lift you up and you can see what direction it goes. Here's the lamp."

Ponderos cupped his hands and Roli stepped onto his palms. Ponderos lifted him effortlessly and Roli disappeared down to the waist in the ceiling.

"Well?"

"Perfectly straight as far as I can see that way," he shuffled round. "And that way... Let me down, quick."

Ponderos lowered the boy and lifted his eyebrows.

"Get away from the hole, in case it sees us."

They moved away and stopped with their backs to the hemispherical plug. Above them, something slid across the hole, a silvery grey hide bulged through slightly and dripped a viscous lubricant into the lower passage. The flexible surface moved slowly past the oval aperture for several minutes, thick liquid dripped from the edge and a ring of gelid stuff collected on the floor beneath the edges of the hole before the creature finally went.

"One of the builders, do you think, Ponderos?" Calistrope murmured. "That is why there are no signs, they can't read."

"I think you're right," Roli said. "That must have been its back end, there were no features, no jaws or eyes or anything."

"So it goes backwards," suggested Ponderos.

"I'd imagine so," Calistrope reached out to rap his knuckles against the tunnel's end. "I mean, if it came this far and changed its mind, it would have to have backed up from here. That's strange."

"And what is that?"

"This wall gives a little. It isn't tunnel wall, not this end part."

Ponderos touched it. "Leathery," he poked it vigorously. "I wonder where it goes beyond here."

"Don't do that," warned Roli. "Something's in there." As he spoke a small tear started near the top and began to lengthen. They backed away. A silvery bullet shaped head poked through and bent this way and that. Small but wicked looking jaws opened and snapped audibly shut. Another head appeared above the first and a second tear started to one side.

"Babies," said Ponderos calmly. "And wicked looking things they are, too. Roli, up again—into the roof. You as well, Calistrope—I don't want to be caught down here with those things snapping around my legs."

Ponderos boosted Roli through the hole in the ceiling and then Calistrope. There was a slurping sound behind Ponderos and he turned to see a thick greasy substance oozing out of the tears which had now spread from side to side. Wriggling and twitching, the tunnel-makers' young slid towards Ponderos.

Calistrope leaned down and held his hand out for Ponderos to grasp. Calistrope pulled the other up to the lip and Ponderos then climbed the rest of the way by himself. "Where's Roli?" he asked as he stood up.

"Reconnoitering," said Calistrope. "That way," he pointed in the direction opposite to that taken by the adult worm. Calistrope picked up the light globe and they followed after—no more than a score of paces and around a curve to where daylight glowed.

This was where Roli had stopped; they looked out over his shoulder.

Directly in front of them was the rough papery grey surface of the wasps' nest. Beneath, on the same narrow ledge they had used before, was a wasp on sentry duty and strewn around it and on other ledges were bits of wasp—limbs, black and yellow chitin and fur. Two long strips had been torn from the side of the nest and wriggling grubs and translucent white eggs were visible. Insects were already repairing the damage from the inside.

"There's been a battle out here," Ponderos said.

"I would guess the worm we saw earlier has reached out of here and stolen a tasty snack," Calistrope stroked his chin. "There are signs of earlier depredations as well. I daresay it has been going on for a long time."

"We have been noticed," Ponderos warned them.

Sentry wasps had been signaled in some way and were crawling into the restricted space between nest and cliff. Glittering eyes stared up at them as the insects closed.

"We'd better follow the worm or go back the way we came, perhaps try one of the other branches."

A few minutes later, they stood at the edge of the hole looking down at the ten or twelve young worms below. Each was two or three spans in length and each was enthusiastically attacking its siblings.

A buzz behind them attracted their attention from the savage little worms. Two wasps were crawling along the tunnel towards them, wings partly spread in the confined space. Ahead, from the far side of the hole in the floor, came a rumbling, rasping sound; movement was just visible in the gloom. The tunnel worm was returning and judging from its young, the creature must have a pair of powerful jaws at this end of the body

Several long seconds passed.

Which way lay the best hope for escape?

Roli and Calistrope raised their swords almost simultaneously and took a step towards the menacing sentinel wasps.

"No," shouted Ponderos. "This way."

In the passage below them, four or five of the infant worms lay twitching—paralyzed by their siblings' venom. Others were already partly eaten.

Ponderos leapt down to the floor below. Roli And Calistrope followed. Swords whirled, cut... snick... snick... snick, three more of the aggressive creatures lay dismembered and dead; some of the newly hatched creatures reared up from feasting on brother or sister to watch the humans, perhaps considering attack, perhaps just caution. A sharp sword dispatched one and dissuaded the others.

By the time the adult worm's head stopped above the opening, they were ten or twelve paces back down the tunnel and ready to run if necessary. The wasps' wings created a high pitched whine as they rushed to the attack but despite their single-minded ferocity, they were outmatched by the worm's armored front end. There was a sense of flickering movement, scraps of wasp fell through the opening to be seized on by the youngsters underneath and then the worm itself thrust its head through the intersection.

Gaping jaws capable of dealing with rock snapped open and closed, tiny black eyes ringed the vicious mouth, and these regarded the men malevolently. The worm wriggled and pushed a little further through the hole, swinging its head back and forth, but it was clear it was not supple enough to make the almost 180-degree turn necessary to reach them.

"Ah," breathed Calistrope when it became clear that they were safe.

"Thank the fates," added Roli.

Ponderos grunted as the worm began to work its way back. "It knows we're here now. It knows these tunnels too; it hollowed them out, after all. Sooner or later it is going to sidle up behind us and that will be that."

"Then our course is obvious," Roli replied. "We get out of here, back to the wasps' nest."

As before, Ponderos boosted them through the hole in the roof and they, in turn, hoisted the big man to the upper level.

Roli leaned out with his arm outstretched. "I can almost touch it from here," he drew his sword and poked the tip into the grey papery wall of the wasps' nest. "It's all damp," he said.

"Well yes. I expect it's where the worm tore it open a little while ago," said Ponderos.

"Well," Roli became excited, "we could cut it open again and jump across, make it down through the inside of the nest—come out at the bottom."

"Very good thinking. As soon as we damage the nest, it will be seething with angry insects."

"No, no it won't," Roli was rather put out. "The guards are all on the outside, once they're grown they never go into the nest again—well hardly ever. There are workers in there, nursemaids, caretakers, cleaners and the queen of course but she'll be near the top."

Calistrope turned to Ponderos, skepticism written large in his expression. "Is he right Ponderos? Would we be safe in there?"

Ponderos shrugged. "I couldn't say. How do you know all this Roli?"

Calistrope's doubt nettled the boy. "Everybody knows that. It's common knowledge, you just pick it up."

"It's not common knowledge with me, young man. I never heard anything like that," Calistrope's tone was sharp.

"When was the last time you busted open a wasps' nest, eh?"

"Well, I don't remember..."

"When was the last time you talked to ordinary people? *Ephemerals*, eh?" Roli spoke the word with distaste. "How would *you* know anything about the *real* world, eh?"

"All right," Ponderos put his hands up, palm out. "That's enough. Squabbling isn't going to get us anywhere," he frowned at Roli, raised his eyebrows at Calistrope and continued before either could respond. "We all have our particular fields of knowledge."

Roli sulking, sat down in the tunnel mouth and let his legs dangle over the drop. Below to right and left, sentry wasps walked stiff-legged along the narrow ledges; above and below, they scrambled over the nest. There were dozens, scores of them, more flew in watchful patterns in the sky above the nest.

"So?" asked Roli. "What are we going to do?"

"We have climbing rope," Calistrope replied. "We'll make it fast up here," he looked for a suitable anchor, "here, through this crack and around this pillar. And we'll climb down the face."

Roli spat and watched the bolus fall between the nest wall and the rock face. He said nothing.

Ponderos asked numbly, "Can we evade the guards?"

"The guards are certainly going to come for us if we start cutting into the nest itself. I suppose we could go back through the tunnel, see if we can find another way."

"Well we can't sit here and wait for the air to freeze," Roli was still angry but a moment later the anger had vanished. "Listen, it's too late now whatever we do."

They all could hear it. The rasp of chitinous scales on rock coming from behind them.

Swiftly Ponderos unwound the rope from around his waist. "This is very smooth," he said, coiling the silken glass fiber on the floor. "No time for knots, we'll have to slide down and risk hand burns," he secured the end and threw the rest out of the tunnel exit. "Wait..." he said as Roli took hold of the rope. "Just a moment..."

Ponderos looked out; left, right, up, down. "Timing is important. We slide down to the first ledge, where the nest is almost touching the rock and we wait there until the worm pokes its head out. That's going to attract the wasps' attention, they may leave *us* alone."

Ponderos looked out once more, looked back into the darkness of the tunnel where a waft of acidic wind blew into their faces. "Go," he said.

Roli took hold of the rope, leaned out over the edge and walked himself down the face. He could not maintain a grip however and his hands started to slip, another downward step and his foot failed to grip and he slid the rest of the way.

"Calistrope, your turn," Calistrope followed his assistant. Hand over hand for two or three ells and then sliding the rest of the way.

Then came Ponderos. He made better progress than the other two but he had more than halfway to go when the worm pushed its head out into the open air.

Calistrope shouted, making frantic but unseen gestures to his friend. "Look out! The worm is here."

The ugly head bent down to seize Ponderos and missed him by a finger's breadth. Again it tried, thrusting out and downward and again it missed but caught hold of the rope. It parted as though it had been cut with a pair of shears. Ponderos came off the face with his legs working in seeming slow motion. In the same instant that Ponderos fell, Calistrope took a turn of the rope around a shard of rock. "Hold on," he shouted as Ponderos hit the edge of the rock shelf and windmilled out into the void.

But he *did* hold on. Calistrope's belay held and Ponderos swung back against the cliff and stunned, let go. His landing was softened by the timely arrival of a sentinel wasp crawling along a lower ledge; the insect's body bent and flattened as Ponderos hit it. Some instinct made his hands grasp as they felt substance under them, his finger's hooked onto the wasp's legs and again, instinct seemed to make the dying insect hold onto the rock.

Ponderos was saved, bruised and battered but alive. He was bemused but conscious enough to loop the end of the rope under his arms so that Calistrope and Roli could haul him back to them.

Ponderos pushed himself up to hands and knees with little yelps of pain. "Think I've cracked a rib," he muttered. "Maybe two or three. I'll not be doing any climbing up *or* down for a while," he got to his feet. "Still, Fortune favors our kind; I would be dead otherwise."

Roli looked up at the worm which had already lost interest in them. Impervious to attack by the wasps, it had again torn open the nest wall, its head and half its body inside the nest. The worm would be laying waste to hatcheries and nurseries while the less fierce insects would be impotent, unable to prevent its attacks.

"Why don't the wasps leave and build a new nest somewhere else?" Roli spoke over his shoulder as he helped Ponderos to a more dignified position.

"Very few insects can think, Roli; they simply don't link cause and effect which is what thinking is for. The ants manage it but only by a sort of collective consciousness."

"Well, however they arrange things, they're well-occupied now," he took his sword and made two deep cuts into the nest wall. He took hold of the flap and tugged at it, bending it out towards him. The wall was as thick as his finger but surprisingly soft and spongy. Roli climbed up to the opening and into the nest, he disappeared for a minute before returning and standing at his new window, "There's a ramp out there, coming up from below—*leading down*, is what I mean. Anyone coming?"

"Very well," agreed Calistrope with resignation. "Cut this flap a little lower so that Ponderos can get through."

Chapter 8

Calistrope helped Ponderos to cross and eased him down the sloping floor inside. They were in a small cell with an opening which, as Roli had said, led to a ramp. Wasps of many shapes and sizes moved up and down the incline on errands which could only be guessed at. Three pale looking wasps were just entering as Calistrope looked around the tiny space, the usual black and yellow bands with which he was familiar were faded, almost grey and cream in color.

"Caretakers," said Roli. "Smaller than the guard insects, see."

Apart from avoiding them, the so-called caretakers ignored the humans. They went straight to the hole which had been cut in the wall and began repairs: cutting loose the flap and then cementing it back into place. It took no more than three minutes but while they worked and the humans—still disregarded—watched them, there was a sudden increase in activity outside the room. Dozens and then scores of insects were all at once trooping upwards, the procession included the unmistakable forms of sentinel wasps.

"Soldiers," said Calistrope, pointing. "You said they wouldn't be inside."

"The worm," said Roli. "It must be doing more damage up there. Perhaps it's getting too close to the Queen."

"Getting too close to us is what I'm worrying about," Calistrope looked wildly around the bare cell for some way of concealing them. "Come on, start tearing up the floor over here. Next to the wall."

Puzzled, Roli came across. "Whatever for?"

"The repairers will try to stop us, they'll hide us from outside."

The ruse seemed to work. Certainly the three maintenance wasps clustered around the companions, attempting to interfere with their depredations and hiding them from view. None of the guards came into the enclosure.

The rush slowed to a few wasps going about their everyday business and they ventured out, leaving the caretakers to tidy up the damage they had inflicted.

"Well. Down that way?" Calistrope pointed to where the floor sloped down and out of sight. As he posed the question five or six small wasps came into view—another contingent of caretakers who seemed to outnumber all the other varieties of insect in the community. Like the previous party, they detoured around the group of humans, taking no notice of the strangers in the nest.

"You see?" Roli pointed out. "The soldiers would bite your head off without a moment's hesitation. Most of the others won't care a jot."

Calistrope nodded, aware of Roli's crowing. He merely followed, supporting Ponderos as they went.

The ramp was a tight spiral with openings leading off into enclosures. As they passed and peered in, they saw storerooms of seeds, fungi and dead rodents which reeked of decay. Others held tall paper cylinders like huge organ pipes, the air smelt sweet and heady with fermentation. Some variety of honey, or wax Calistrope guessed. There were still more rooms which were completely bare—not in use as yet.

Light filtered through certain areas of wall which had been left especially thin. The illumination was dim for human eyes but sufficient when they had become used to it.

"Shades," said Roli, halting. Two insects came round the central pillar which supported the spiraling ramp; brilliant yellow, dense black. "Guards."

Calistrope let go of Ponderos and drew out his sword. Before the wasps could react, he had confronted them and hacked viciously at the head of the nearer of the two, he sheared off one bulbous eye and the jaws. Roli followed him in and decapitated the injured wasp while Calistrope closed with the second.

The wasp snapped at him, taking hold of the glass sword and trying to shake it from his hand. The blade was too smooth, the wasp could not retain its grasp and Calistrope lunged as soon as it slid free. The point went into the wasp's mouth and came out of the top of its skull; bizarrely, it inflicted no damage and this time, shaking its head, the wasp pulled the sword from Calistrope's hand.

Cursing, he kicked out at the weaving carapace and the wasp backed off with Calistrope's sword securely lodged in its head.

Roli had gone beyond the wasp while it had been engaged with Calistrope to see if any more followed. The two were alone, he found and turning back, he slashed at the wasp's rear end, cutting of the deadly sting and its sack of venom. While the wasp turned its head to find its new aggressor, Calistrope leapt close and pulled his sword free. This time, the weapon must have severed some nervous tissue; the insect collapsed in a tangle of legs. The wings buzzed three or four times and stilled.

"I thought we faced our end, just then," Calistrope said, sheathing the glass sword.

"Practice," said Roli. "We've had quite a lot of practice at looking after ourselves."

"Yes," Calistrope nodded. "We have."

Ponderos had stumbled to the side of the corridor when the fight began and now Calistrope supported him again. They began the descent and two maintenance workers passed them to pick up the remains of the guards.

"That's uncanny. How do they know when to come?"

"Or where? They started in on repairing our entrance before we had left the room."

"Calistrope," Ponderos paused a few minutes later, as they were passing by one of the empty rooms—a space which opened up towards the nest's central axis. "How near to the bottom are we?"

Ponderos shrugged. "Roli, have you any idea?"

"Near the bottom, I'd say. Perhaps three, four floors, five."

"Then this is where we must do it."

"Do what?" Calistrope eased his friend's arm from around his neck and stretched his back.

"We should set fire to the nest before we leave."

Calistrope frowned. "Whatever for?"

"We have to come back this way. Do we have to hope that the worm will attack them again at just the right time?"

"Come back this way?" Calistrope had not given the matter of return any thought at all. "Well, yes, I suppose we do." The concept of *return* seemed almost unreal.

"If we set fire now, then we don't have the problem—and don't forget those villagers, too. With the nest gone, they will be able to trade with the coast again, their lives will change for the better."

"I can't see them doing anything like that again. They're too bound up with their imagined riotous living."

"Don't be so hard on them. When they realize it's possible, they will change."

"Very well then. Let me have that flame of yours."

Ponderos felt—very carefully—in several pockets before he found what Calistrope wanted. Moving his arms carefully and grunting at his hurts, he pulled out a small cylinder. Calistrope took his knife and crouched, he began to cut and tear long strips from the floor. A little while later, he gave up and sat back on his haunches. "No. It's no use Ponderos. It's too damp. Won't burn."

"Then we'll have to go back, higher. I expect condensation and other liquids run down the spiral and soak into the lower parts of the nest. It will be drier further up," Ponderos lurched to his feet. "Give me the flame."

"Don't be silly," said Calistrope, "you aren't fit enough. Stay here with Roli and I'll go."

Calistrope left the others and began to climb back up the ramp. Somehow, he guessed, worker wasps had been alerted to the damage he had inflicted on the nest; he had climbed past two floors when a line of four of the insects filed past him and continued downwards. Calistrope turned and followed them. They stopped outside the enclosure where Roli and Ponderos were hiding; inside, the insects crowded the humans to one side and began to chew with their mandibles at the broken floor, as they worked each little bit into a sort of paste, they patted it down and smoothed it.

As before, the workers would hide his friends from insects with more serious intent.

Calistrope looked at the others. "There," he said and grinned. "Protection". He left them to it and ascended, running up the ramp. He passed the place where the workers had appeared and carried on until he was out of breath before stopping to test the floor and walls. Finally, Calistrope was satisfied that the material was really dry and would burn fiercely.

He was still on the ramp and worked quickly to tear enough papery scraps up to start a fire. He uncapped Ponderos' little cylinder, inside a small blue flame flickered, as it had done for the countless years that Calistrope could remember. He piled the scraps in the angle between floor and wall and set fire to them.

A worker came by, two, three, several, alerted by the smell of smoke perhaps. Calistrope had to keep pushing them away to allow the flames to get hold and even when they were roaring up the wall, fed by a growing updraft of air, the insects attempted to extinguish it by smothering the flames with their own bodies. Had there been more of them, the wasps would have succeeded but a great number must have been trying vainly to repair the damage to the egg stores made by the worm.

Satisfied the fire would not be put out, Calistrope tramped back down to his friends and supporting Ponderos between them, they made haste down the last four floors or so to reach the bottom of the nest where the main exit and entrance was.

They came to a final turn of the ramp and Roli, slightly in front, stopped and backed up, dragging Ponderos' bulk with him. "Soldiers," he said. "Guarding the opening."

"How many?" asked Calistrope.

Roli let go of Ponderos and sidled round the curve again. "Five," he said a moment later.

"That's too many. Especially with Ponderos unable to fight."

"Oh come on..." started Ponderos.

"No my friend, you're in no condition..."

"Will you listen? I was going to point out we have to cut our way out of this thing anyway, the main entrance, as I remember, is over the river... unless you've got any ideas about wings? And we'd best choose a store place on the outside or we'll still be over water."

"Wings? Hmm," Calistrope shut his mouth and nodded. They backed up a dozen paces or so and found a store stacked with oval plates of some shiny material. They pushed some of the stacks over and went to the wall. They set to work, the soggy, water-logged paper was quite difficult to cut but at length, they had an opening large enough to see the river bank through and perhaps, the height of a man below them.

"You know what this stuff is?" asked Roli, examining one of the pale yellow plates. "It's wax. Make a nice fire with this."

"Fine. The only fault with that idea is that it's just a little late."

Roli went first, jumping to the river bank and steadying Ponderos as Calistrope lowered him to the ground.

Down at the side of the river, Roli drew a great breath of fresh air. "Let's go before we draw any more unwelcome attention."

They hurried off until two minutes later, Calistrope stopped them. "We're going the wrong way."

"Don't be... how can we be?" Roli frowned.

"Look up. No worm—if it's still there—but no tunnel entrance either, no hole in the nest. We've cut our way out on the other side of the river. It's this way."

They about turned, walked under the nest again and out the other side. A few minutes after emerging from the nest's shadow, they could see part way around the curving wall—there was the worm fighting off the aerial attacks of sentinel wasps; further on still and they could see where Calistrope's fire had taken hold and was burning out of control. A huge plume of greasy black smoke rose in billows into the dark sky.

"Ponderos, you mentioned wings back there," Calistrope's voice was ruminative.

"I did?"

"Suppose we could catch some wasps and train them to carry us..."

Both Roli and Ponderos stopped and looked at their friend with consternation.

"Perhaps not wasps," Calistrope continued. "Perhaps something less dangerous but big enough to carry us while they..." he noticed their expressions. "... You don't think it's a good idea?"

"I need to rest awhile, Calistrope," Ponderos was firm. "I still hurt all over. Now you're making my brain hurt as well."

"Me, too," added Roli. "I'm tired."

Calistrope sighed. "I suppose there's no reason why we shouldn't stop for a while," he looked around. "Not a lot of choice though," they stood aside as a swarm of small hoppers skittered along the hard beaten trail, the swarm was followed by a pair of beetles intent on picking up and munching the slower individuals. "The bank is very narrow here."

The river ran hard up against the valley wall at this point and the game trail they followed had become narrow and constricted. They rested awhile, fending off the attentions of a number of hungry creatures before Ponderos decided the aches and pains of walking were easier to take than constant hostilities.

They continued on slowly until they came to a place where the river became wide and shallow enough to cross without getting wet above the knees. On the southern and kindlier side of the water they began to look for a suitable place to make camp. They threaded their way through an area of large boulders and rounded a final spur of rock.

"What's that?" asked Ponderos. A tall spire was visible in the distance.

"How should I know what it is?" Calistrope grumbled. "Why don't you look at your map for a while and tell *me* what everything is?"

"Because you prefer to tell us."

"Well. That's a good enough reason, I suppose," Calistrope searched his pockets for his copy of the map, checked his cuffs. "Do you have my map Roli?"

"Try your little bag."

Calistrope rooted around in his bag. "I wouldn't have put it in here, too many other... aha, here it is," he opened the map and traced their route. "The Exhibition?"

The Exhibition was deceptively far off. The spire they had seen swelled to grander proportions, grew in height as they approached. It took on shape and form, it became a statue. A woman in flowing robes and a crown. She held her arm up above her head; she carried a cone shaped torch with a flame molded from some translucent material.

They came to halt a hundred paces away, their heads tipped back until their necks creaked.

Calistrope cocked his head to one side. "She's not upright."

"Ah, you recognize her?" Ponderos chuckled. "But I think you're right, she leans a little to the left."

"Is this the Exhibition, then."

"An exhibit, I think Roli," Ponderos pointed along the river bank. "See, there's something further along *and* beyond that as well."

"We should investigate these things Ponderos, they must be unique."

"Calistrope, if you think I'm going to put one more foot in front of the other before I sit down for an hour or two, before eating and drinking my fill, then you can think again."

"That goes for me, too," said Roli.

"Oh no it doesn't," Ponderos did not mince words. "You are going down to the river to catch six or seven crayfish and a hatful of water for tea and Calistrope is going to help me bind my ribs. Are my words exact? Do I need to explain anything? No? Good."

So Roli spent half an hour turning over stones at the edge of the river and ten minutes collecting driftwood for a fire. He filled Calistrope's collapsible panikin with water for cooking and the shell which Ponderos used for brewing tea, set them on hearth stones to boil and at last, sat down. "There. It's done."

"Me, too." Calistrope helped Ponderos with his shirt and leather vest and sat down himself.

They ate. Drank aromatic tea. "Oh, that was excellent, excellent. Those crayfish, Roli, some of the best I've had. Calistrope? What do you say?"

"Very tasty Roli. I believe I will sit here a little longer, there's no point in risking indigestion."

"None at all."

Roli, by nature rather more restless than his older companions, roamed the shore. Ponderos and Calistrope were content to watch the water streaming past where high-stepping insects picked their way from one stone to another looking for tasty tidbits of their own in the magenta tinted foam and bubbles.

It was all very peaceful. Until, of course, Roli disturbed them with urgent cries.

"Now what?" asked Calistrope with resignation. He stood up and looked up the bank's rise to where Roli stood with legs and arms spread out. "Now what?" he said more loudly.

In answer, Roli made a pounding motion with his right fist. There was dull thump, as though he had hit a bass drum.

Calistrope and Ponderos approached cautiously. It appeared that Roli was leaning his weight against thin air. It proved to be a barrier, a barrier so clear and clean that it could be sensed only by touch—except at ground level, Calistrope noted. Where the unseen barrier touched the ground, there was a sharp edge to the sand where it had piled up against it a little.

The barrier was non-reflective, non-refractive; it had no texture discernible, a finger slipped along the surface without registering sensation of any sort. Smooth, transparent, impassable. Roli had simply walked right into it.

"Impossible," Ponderos decided. He shook his head and slammed his palm against the unseen surface with all his might. The blow produced exactly the same drum-skin noise as before.

"No, no," Calistrope smiled. "It's here isn't it? So it is not impossible. You and I—even Roli, here—are accustomed to seeing apparent impossibilities. We call it magic."

Ponderos sniffed. "There's no magic here. No smell of it," he closed his eyes for a moment. "No, I can't feel a thing. No magic. This is just…"

"There's a sign over here," Roli had walked a little further along, around the barrier's curve. "Can't read it though."

When they came to it, a small rectangular sign set at ground level, they saw it bore a single word composed of characters which none of them had ever seen before. Strange cursive lines with a half melted look to them, quite unknown.

It came as a minor shock to Calistrope and Ponderos. Apart from minor differences in dialect, speech and reading-writing were the same everywhere, understandable communications between human beings had long ago become instinctive. It was almost impossible to invent a new spoken or written word that could not be comprehended by all or almost everybody else.

They continued on and eventually discovered the barrier to be circular, a protective case right around the majestic figure within. A great bell-jar placed over the statue by some giant hand to protect it from the elements.

"Here is another sign," Ponderos nodded at the small plaque. "And readable this time though it's still gibberish."

N'York, the sign said. As meaningless as before.

"I suppose it could be a place name," Ponderos surmised. "They can sometimes seem irrational."

But Calistrope was considering other aspects. He did not reply.

"This is more recent than the Ants' map suggests, I suspect," Ponderos suggested. "Look at the creases in her robes—as sharp as the day they were cut by the stonemason's chisel. Even protected from wind and rain, they'd not stay as sharp as that, surely..."

"The map—at least the original—was made long before the world stopped turning," Calistrope said. "When the sun shone white."

"So the Ants told you."

"I've no reason to distrust them, I'm not certain that ants *can* lie—that takes a human being, I think. Besides, it isn't stone that the statue's made from. I believe it to be metal."

"Metal?" Ponderos was incredulous. "Come now Calistrope, that's taking things too far."

"Well we'll see. Let us look at this next one. It seems to be a building."

They walked away from the statue. The distance was a furlong or two to the building which took on a more and more wondrous appearance as they approached. So marvelous in fact, that the nearer they came, the slower they walked.

"That is beautiful," breathed Calistrope. "The statue is inspiring but this is... this is pure beauty."

For once Roli said nothing, both he and Ponderos were as stunned as Calistrope.

The structure was built from white marble with pastel hued veins of blue and pink and green running through it. Tall archways gave entrance to the interior which was shadowed but gave hint of intricate stone carvings and sweeping arabesques of silver inlay on the floors. The roof: sheets of burnished copper which reflected the burning rays of some unseen sun, slender spires topped with the heads of serene gods and goddesses. Despite the decoration, the architecture had a simplicity which defied time—it might have been created since the world ceased its turning or could just as easily date back to the great eras of *Dispersal* and the *Rekindling* of civilization.

The astonishing building was reflected perfectly in a pool of still water which lay before it, between it and the circular barrier which surrounded and protected it. The ground around the building and the pool was covered in a dense green of what they assumed was a sort of moss, a variety with short narrow leaves like miniature sword blades.

"And another sign board," said Roli, first to break their silence. "Unreadable, too."

On a tour around the building which was almost as incredible from the sides and rear as from the front, they encountered other signs in differing alphabets. One of them was lettered in familiar script, so mundane that it had no name and seemed remarkably out of place next to this exotic edifice. *The Tomb of the wife of Al Jehan*, it told them.

Calistrope frowned. "A tomb," he said to himself. But Ponderos, less introspective, called their attention to the sand which was blown by a freshening breeze. The thin film of dust was sliding down to the ground leaving the surface of the barrier unstained and clear. It was, however, sliding down the surface of a hemisphere which evidently closed above the building.

Ponderos wondered if the barrier was in fact a globe, penetrating underground as far below as its height above.

Calistrope was still looked at the sign. "I wonder who this Al Jehan was," he murmured. "And who was his wife. Why so grand a... Roli, I am out of touch with such matters, what happens to people when they die?"

Roli pursed his lips, shrugged. "Sometimes they are buried though more often burned."

"A tomb though. What is the purpose of a tomb?"

"To keep the memory alive? I don't know," Roli kicked at a knob of rock. "In my family, we counted ourselves lucky if we could find enough to bury," he leaned back against the barrier, his hands deep in the pockets of his surcoat. "This is morbid stuff Calistrope. Death is not fit subject for discuss..." Roli fell suddenly backwards onto the greenery which came up to the barrier's perimeter.

Calistrope and Ponderos rushed forward to help him up and stopped just as quickly. The wind had abruptly died, the sound of rushing waters had stilled, the myriad squeaks and chirps of insect life were silenced.

From the pool in front of the mausoleum, the sound of a fish jumping left a widening ring of ripples on the surface which shattered the perfect reflection.

Somehow they were on the inside of the barrier while outside, beyond its invisible locus, the world was compressed, as though seen through a distorting lens. It flickered as they moved, like a scene seen though the gaps in a board fence and overhead, the clouds raced across a sky stippled with black and silver bars. The sun alternated between the timeworn maroon bloat and a blinding disc of white.

CHAPTER 9

To one side, the great statue looked down at them, her calm visage holding an enigmatic smile. To the other was the great building which had—on the outside—stood half a league or more in the distance; here it was no more than a furlong from them, an effect of crossing the barrier between dimensions.

For a few minutes they stood and looked at the Tomb of Al Jehan's wife then, by common consent, walked on to the next building which now was revealed as a low pyramidal structure, perhaps three chains on a side. Even though it was low in proportion to its spread, it grew in stature until it dwarfed the building they had just left. A single portal was visible on the triangular side which faced the river. A narrow slot cut straight into the wall, internal radiance flooded out through the opening laying a long, straight path across the sand.

"Another tomb?" wondered Ponderos.

Calistrope shrugged. "Who knows?"

Attached to the sloping face just outside the entrance was a sign. In mundane characters it read: *the Palace of Turain the God.*

"Huh!" Roli snorted, looking up at the stark and unadorned slabs of sandstone, chisel marks still evident in the stone facing on the sloping walls. "Well. Turain the God certainly prefers his palace plain. Shall we go inside?"

Calistrope shrugged once more. "Why not? Another hour or two is not going to matter much one way or another."

They passed through the entrance, so narrow that perforce, they walked single file. Each of them gave an involuntary gasp of amazement as they reached the interior threshold. "Not so plain," said Calistrope, his eyesight blurring with tears until they became accustomed to the brilliance. Light bathed the whole interior in a creamy-white, shadowless luminescence. "And there," he added when he could see plainly once more, "Turain the God."

At the geometric centre of the hollow pyramid, on a raised dais, a great gilded statue sat indolently upon an equally massive throne. Beneath the gold leaf, the figure was naked, a huge belly swelled over massive thighs, great dugs drooped over the greater belly and had not been for the obvious signs of masculinity, the statue could well have been that of a pregnant female deity.

In contrast to the rude, unfinished state of the exterior, the inside surfaces of the pyramidal palace were covered in white and pink alabaster slabs. Faces—both angelic and demonic—were carved along the tremendous arches which supported the enormous plates of masonry. The floor space was covered with square and rectangular courts filled with colored gravel.

The pebbles seemed to be gemstones, sometimes rough and dull, sometimes polished and sometimes cut and flashing like rubies and diamonds. Colors ran the gamut of the spectrum: red and blue, white and yellow, green, purple, indigo, black.

The area immediately surrounding the statue and its dais was bare, a border of plain white sand some two or three ells in width. Above them loomed Turain the God, the statue's head halfway to the high ceiling. The dais was at waist height, the throne supported on a smaller platform upon the dais; ten blue-painted toenails faced them, the largest the size of a man's hand print, one foot was a little in advance of the other.

Behind the glittering toes, a pair of gold bangles encircled each ankle from which rose a pair of shins to knees like cauldrons and thighs like tree trunks. From there, the eye traveled up and up, across the mound of belly, the puffy flesh of the chest, the fat wrinkled neck and to the severe face of Turain the God.

Turain looked sleepily down at them from slanted eyes all but enclosed by fleshy lids.

"Shall we go closer?" Ponderos almost whispered so overcome was he by the richness and the brilliance.

Hands rested on each of the throne's arms. Fingers encased in rings encrusted with jewels grasped the rounded ends. One of the fingers, carrying a ring with a stone of clear translucent blue, twitched.

"Um," began Calistrope and stepped back a pace.

"Er," said Ponderos and followed suit.

"Ouch," yelped Roli springing to one side as the hand closed on the space he had occupied a heartbeat before.

All three of them separated and backed away.

"Ha ha ha!" The God's deep laugh rumbled away and echoed throughout the cavernous building like thunder. "Ha ha." Turain bent forward, arm outstretched, finger straining forward. Just beyond his farthest reach, Ponderos stood firm. By the width of a hand, Turain was just unable to prod the Mage in his muscular stomach.

"Well well," said the God. "After all this time," he boomed.

Ponderos' gaze traveled up the finger, the forearm, the flaccid biceps and then to the great jowly face grinning down at him.

"Worshipers. Real, live people come to worship me." Turain labored to reach Ponderos. The finger moved nearer by a knuckle. "Nearer little man. Come nearer and know what it is to have a God touch you."

Ponderos remained where he was and strain as he might, Turain could not reach him without getting off his throne, something he seemed loath to do—perhaps because of his monumental weight. After a moment or two Turain relaxed and Ponderos moved back another step or two, over the low curb and onto one of the squares filled with gems. Calistrope and Roli did the same, moving back and sidling up to stand next to Ponderos.

"I have to admit to you that our allegiance is to another persuasion entirely."

Turain frowned and it was though dark storm clouds gathered over them, then his expression cleared, bright sunlight shone from a corner of the lowering skies. "That is of no moment. You are here, that is what matters. Devotion to some other gloomy deity who won't disturb his slumbers by looking over his demesne—how can you compare such a one to me?"

Turain leaned forward once more. "My worshipers feel my love for them, I care for them, nurture them. Come, let me but touch one of you and you will *know* what I say is the truth."

"Why should you want our poor devotion?" Calistrope edged sideways, into Ponderos hoping his friend would take the hint and they could leave.

Turain's eyebrows lifted towards the golden hairline with its artful border of curls. "Evangelism. I need more than you three to worship me. Without a following, I am chained here. Go from here and bring me converts, your reward will be great, more than your small minds could possibly envision."

Calistrope had met Gods before.

A world with a history as long as Earth's accumulates Gods by the dozen, by the score. Whatever event triggers the creation of a God or elevates a person to God-hood is, fortunately, a rare one. However, multiply that rarity by the millions of epochs of an aged world's life and it must have occurred hundreds, thousands of times.

Gods, from the small strutting self-important kind to the great aloof beings who can barely comprehend the verities of physical life—Calistrope had met enough. And he did not care to be coerced into proselytizing for any of them.

Roli, next to Ponderos, whispered to him. Ponderos nodded and leaned towards Calistrope. "Keep Turain talking," he whispered and Calistrope was left to keep the conversation afloat alone.

"What do you need a congregation for?" he asked. "The truly ancient Gods think their own thoughts. They do not wish communion with the likes of us poor mortals—um, souls."

"Souls? Look around you man. Look at the souls of the millions upon millions who once worshipped me. They sleep here now, dreaming beatific dreams for all eternity. No more toil and hardship, eternal bliss is their lot."

Calistrope could think of little that he would care less for. However, he kept the thought to himself. "Souls?" he asked. "What souls?"

"All about you. The baubles that even now, you tread on so thoughtlessly. They were my worshippers and have come into their own reward."

With alacrity, Calistrope stepped off the blue gems under his feet. "Souls?" he said in wonderment.

"Souls. You live, little man, then you die. Without a patron such as myself, what happens? Pff! Your soul flits away like a moth and expires. Here you will sleep and dream forever."

Calistrope shook his head. "I have already lived more lives than I can remember," he said. There were subdued sounds from behind the dais; a glimpse of movement. "And they have all been filled with more interesting things to do than dream."

Turain did not answer him. The God's eyes seemed focused on eternity, his jaw gaped.

"Turain?" Calistrope went closer. There were more sounds from the rear of the dais and Turain's eyes snapped wide open, Calistrope could feel their blaze like hot sun upon his skin. The hand reached out faster than a bolt of lightning, the tip of the God's index finger brushed against his chest, light flooded Calistrope's brain.

Joy and happiness, ineffable pleasure, sublime contentment... brilliance, radiance, warmth. It visibly streamed towards him from Turain—a beautiful youth whose smile was like the springtime sun. Tenderness enfolded Calistrope; love, compassion, sweeter than a mother's for her new-born infant enveloped him, buoyed him up.

Here was Calistrope's heart's desire, everything he had ever sought after, everything he would ever need.

Calistrope was bathed in the warm glow, the beneficent rays of a young sun caressing his body, his mind, his soul... and it all suddenly died away...

Darkness, cold, loneliness. A loneliness such as he had never felt before came over Calistrope. He wept great tears of grief, rivers of anguish. He lay on the hard ground of that brilliantly lit place and cried in the utter desolation of the darkness of the God's going.

"Calistrope. Cal..." A warm, hard muscled arm cradled his head. A familiar hand stroked his brow. "Whatever is it that ails you my friend?"

Calistrope looked up, silhouetted against the brightness was the dark shape of a familiar face, a friend who had loved him since long before their present memories began.

"It's Ponderos," said the friend.

"Ponderos," Calistrope sighed and with a great effort, pulled himself to a sitting position. He looked up at the now still statue of Turain and shivered.

"It's all right Calistrope. We found the key and turned it off."

"Off?" Calistrope's brow wrinkled. He touched me Ponderos. He poured his love into me. It was like... like... I can't explain it Ponderos, I can't describe it. Now that it's gone, it's like the greatest loss I've ever suffered."

"It was an automaton, Calistrope."

Calistrope shook his head. "All that love, just for the taking."

"Not real Calistrope," Ponderos, his voice harsh, wrestled Calistrope to his feet and together, he and Roli marched him around the side of the dais to the back. "Not real, Calistrope, look."

Calistrope was still on the edge of despair but he allowed himself to be manhandled and pushed onto his knees beside a hole torn into the back of the dais.

"Roli noticed it first. The statue is part of the throne—or vice versa. Turain couldn't leave his seat, it's all a clever working model."

Calistrope peered into the hole where a panel had been torn away. Inside, the dais was hollow. Pipes sprouted from the ground and connected to pumps and cylinders which were, in turn, connected to wheels and gears and levers. More tubes ran up the inside of a dark shell—what could only be the torso of the seated God on the throne above them.

On a casing, just inside the opening, was a handle. It rested in an upright position. Roli took hold of it and wrenched it downward, it turned on pivots through 180 degrees. There was a sigh of in-drawn breath from above them, an exhalation...

Calistrope's eyes swiveled upwards in their sockets and he slumped forward. Softness engulfed him, tender thoughts stroked his mind, loving... "Off," he groaned. "Turn it off for *God's* sake, turn it off..."

The sensations faded and he opened his eyes once more. His head was haunted, his mind tormented by the remembrance of that suffocating love, the terrible certainty that here *was* the one true God.

"Can you break it Ponderos? Break it so that it can never be used again," Calistrope sat down with his back against the side of the dais and when he heard the shriek of tearing metal, he nodded. "Thank you my friend."

Later, as they supported him to the doorway, Calistrope asked: "What's a penny?"

Neither Ponderos nor Roli could give him an answer.

"Something I heard once," he told them. "A priest, I think. I'd stolen a jewel for him. "God's are ten a penny, nowadays." He said."

Outside, after some time had gone by, Roli went to the pool in front of Al Jehan's Monument and caught three of the silvery fish. Baked, they proved very good to eat.

Calistrope sat and ate what was given him and drank when the cup came around. *All those souls,* he mused. *As lovely as gems and as hard. What would happen to them now, now that their God was dead? What was there to inspire their endless dreams?*

While Roli slept and the hours passed by and the curious piebald moon rode the skies of the exhibition space, Calistrope sat and told Ponderos of what he had experienced.

Ponderos, brow wrinkled, tried to make his friend realize that it was all a sham. "This is an exhibition, Calistrope, of ancient monuments. There was no God in there, just a clever model."

"I felt Turain's touch, Ponderos," Calistrope reached over and placed his hands on either side of Ponderos' skull. "Inside. I spoke to him..."

"We all spoke to him."

"... and him to me. Terrible and beautiful, Ponderos. Incredible."

"Ersatz emotions, ersatz feelings. They were projected by the machinery underneath the throne, so that whoever the automaton touched could feel what the power of a God felt like."

"Well," said Calistrope, only partly convinced. "Perhaps you are right. I hope you are."

A fish leapt from the water at their side and splashed home again. The sudden noise disturbed Roli and the lad sat up, his hair disheveled and eyes puffy. He shuffled over to the fire and poked about in the ashes until he found a few fragments of the fish they'd baked between the hearth stones.

"Well?" he asked between swallows. "What do we do now? Anyone—" he picked a flake of white fish meat from between his teeth, "know how to get out of here?"

"I've no idea at the moment," said Calistrope. "Perhaps the same way we got in here, by wanting to."

"However we do it," said Ponderos, "it would be better to walk east from here until we come to the end of this little cosmos. Distances are not so great in here; we would save ourselves some effort."

Calistrope raised his eyebrows. "I never thought to hear *you* advocate an easy way, my friend."

"That tumble from the cliffs has aged me, Calistrope. While I have to favor these ribs, anyway."

Roli grunted. "An easy way is the way to go," he fished in his pocket and pulled out a grimy kerchief on which to wipe his greasy fingers. A shower of clear blue stones fell from the folds as he shook it out. "Hmm. Forgotten those," Roli began to pick them up.

Calistrope waited until he had picked up every one he could find. "You'd better put them back where you found them," he said.

Roli looked at him oddly. "Put them back? There's a Guildmaster's ransom here Calistrope. You should be pleased with my foresight, we'll all be rich men when we return."

"They're souls Roli, not gems."

"Come now Calistrope, They may not be sapphires but I'd thought we'd cleared all that up. Not souls again."

Calistrope shook his head. "Whatever. They are not sapphires, Roli. Have you never seen a sapphire?"

"Of course not. A few copper flakes was the best haul I ever made."

Calistrope fumbled in his bag and brought out a flashing blue stone which caught the mixture of silver moonlight and the magenta sunlight and threw it back in a score of different directions and blues. "That's a sapphire. Cut, of course and polished," he handed it to Roli who compared it with those from Turain's palace. Reluctantly and somewhat crestfallen, he handed it back.

"Keep it," said Calistrope and Roli was at a loss. "I can always make another."

Eventually, Roli settled on delight as the pre-eminent emotion and dropped the other stones into the moss and short leaves.

Ponderos broke in. "Shall we go?"

"*Oh no.*" The voice was not Calistrope's nor Roli's but that of a sudden newcomer who's form wavered like a coil of smoke on a still day. As they turned to regard the newcomer, the figure strengthened, grew firm, became that of a man in his middle years, a man with a thin acetic face and long somewhat unkempt hair. He was dressed in a blue robe which both matched his eyes and the blue stones which Roli had thrown away a minute or two before.

"No," said the man again, his voice more vigorous than before. "Certainly you have done us a service but having gone this far, surely you cannot go without finishing the task you began." What started as a threat ended almost as a plea.

"And what task is that?" asked Ponderos, a dangerous edge to his voice.

"You have freed twenty seven of us. You must free the rest who still sleep and dream the insipid fancies foisted upon us by Turain.

"And how, pray, would we do that? Hmm? Twenty-seven of you out here, how many millions of you in there?" Ponderos asked as he saw the vaporous forms of other men and women burgeoning from the fallen soul-stones. "In the Palace of Turain the God?"

"There must be a way." The shade almost wept. "There must."

"I can think of none," Ponderos was cool. "Whatever we did, it would be a grain of sand on a beach. A nothing. If we labored a, er, a lifetime, it would still be nothing."

Calistrope laid a hand on his arm. "Let us think about it Ponderos, at least. Let us sit down here and think. Perhaps there is a way," he looked at the released soul. "Sir, what is your name? Do such as yourselves have names?"

They sat down. The shades gathered about them.

"I am Arctorius, from the Delphine."

"And I am pleased to make your acquaintance. I am Calistrope," Calistrope introduced the others and then turned to Roli. "Roli, have you more of the stones on your person?"

"Well, yes."

"Then give one to our ectoplasmic friend here."

Roli took out a green stone and offered it. Arctorius took it and looked at it. "From the Alamatera."

"Beside the point," said Calistrope. "The point is, that you can hold it, you have enough substance to carry the stones."

The other nodded.

"Then each of you go back into the palace and bring out a double handful. Wait until they sublime or whatever you call it and let each one who returns bring out two handfuls. It will take a long time to—to resuscitate the many millions but it can be done and with no great effort from any of you."

"We cannot go in there. The light will condense the souls into hard stones again. That is what it is there for."

"The light?"

The other nodded slowly.

"Hmm. I wonder if the stones float. Roli..."

"Why?" asked Ponderos.

"Perhaps we could float them all out with water."

"And where would the water come from?"

"That's a different problem. Roli..."

"No it isn't, Calistrope. It's the same problem."

"Well, there is a certain logic in what you say. Still..." Calistrope thought for some time and then grinned. "Another solution occurs. If these, er—evaporated? If these souls can carry the soul stones, are they material enough to carry ordinary stone? Would you try it? Lift that one there, the flat one."

Arctorius bent and took hold of the stone. He straightened up, lifted the slab."

"Good," said Calistrope and grinned again. "The solution then, is simple. The roof of the pyramid is formed from slabs of stone, so we lift a slab and let natural light into the palace. The natural light will resuscitate your fellows—at least, I think so. Roli?"

Roli turned, a question in his expression.

"Be so good as to take two stones and put them on the ground. Keep your hand over one of them."

Roli did as he was bid and Calistrope put his own kerchief—considerably cleaner than Roli's—over the lad's hand. "Now we wait."

They waited. A streamer of white vapor eventually curled up from the uncovered stone, the vapor darkened, took on form, color; a lovely young woman looked down at them with sparkling but puzzled eyes.

Calistrope took the square of linen off the other gem which, in due course, became a young man with an age and racial aspects similar to those of the woman.

"You see?" asked Calistrope, looking back at the main group. "Natural light. That is what brings you back to life."

"You have a clever mind," said the speaker for the souls.

"Indeed I have," Calistrope replied, his grin a trifle too wolfish to be entirely trusted. "Now. I said we will lift the slabs, but the *we* was purely rhetorical. *You* will lift the slabs—although my muscular friend here, will, I am certain, be happy to lift the first one for you. Will you do that, Ponderos?"

"Naturally. Follow me, Arctorius." Ponderos crossed to the pyramid to do as Calistrope had asked. "Your deductions were brilliant, Calistrope. As always, of course," he said as he passed by Calistrope.

Ponderos climbed part way up the twenty degree slope and began checking the stones which faced it. He found a slab that seemed less secure than most and slowly worked it free, letting it slide down the slope to the ground. Another followed it and another. Light from within shone on his face.

"Quite enough, Ponderos," Calistrope called, hoping that what he had seen had gone unnoticed.

Straightening up, Ponderos waved and slid down the slope, jumping over the several squares of stone that had preceded him.

"Now," said Calistrope. "Your turn." And as first one, then another, began to scramble up the slope, Calistrope ushered his two friends away with some urgency. "Time we left, too," he told them.

"Calistrope, the light inside the palace is really very strong. It might swamp the daylight on the outside."

"That is a possibility. A very real possibility and one which I have taken into account. Ponderos, I would prefer to leave quite soon."

There was a sort of long, drawn-out ping from above them. Calistrope guessed it was the sound made by a soul being reduced to a small, hard stone.

"In fact, I wish to leave immediately."

Roli had heard the start of the conversation and had not waited for its outcome. He was already halfway to the barrier when the sound of conversation among the reconstituted souls changed from *heated* to *enraged*. Ponderos and Calistrope lost no time in catching up with him.

At the barrier, they stood with hands against the unseen surface. "Now, *want* to get out of here with all your strength." The crowd of souls was coming nearer. "Concentrate. All else is inconsequential."

In the end, it was not a matter of mental muscle; rather, it was more the way in which the problem was considered. Roli was first to find the trick. Perhaps his past history of thievery helped or perhaps it was the familiar sound of angry voices in pursuit or even the combination of both which made him take the mental side-step *past* the barrier rather than *through* it.

Moments later, Calistrope and then Ponderos joined him and turned to look back through the boundary. Inside, the preserved world was as it had been when they first came upon it: a tall statue with a serene countenance, a beautiful mausoleum reflected in a placid sheet of water, a large low pyramid.

They walked parallel with the river, along the bank towards Turain's Palace and by chance, Roli chose that moment to look back over his shoulder. He plucked wildly at Calistrope's sleeve and then pulled Ponderos to a halt. "Look," he gasped at last and pointed.

Little more than a chain away from them, directly in front of Al Jehan's Mausoleum, three figures stood: a tall spare fellow in a midnight blue surcoat, a slightly shorter but much broader man and a youth. At the point where they, themselves, had first slipped through the barrier, the three others contrived to pass through also. Inside, they were visible for a few moments against the light from the placid pool, then they faded from view.

Calistrope cleared his throat and turned resolutely away and began to walk. Ponderos and then Roli followed after. They walked for an hour, passing Turain's Palace, which stood within its shell, unaltered: plain, craggy, unadorned. Intact.

Old days came and went. The valley they traveled along—sometimes narrow, sometimes with many leagues separating the high walls—meandered onward towards the East.

CHAPTER 10

The mesa had actually been in view for some time, perhaps as long as an hour, before anyone noticed it. It was an ancient volcanic core rearing up from the river—in actuality, a vertical sided island, the river dividing and foaming around its base. It was black basaltic rock, the sides cracked and flawed by the freezings and thawings of a geologic age. All manner of vegetation grew in the crevices and along the ledges and at the top was a fortified community, its castellated walls forming a lighter colored crown to the conical hill.

A line which zigged and zagged down the side resolved itself into a stepped foot path. The path ended at a rickety bridge of stone bulwarks and wooden floor planks that crossed the river. One of the spans was supported by an overhead gantry of timber poles and counter-balances. A pair of dwarves stood at the bridge, ready to raise it should unwanted visitors chance by.

At the very top, a tall chimney rose above the walls, and a waft of smoke or steam rose upward until a crosswind whisked it away in tattered streamers to the north.

"This must be the place," said Ponderos after staring at it for some time. "The map is inaccurate."

"I cannot believe that," Calistrope looked from his map to the water-bound hill. "We are not yet halfway to where Schune should be."

"Is this place marked?" asked Ponderos, his finger stabbed at the map. "No, indeed it is not. Even though lesser landmarks are shown, God's Finger for example. We passed it before coming to that place with the magic lantern, you remember?"

"Yes, yes. I remember."

An interesting phenomenon, no more, yet that was marked, this is not and Schune is marked only as an afterthought."

"Suppose," said Roli quietly, "that we visit this place. If it is not Schune then we can continue; if so, then our journey is shorter than we had expected, that is all."

Calistrope looked at Ponderos and Ponderos stared back. Ponderos was the first to smile; Calistrope, the first to speak.

"Roli is, of course, quite right. The solution is a simple one. Was I not wise to choose him as my apprentice?"

"Undeniably."

The bridge's rickety appearance was no more than appearance. The wooden planks were reinforced glass, the counterweighted section was operated by a small humming motor and the two dwarves which guarded the bridge were a pair of cunningly made automata which smiled and greeted them as they reached the island side.

Nor did they have to climb the forty ells to the top, a large open sided cage hung on a thick rope and wound them slowly to the top when they had all stepped inside. As the cage rose, the white foam of the river below reflected more and more of the sun's color until it seemed a river tainted with blood. The air also grew noticeably cooler and each of them wrapped their cloak around themselves.

The cage lifted them through a square hole in an alcove of the outer wall. A stout glass-fiber trapdoor thudded closed underneath them and the cage was lowered to the ground.

"Greetings to all of you," said a person who was obviously waiting for them. He wore bright clothes—a red jacket and yellow trousers, he smiled, bowed. "We get very few travelers here since the wasps built their nest upriver. May I inquire where you have traveled from?"

"Sachavesku," Calistrope answered.

"From...! That is west of here, I believe. West and south."

"Indeed it is. The nest you mentioned is gone."

"I'm pleased to hear it. Trade has dwindled to nothing over the past generation. Come this way please."

The man who had welcomed them clapped a wide-brimmed hat back on his head, and took them over a courtyard to where an avenue opened. Judging from its length, it ran entirely across the small township.

"The Street of Heroes," he said with a flourish. "Along here you will find craftsmen if you need new boots or a cloak, bakers if you are hungry and an inn if you are tired— the inn also boasts an excellent dining room, fine ales and wines, too. To the left, as you go, is the shambles and to the right, the fishmongers."

"Thank you for your welcome," said Calistrope. "I look forward to all your town has to offer. May I know what it is called?"

"This is Peronsade," replied their guide. "I am Mayor, official Hospitaller and Master of Banquets so I urge you to enjoy yourselves. On the other hand, I am Mayor, Prosecutor General and Jailer so beware of offending the citizenry."

"We shall bear all this in mind. Thank you Sir."

The Mayor left them and they walked along the street which had small trees planted in tubs along both sides of its length.

"Well, it's a pleasant enough place," Calistrope looked forward and back, to right and left. "But not Schune."

"How can you say that? Perhaps the old name is forgotten and has been supplanted," Ponderos shook his head. "We must make inquiries before we can be certain."

They began to walk. The Street was long enough for only a handful of heroes though there were no signs anywhere to tell them which heroes were honored. A few minutes later they came abreast of the side streets. Their noses confirmed the trades to right and left—the smell of flesh and the smell of fish, respectively.

A little further on, they came to the Inn: a tall building of four stories and two gables with a frontage as wide as two small shops. Land was clearly at a premium in a place like Peronsade, presumably it cost far less to build upward than outward.

They turned into the doorway where a counter of polished planks of black hawthorn confronted them, a white glass bell was the only item on the counter. Calistrope tapped it with a fingernail, a clear mellow note rang out and instantly a figure appeared.

"Ha. Good day gentlemen," said the Mayor. "Permit me to introduce myself: Lang Wonethop, Landlord of the *Gad fly*. May I offer you bed and board?"

"Board," said Calistrope.

"Bed," replied Roli.

"Board and bed," said Ponderos. "In that order."

"Very well, Sir. A copper sequin each, if you please and if you wish to stay longer, I can provide an abatement on the tariff. As to board, a main meal will be served at the eighteenth hour or light refreshment at once. I might add that all beverages—and they are all excellent—are brewed here, under my supervision. Wines as well, of course. Fermented from selected fruits of the neighborhood."

"How long is it to the eighteenth hour?" Ponderos asked.

"Aha, travelers. Easy to become out of touch with the clock. Now, it stands at a third before seventeen. A little over an hour to dinner time."

They chose rooms on the highest floor for the view afforded by the windows. A view of the valley and the racing waters which lay ahead of them. "Think," said Calistrope, throwing open the window, "if we had wings like wasps, how easy to fly along there."

"I have heard this before, it makes no more sense now than it did before," grumbled Ponderos. "I am going to bathe in the hot tub in my room then eat myself into a daze. How, in the name of Fate, do they get hot water up here? Eh?"

This was only one of the many mysteries of Peronsade. There were the constant streams of water that ran along the gutters in every street, the lights which lined the pavements to relieve the gloom on cloudy days and more lights fixed to the ceilings of the corridors and on the staircases.

The dining room took up most of the ground floor with a kitchen occupying a walled-off corner and a pantry and storehouse. A beer cellar—they discovered later—was in a basement level below street level

The ceiling was made of roughly adzed boards supported on great beams as thick as a man's waist. The unshaped trunks of nine great trees supported the inn, founded on the rock floor of the basement and extending upward to the roof beams above. Generations of diners' exhalations and the steamy fumes from their dinners had stained the woodwork a rich dark brown which flavored the very air with pungencies from a thousand different dishes.

Narrow windows along front and back let in red light though the high buildings on either side of the streets outside reduced this to a glimmer and a dozen globes had been fixed to the ceiling to augment this with a creamy light.

The companions perused the menus and ate nuts and dried beans and drank tiny glasses of appetizing liqueurs before deciding on their food.

The meal was excellent. Following a soup course—a bowl of thick vegetable broth flavored with chopped anchovies—they ordered the main course. As usual, Calistrope made a capricious selection of dishes: nuts marinated in vinegar, preserved eggs, leeks boiled in salt water and a bottle of wine dry enough to pucker the lips on the hobgoblin's effigy carved into the wooden cornice above him.

Ponderos went for bulk, three tenderly baked crabs in a piquant sauce and a mound of sliced and roasted turnips with fried beans. Roli ordered a panful of shrimp and a plate of red watercress. Both he and Ponderos had a jug of sweet beer.

"Now that," said Ponderos twenty minutes later, "was what I call real food. I shall keep these shells to use for plates on our travels hereafter."

"Then, you are persuaded that this is not the place our maps call Schune?"

"Not at all. Our travels will include a return to Sachavesku surely?" a man-shaped automaton had come to the table. "... Ah yes?"

The half-size humanoid shape was made of dull, copper colored glass with silver eyeballs and long, jointed, metallic fingers. "Would the gentlemen care for puddings or refreshing drinks?" There was no mouth to speak with but words trilled from a cone-shaped orifice at the top of the spherical head. It was dressed in sober white and dark brown clothes, as self-effacing and as deferent as the most expert of waiters.

"Pudding," Ponderos spoke before anyone else could utter a word. "What is there?"

"Rice flavored with brandy pears in cold sauce suet dumplings in plum sauce biscuits of almond..."

"Dumplings," Ponderos cut off the unpunctuated recital as soon as he caught the word *dumplings*. " Dumplings in plum sauce."

"As you wish Sir what of the other two gentlemen please."

"Another beer," Roli said.

"What refreshing drinks are there?" asked Calistrope.

"Green tea, persimmon tea with butter roasted bean, tea sour plantain, tea hot lemon and infusion of nettles with pepper and green apple..."

"Bean tea." Had Ponderos and Roli laid bets, both would have lost their stake. Bean tea, they would have thought, could not have stood a chance against sour plantain or even pepper-nettle tea.

When the servitor returned with their orders—exactly right, balanced on a tray and each offered to exactly the right person—Calistrope asked it about Peronsade.

"Has the town always had this name?"

"I have heard no other spoken of."

"Do you know of a city called Schune?"

"I have not heard of such a place."

"Is there anywhere here in Peronsade from where the world can be moved?" Ponderos asked, a trifle bleary after his vast meal. He belched. "Pardon."

"Of course," replied the mechanical servitor.

Calistrope's jaw dropped, Ponderos shot him a glance of triumph.

"Whereabouts is this place?"

"At the residence of Somta Pantel."

"Thank you," said Ponderos and began to ladle thick cream over his bowl of dumplings and plum sauce. When the automaton had gone, he grinned at Calistrope. "You may congratulate me at your convenience."

"Well, yes. My congratulations, Ponderos. I did not imagine it to be so simple."

"You must learn that not everything is difficult, Calistrope," Ponderos finished his dumplings and put down his spoon. "Now, I am off to my bed, after a meal of these proportions, my digestion works best in a horizontal position."

Calistrope found an opportunity to speak again to the servitor about finding the home of Somta Pantel.

"Ask any of us," it said, eyes sparkling in the dimness. "All of us know all of us know whatever the others do."

The companions slept, woke, took breakfast. They stood on the street outside the *Gad Fly*.

"So, we go to talk to this Somta Pantel?" Roli asked.

"In due course Roli. Our host said we could have new boots made if we needed them. Mine," Ponderos lifted his right foot to show how the heel was worn away, "are almost finished."

Calistrope looked along the street in both directions, pointed, "There is a boot maker," he pointed up the street where, above a narrow window, a wooden sign had been cut in the shape of a high boot. *Bunda Freng* it said and underneath in small red lettering: *high quality footwear*.

They crossed the narrow roadway and while Ponderos went inside to be measured and to pay, Calistrope and Roli wandered along in front of the shops. Without exception, all were narrow fronted with living accommodation above on one or two stories. Here and there, gratings in the paved sidewalks showed where cellars had been dug out to provide extra space.

Ponderos rejoined them. "They will be ready at the sixteenth hour," he told them and showed them his receipt: an oblong of green cardboard with the number *16* written in red ink. They continued along the street, looking in windows which displayed everything from artwork to vegetables, books to wines. A steady stream of townsfolk passed them or overtook them. Most spared a moment to nod or to say a word of greeting, even to gesture at a wine merchant and comment on the day's prices or to look at the sky and mention the possibility of rain.

"Rain?" asked Ponderos after the last observation. He looked up and felt a spot of moisture on his face. "The fellow's right?"

"It was a woman," Roli pointed out.

"Then she's right. Where is it coming from? The sky is cloudless."

"The vapor from that chimney must be steam," said Calistrope, nodding to the tallest building of Peronsade. If the weather up here, or up there, for it must be fifty ells high, is cool, the town will have rain."

"Steam?"

"Excuse me," Calistrope spoke to one of the little mechanicals which walked purposefully along the street at intervals.

"Sir you require directions to the house of Somta Pantel."

"That is so."

"One moment." The mechanical bent, picked up a leaf which had blown into the street and popped it through a door in its chest. "Follow me."

They followed it as it paced along on short legs, stopping every minute or two to pick up a piece of debris, a dead insect or to move a stick which was blocking the water flow in the gutters.

"Here is the house of Somta Pantel press the knob at the center of the door." The street cleaner left them, it picked up a fallen scrap of paper and disposed of it, went on about its business.

Calistrope pressed the large knob at the center of the large black door. A chime full of rich overtones sounded within the house. Presently, the door opened and a stout man with flowing white hair and a curiously blank look stood there.

"Yes? Ah!" Comprehension flowed across his features. "Calistrope and Ponderos and Roli. They told me you would wish to speak to me. Please enter." Pantel stood to one side to give them room and closed the door with a bang when they were all inside.

They stood in the hall, long and narrow and with a number of doors opening off each side, each one was a shiny black set in a frame of similar material. The walls were contrastingly white with a line of glow globes along each wall to provide a brilliant light.

"You wish to talk about moving worlds they said. How exactly can I help you?"

"The sun is shrinking and the world gets colder. At some time..."

"Yes, yes. The Freeze. The End of all things."

"But it need not be so. Is there a place we might talk more comfortably?"

"There is of course. First, I wish to confirm that I am not about to be harangued by a visitation of religious fanatics."

"Religious? No, no. I don't think we could be described as such. Ponderos and myself are mages from Sachavesku, Roli is my apprentice."

"So it's magic, not religious zealots?"

Calistrope looked disappointed. "Magic is merely a word, a name. Anything that is not understood can be called magic."

"Well it's true enough. Come on then. This way."

Somta Pantel led them down the hall to the last door on the right. He opened it and ushered them in ahead of himself. The room was large though its exact dimensions were difficult to make out because it was only dimly lit by seven large globes of various colors. They hung at head height and many—in fact, Calistrope realized, all but one of them—had tiny globes accompanying them. Several seconds later, as Pantel indicated chairs, Calistrope realized what he was seeing.

"This is an orrery."

"Just so," laughed Pantel, pleased that at least one of his guests recognized the contrivance. "Since we are to talk of moving worlds, I thought this must be the most appropriate place to talk about it.

And Calistrope began to see how large the room really was. Pantel was very wealthy or wielded great influence, so much horizontal space in Peronsade must be expensive.

"Bluta," said Ponderos. "Neptorn, Juba, Earth, Sadtun, Marr. And what is that one? Ah yes, the cinder world."

"Quite so. There used to be a ninth, you know? Merca. Very close to the sun, vaporized when the sun expanded, became part of the star itself. Relative to the far stars, each planet you see occupies its proper position."

"And the sun itself?"

"If turned off, it is easier to see the worlds, Pim," he addressed a mechanical which evidently controlled the astronomical display, "Switch on the sun, low brightness."

An irregular cloud, roughly spherical formed at the center of the orrery. Its nebulous outer edge seemed to brush the world of Marr.

"Now, what was it you wished to speak of?"

"The sun is shrinking and as it becomes smaller, the Earth will get colder."

"Indeed that is so. Pim, take us forward a million old years."

The dim red cloud began to collapse in on itself. The worlds became blurs as they moved and spun through astronomical distances in seconds. When the shifting stopped, the sun was a cold hard point of light at the center, the moonless Earth, which by chance, had stopped farthest from them, reflected a tiny gleam of off-white light.

"What temperature would there be on the Earth?"

"Three degrees," sang the musical warble of the little automaton. "Three degrees above the ultimate chill."

"It need not happen, you said."

"No," said Calistrope. "It need not. The world can be made to spiral back towards the center . To its old orbit or closer if needs be, so the sun will continue to warm it."

Somta Pantel frowned. "What you say is true. When the sun grew old before its time and began to wax, the Earth was pushed out beyond Sadtun to save it. Doubtless, it could be sent back again."

"It *could* be done?"

"I don't doubt it. The engines must be restarted, the direction computed and thrust applied. Pim, how much thrust could be employed and for how long, to do what we have been discussing?"

"I cannot perform the computation so quickly nor alone."

"I will have it done, my friends. Come back in... how long Pim?"

"Fifty thousand seconds."

"Fifty—how long is that in hours?" Ponderos asked. "Or days."

"About fourteen hours. Come back after your next sleep," advised Pantel.

Calistrope stood up. "Thank you for considering what we had to say."

"Not at all, gentlemen. It is an interesting idea, it has captured my attention."

Calistrope noticed Pantel's eyes again. There was the same silvery flicker between his eyelids that characterized the automata and his left hand, the Mage noticed, was made of the same many segmented fingers which the little mechanicals employed. As Somta Pantel aged he was replacing those parts which wore out with mechanical prostheses.

"Did you create these automata?" he asked.

Pantel smiled. "Indeed, yes. This community was built by them many years ago now. Without them, it would be just a primitive little hill fort, like many you see."

"And the power used here; the lights, the heating, water..."

"Is galvanic. We drilled a deep well with a very clever machine. Water from the river falls to the hot rocks far below."

"And rises as steam to turn the machines which make your power."

"You know about this?" Pantel was surprised.

"I have read about it. Conducted a few experiments even. The steam generation, the principal, is said to be used in the water and air regeneration plants of course but galvanism, on this scale, it is a great achievement."

"Thank you."

"Also, I presume the hot water in the houses, the water washing the streets—these are, so to speak, by-products?"

"Exactly."

"And the mechanicals, they are powered by galvanic fluxes? I take it you made them."

"Every word is true," he said then to the automaton he referred to as Pim: "Pim, will you show these gentlemen out? I have to think about the problem they have set me."

Calistrope, Ponderos and Roli explored the small town. They took a light meal at a cafe which also served interesting liqueurs, an armorer sharpened their swords on a carborundum wheel, a map maker showed them maps on which Peronsade was shown but Schune was not—at least not at the location that the ants had marked.

Then it was time for a larger meal and since they were more refreshed than before, they stayed in the dining room of the *Gad Fly* as tables were rearranged and a small stage assembled.

The *Gad Fly* provided entertainment for its patrons.

The first performance was given by a conjuror, a talented young man who had an obvious following among the somewhat older women of the town. He made jewelry disappear and found it in unlikely places on the persons of the more mature ladies among the audience. While watching him carefully Calistrope absent-mindedly made a bowl of green cherries fade slowly away; Roli found the cherries later, in the left hand pocket of his tunic. They never did find where the bowl went to.

After the conjurer came a musician. *Diamante*, he called himself and he played a tall narrow harp with a round sound box between his feet. Diamante's voice might have benefited from some training but the solos he played on his harp were the stuff of sheer fantasy. The man was simply lost to the world when he played, the end of each melody coming unexpectedly and leaving him as startled as his audience.

At length they retired to bed and were called early the next morning by a wake-up boy with a list of times and room numbers. Following breakfast, they made their way once more to the house of the roboticist.

"It is done," Somta Pantel told them. "Come, watch."

In the hall with the orrery, they sat once more and Pim made the model solar system follow its calculations. The Earth swung along its path, turning so that one face only confronted the misshapen sun. Gradually its velocity was slowed; as its primary shrank, so it fell slowly inwards, spiraling past first Sadtun and then Marr. Finally, it took up a stable orbit around the sun, which was now a dirty white point at the system center .

"Four hundred and twenty eight thousand years, Calistrope. In approximate terms, the Earth will have to be slowed by three leagues a second."

"So it can be done."

"I don't see how. To bring about this change would require the same amount of energy that the sun squanders in something like one hundred days."

"But the engines—it was done before!"

"True. Spread over almost half a million old years, it is possible to handle that sort of energy, but no one knows where these engines are. Nor can *I* see where so much energy can be found."

"But the engines are here. Surely? You said—"

"No, Sir. They are not. *I* did not."

"No," Calistrope thought back over what had been discussed. "You didn't. I inferred—wrongly. We mistakenly thought Peronsade to be the place where these engines are. Well, we must continue our journey."

☙

Ponderos visited the boot makers.

"Oh yes, Sir," said the boot maker, inspecting the receipt. "Ready at the sixteenth hour. Tomorrow."

"Today," said Ponderos quietly.

"But—"

"Today. *Now.*"

"But I cannot make them while you wait."

"What have you ready? In stock?"

"Well. How do feel about red leather?"

"No. It's not my color."

The boot maker opened a floor-to-ceiling cupboard filled with footwear. "Blue? Purple? No, I suppose not." The pile of boots behind him grew as he sorted through the cupboard's contents. "Aha. Green? A very dark green?"

"Not black?"

"No. I have no black ones."

"Very well."

The companions were let down the side of the cliff. On the bridge, the two mechanicals lifted their hands. "Fare you well," said one.

"Thank you," Calistrope replied and they resumed their journey.

At one point a distant vista was visible. The valley was very broad here with the river divided and subdivided into countless channels of racing waters. At the farthest reach of the eye and dwarfed by distance, a solitary mountain thrust upward from beyond the horizon.

Calistrope pointed. "Schune," he averred. "The City of Schune is built upon the slopes of that mountain or perhaps in the foothills, we need not be obsessed with exactness for the moment but that is our destination."

"Unless the map lies to us," Ponderos was thinking of the journey which still lay ahead, a journey which he had been convinced until a few hours ago, was over. He was presently in a gloomy mood.

The remark irritated Calistrope for the sight—however distant—of their destination had cheered him and here was his friend pouring ice-water on his enthusiasm. "Ponderos, I am tempted to believe you were born a paranoid."

"Oh no," Ponderos replied with a shake of his head. "It is a habit I have learned from careful observation. In circumstances such as these, it is a most healthy attitude."

"Nonsense," Calistrope admonished. "The weather is fine, the view exhilarating. Look at these fine blooms along the wayside."

"Flowers? Bah!" Ponderos sneered as he walked on, leaving Calistrope bending over a stand of blood-red blooms growing at the top of leafless rods behind him. "My stomach rumbles, Calistrope! I have just pampered it with fine foods and great wines, and now it protests at what is to come. There are times when I wish I was back in Sachavescu! There is small eating place in a cellar hard by Bart's, do you remember it?"

"Well..." Calistrope began as he straightened up. He felt a tug at his collar and shoulders. His coat tightened under the armpits, his feet left the ground.

"They baked calamares in a black sauce made of the squid's own ink," Ponderos continued without a backwards glance. "*That* was a dish worth waiting for! I took it rarely so it would never become too commonplace to me."

There was a sigh of wind over membranes, and then the feel of wings dipping and thrusting. Calistrope looked up at the underside of the huge moth which was bearing him up and away from his comrades."

"Ponderos!" he called, his voice weak with surprise.

Chapter 11

Calistrope's heart pounded and his breath came in short gasps; vital seconds came and went before the shock abated. He cried out and more time passed before either of his friends thought to look upward. At last, they finally spied him—a black silhouette against the sun's magenta sprawl.

Calistrope could see them pointing and gesticulating. Perhaps Ponderos attempted some magic but with no effect—the ether was as empty and as flat as stale beer.

The moth's huge wings—an ell or more in length—beat steadily, the ground dropped away, Ponderos and Roli were minuscule smudges, smudges with pale dots for faces. Then Calistrope was alone, hanging by the shoulders of his coat beneath the insect. The air sighed past him, growing thinner and the hum from the creature's tracheal bellows deepened.

Soon the cold began to eat into Calistrope's body and his autonomic systems closed down one by one, conserving heat and energy. The last to go was vision, a black space which swallowed the last of consciousness.

The great expanses of dirty snow glittering with a hundred shades of dark vermilion went unseen as the moth rose above the continental edge. Here was the litter of eons: crumbling mounds which had once been ancient cities, wandering furrows ploughed by long-dried rivers, great blocks of ice shining like monolithic rubies. Far to the southeast was the sugar loaf shape of a mountain with its tell-tale plume of vapor, clear in the thin air: Schune, where the world's engines were.

The moth, struggling a little with the weight of its prize, flew parallel with the rift until it reached a place where one of the old rivers had once poured over the continental edge, a hanging valley notched deep into the southern wall. The moth relaxed its efforts and lost height, gliding into the high valley with no more than a twitch of wings.

As the air thickened, Calistrope revived and began to shiver violently. He recalled his predicament and looked down in time to see the greater rift disappear as they swept into the breach cut into the southern wall. The floor of the new valley sped by beneath his boots; a silver watercourse wound along its length with great cushions of moss and pockets of brush and small trees to either side.

Where they had entered the valley, the walls were half a league apart at the top, narrowing to a chain or so where the river leapt into space. The moth headed up the valley which closed in rapidly, its sides becoming rocky and precipitous, lined with cracks and fissures. The insect slowed and dropped towards one of these, alighting clumsily on a ledge before a narrow entrance, it dragged its catch inside. Calistrope was still half frozen and numb, incapable of movement, he could do nothing when he was lifted and suspended from a rocky projection by a cord around his chest.

He hung there, turning slowly as the insect backed away to inspect its work. With a tremendous effort, Calistrope raised his arms and fumbled awkwardly with the silk cord securing him. The movement alarmed the moth and it reared up, with its forelegs it clasped Calistrope's body to it, he felt the creature's ovipositor slide forward. In a fit of revulsion, despite the cold and stiffness, the Mage found the energy to writhe in the stick-like embrace.

The insect clung to him, legs hooked into the clothes below his arms, its wings vibrating to maintain balance. The long sharp tube sought for purchase, found it, thrust, plunged home. Calistrope knew total horror as he felt the pressure against his side, felt the pulse of eggs being expelled.

The moth shuddered with the ecstasy of procreation and the tube was retracted. One last task—Calistrope's body was made to spin, silk threads jetted from the moth's clustered spinnerets and wrapped him from chest to ankles. The moth left him to hang, twisting first one way then the other.

Calistrope felt physically sick. Somewhere inside him a cluster of eggs nestled, a few days from now, ravenous grubs would hatch and feast upon his insides. His end would be indescribable, a hollowed out husk filled with wriggling worms. Merciful oblivion overtook the Mage; his mind, unable to contemplate such a revolting fate, such stark horror, simply withdrew.

The cocoon conserved the Mage's body heat, and so from numbingly cold he grew uncomfortably hot—and in this state he awoke again with sweat streaming down his face and trickling along his limbs, torturing his nerves with its tickling. At least he could move easily now and his arms, he discovered, were still unbound. Calistrope knew hope, at least he could take his own life before the brood did it for him,

The silk covering was quite loose, and with a little struggle, Calistrope pushed the cocoon downward until he could reach into a pocket. He drew out a small clasp knife, opened it, and began to cut. The silk strands parted easily and when he was free of the cocoon, he braced himself before cutting the cord which suspended him.

The drop was rather less than he had expected and he landed awkwardly, spraining an ankle before rolling down a steep slope onto a pile of brittle bones and debris. Calistrope hobbled towards the cave mouth and looked out. No insect guardian, he was free to go and even though he was determined to kill himself, Calistrope preferred to do so in such a manner that his remains would not be food for grubs. Perhaps near the small river, so his body would be swept over the edge to the floor of the rift a league or more below.

A new thought struck him. Where had the eggs been laid? Even now, warmed and with restored sensibilities, he could feel no wound. Presumably the insect secreted some sort of anesthetic, if so and if the eggs were near the surface or in some non-vital part of his body, then it might be possible for him to cut the clutch out. A risk but any risk was worth the attempt in this case.

Calistrope stripped himself naked and with some effort, contrived to touch every bit of his skin. Nothing. No cut, no incision, no sign of violation. Puzzled and not entirely at ease with the discovery, Calistrope dressed himself and picked up his bag, still with him after all the leagues, through all the adventures the three of them had shared along the way. He slung the bag from his shoulder and there was the *clink* of something falling to the floor.

The Mage stooped down and looked for whatever might have fallen. A tiny gleam caught his eye, a key! The key to his manse, tiny but imbued with surprising power. Calistrope dropped it back into his bag and discovered where the moth had deposited its eggs—in the side of the bag was a finger sized hole, within were seven round yellow-white eggs.

With grim amusement, Calistrope limped across the cave floor and clambered down outside. He gathered dried twigs and tinder along the base of the cliffs and presently found a place to set a fire. The Mage took out a small pan from his bag, and certain condiments; the eggs, he decided, would be best scrambled.

Feeling surpassingly cheerful and light headed now that the awful prospect of death by ingestion had receded, Calistrope considered his future. A trickle of water dripped from a stony point on the cliff nearby, he washed his pannikin, filled it and set it to boil for tea.

First, there was his injured ankle to take care of; he bound it and wished for the barest breath of magical power—time was the only physician for the moment.

Second on the agenda was his future. Here, time was irrelevant, he supposed. Ponderos had a copy of the map, he and Roli would go on to complete the task. Unless he could climb down the almost sheer sides of the rift valley amazingly quickly, he would simply be left behind. However, left behind or not; he would have to take that route if it took him a week.

Over the next day or so, Calistrope explored his surroundings. For a person of hermetic leaning, the place was idyllic. A lacework of streamlets wove their ways across the hummocky valley bottom, cascading over rocks, sliding beneath stunted alders and willows until they emptied into the main watercourse through the valley. This was almost a small river, by turns splashing over shingle and small boulders or running deep and tranquil through still pools where lazy fish sucked drowning flies from the surface.

Patches of scrub wood—oak, alder, hazel—punctuated its course and threw shade where fat eels swam idly against the current. Fishing was easy, turning over stones exposed succulent crayfish and larvae; silver fish could be driven into the shallows and picked out of the water and eels might be taken with a basket woven of reeds and willow.

He saw the moth which had brought him here—or its fellow—at regular intervals. The pair of them carried smaller insects or more occasionally, reptiles or a rodent, back to the cave which even now, Calistrope could not pass without a shudder. Neither of the moths showed any interest in him although he was always wary of them.

If only man had been given wings… came the thought and took him back to the half-joking comments he had exchanged with Ponderos about training wasps to carry them. Here was the germ of an idea; could he capture one of the moths responsible for his being marooned and persuade it to return him? Calistrope imagined bridle and saddle, coercing the insect into wearing them, learning to guide it as if it were a land-bound dray-beetle.

The task would be a daunting one even when his ankle was strong again but he continued to plan the attempt until the lizard landed in his dinner.

The lizard appeared to be fat and baked in clay, would provide a succulent meal. Calistrope's impression was wrong, however. When he caught it, the lizard was as thin as a snake, the appearance of plumpness coming from the large flaps of skin stretched between fore and hind legs. Calistrope tossed it away and was surprised to see it take flight or, to be more exact, to glide away and land on an outcrop where it spread its pseudo wings to soak up the sun's meager warmth.

The Mage sat by his fire for a long time after that, feeding sticks to the blaze and looking from his cloak to the basking lizard. At length, he got to his feet and hobbled over to one of the numerous streamlets to collect several large leathery leaves and a handful of thin pliable willow twigs. He sat down again and began to fashion a model.

That first one did not work well; not at all, in fact. But as his ankle healed, Calistrope persevered and by the time he could walk without limping, he had constructed seven experimental models; each one more successful than the last.

Satisfied with his progress, Calistrope went down to the river and walked along its bank, searching each patch of trees for poles which were long enough and straight enough for his purposes. There was enough line in his bag and—probably—enough material in his cloak to make a gliding machine.

Aha! A willow tree with tall, straight growth springing up from its roots. Calistrope used his fighting knife to cut five or six lengths and a bundle of springy withes which could be woven into a framework. He set off back to his camp with vigorous step.

Perhaps, with the thought of escaping this eyrie, his mind was less cautious than usual. He was alerted by the flap of membranous wings above him but too late to avoid being seized by the coat in exactly the same way as before.

This time, the outcome was different. This time it was less of a shock and he had a weapon: the willow poles. Calistrope dropped everything except for one pole and with this he delivered a series of crushing blows to the insect's thorax. The chitinous cage which protected the wing muscles split. More blows damaged the creature's vitals and insect body fluids leaked from the casing as Calistrope continued his attack. The moth eventually dropped him and flew on, its wing beats no more than reflexive spasms until it came to the ground, wings outspread, ten or twelve ells from where Calistrope had tumbled to earth. It twitched and struggled for some time before expiring completely.

Calistrope went back down to the river to wash himself and his clothes free of the bitter and sticky fluids which had escaped from the moth's viscera. Shivering violently but cheerful after the defeat of the insect, he went back to his fire and used most of his stock of firewood to build up a warming blaze.

Once warmed and dried, Calistrope went back to gather up the poles and withes he had dropped. He stopped at the side of the insect and studied it and realized this one was male. It possessed remarkably complicated procreative organs at the rear end and it was noticeably smaller than the moth which had abducted him. Perhaps this was another reason for his successful escape from its clutches.

As he stood there, looking at the creature and at the breadth of its spread wings, Calistrope had the distinct impression that his inner, subconscious mind was struggling to make itself heard. What did these tantalizing half images mean?

A slight wind was tugging at the moth's stiffening carcass and rather than seeing it blown away, Calistrope placed stones on the tips of the wings and on the thorax to anchor it down in case he wished to study it later.

He collected up his materials and returned to the sheltered niche and his fire. He set out the poles and trimmed away the stubs of branches, he measured and marked where the great semicircle of his cloak would have to be cut. The final stage lay before him and Calistrope decided to see to renewing his wood pile and collecting for his larder so he could work on undisturbed by bodily needs. Later, when he had cooked his meal and the air was redolent with the odors of food, the flying lizard returned. It nosed about, searching out fragments of food and ignoring Calistrope's presence entirely.

Calistrope observed the animal closely, this would be his last chance to learn the art of flying from nature. He noted how the thin folds of skin were attached close to the creature's feet and how the long muscular tail had a raised ridge of cartilage along its length. This, surmised Calistrope would steer the reptile in flight. He had assumed that steering would be controlled by posture while flying but this way might be easier, he wondered how to emulate the feature in his own design.

The Mage suddenly stood, his cooking pan rattling off the hearth stones and frightening the lizard off. His forebrain had just caught up with what his unconscious had been trying to tell it for hours.

Leaving the fallen food for the lizard to scavenge, Calistrope rushed back down to the dead moth and looked at it as closely as he had examined the lizard. A minute or so later, he strode back to the fire and took the prepared wood and twigs back to the moth.

Calistrope worked like one demented. Over the next several hours he cut away parts of the dead moth's body, he opened up the great veins which in life, stiffened the wings and worked the willow poles into the vessels. He improvised fastenings and slings, guy ropes, steering surfaces. At the end, he had a winged apparatus which he then fastened to his shoulders.

Without further pause to consider, Calistrope climbed to an outcrop of rock and leapt. If not instant flight, it was certainly not ignoble descent. Calistrope adjusted and fiddled and tried again. A glide: a dozen paces from his launch point.

The problems became fascinations. Experiment after experiment drove him on. Longer and longer glides rewarded him. At one point the wind caught him and almost without thought, Calistrope reacted to it, turning into the breeze, using it, climbing, extending his flight path. The river passed by below, bushes and trees like balls of green fuzz, bare rocks—the knees and elbows of the world's skeleton, then he was losing height, skimming a bush, running, catching his toe in a hole, falling forwards.

Calistrope whooped like a youngster. He had flown, maybe two chains: three, four minutes' trudge over the puckered ground squeezed down to a few long seconds' flying time.

The moment was significant.

He was also on the wrong side of the river. He could ford the flow or... Calistrope found a suitable pile of rocks and climbed to the top. He launched himself, glided carefully across the stream and alighted. He did not wish to exhaust his good fortune too soon, he took of his apparatus and carried it up to the campsite where exhausted by both hard work and elation, he sat down next to the dead embers of the fire.

Calistrope was hungry and thirsty too. He picked through what remained of his larder—a cache of stones on a three legged platform of woven branches—it was empty. He stood up, sat down again and stood up once more, walked back and forth a few paces. Calistrope was tired but the exhilaration he felt over his success would not let him rest. Eventually, he took up his scoop net and went fishing.

In a shadowed pool at the side of the river, eels performed their never-ending dance—coiling and circling, interweaving their patterns. If he moved fast enough, Calistrope could catch one every three or four tries. He persevered long enough to catch three—a good meal and a change from the taste of the more easily caught crustaceans. The Mage picked a handful of crisp watercress from the shallows and he dug a pair of tubers from the muddy bank. Earlier experimentation had proved them to be tart of flavor and crisp if not overcooked.

The forced change in pace provided Calistrope with time to consider his new machine; small changes in design would improve certain handling difficulties, others would make it more robust. Too, there was the immediate future to think of: how far had Ponderos and Roli traveled over the past—Calistrope estimated—six or seven days? Suppose they had covered thirty or more leagues, how did such a distance appear from above? How fast might he himself cover such a distance through the air?

Calistrope awoke with a start, the fact that he had fallen asleep unintentionally told him how tired he had been. The fire was no more than a few glowing coals and nosing around was the lizard—somehow aware it had been elevated to the rank of *talisman* and therefore safe from harm.

With a smile at the creature which had shown him the way out, Calistrope stood up and stretched. He walked across to his flying apparatus and began those modifications he had envisaged. He saw places where the bindings had chafed, he reinforced these to reduce movement and then he made more training flights until it was clear he was as ready as he ever would be.

The place which Calistrope had chosen for the final launch was a spur of rock where alternate freezing and thawing had eroded a series of steps down one side. He carried his equipment to the top and stared down the length of the valley, he was certain the vantage was high enough to give a flight path which would take him to the end.

Calistrope donned his cloak and wrapped it around him—thankful it had not been necessary to cut it up. He took up the gliding apparatus which he attached to his shoulders and looked for the last time around the now familiar contours of the valley.

A great breath of anticipation. Three, four, five steps and a jump. Calistrope was airborne, a slight cross wind to adjust for, a cloud across the sun, darkening the light a little. A cloud? Up here? A solid thump as something collided with him and clung tightly.

Whatever it was bore him steadily to the ground, too much weight for his wings to lift. Calistrope swung himself to left and right in an effort to dislodge whatever was there. He looked up, a second pair of dusty brown wings stretched above his own. It took a few moments to realize what he was seeing: another moth—probably the original insect and mate to the one whose wings he had usurped.

There was nothing he could do, no way to beat off the insect, no way to avoid the ground which was rising towards him at a great rate. As his feet touched down, Calistrope released the knots which secured his wings and ducked. The moth and the remains of her mate continued on until it came to ground. The upper insect was certainly attacking Calistrope's apparatus, pulling at the wing roots and tearing great holes in the flying surfaces.

With no weapon, Calistrope dared not try to drive the female off, he was doomed to watch the destruction of his creation. At length the creature flew off and Calistrope, free to look at the damage, knew it was beyond repair. *Why?* He wondered gloomily. *What had caused such behavior? Had the moth considered his flight to be an invasion of its territory? Perhaps it believed its mate to have been unfaithful or lax in its care for their young.*

Not that it mattered. Calistrope clenched his fists. The female had ruined his flying machine and the female would have to be stalked and taken as a replacement. Calistrope was determined, alternatives did not merit consideration.

He visited the cave where the moth's young were hatching, it was the first time he had been close to it since escaping. The place was larger than he remembered and far more noisome, the reek of decomposing meat was overpowering. There were disquieting sounds and repulsive movements among the living hatcheries which hung from the roof along the right hand wall.

There was room for no more debate. Calistrope's first thought—of taking up quarters here to wait for the moth's return—was untenable. The thought of sharing this space with rotting carcasses and ravenous grubs revolted him beyond all reason.

Instead, Calistrope cut wood from nearby bushes and wedged them loosely across the entrance. He knotted a long length of twine to the branches and brought the other end down and along to where his camp was established. The Mage tied it to a sapling which he wedged between two stones and sat down to wait patiently. The lizard climbed on his knee and he tickled its chin.

Presently, the sapling was disturbed and Calistrope put the lizard down. A sharpened pole in one hand, a sword in the other, he went back to the moth's lair. The barrier was gone, its remains were a loose pile of sticks below the opening; there was a sense of movement within.

He approached the entrance, climbed the mound of debris below and crept inside. With his weapons stretched out protectively in front of him, Calistrope waited for his eyes to adjust to the gloom. At the same time the insect became aware of the intruder and turned away from the task of spinning a cocoon.

Calistrope had no idea what the moth might bring to bear against him, he tried to be ready to rebuff stings from the tail end as well as bites from the head. It was the latter he had to contend with, a pair of massive mandibles with wickedly serrated cutting edges sharp enough to snip a human limb.

However, the moth was unused to combat, and Calistrope's spear sank into an eye. While the creature was slowed down by nervous shock, he cut through the mouth parts to render it more or less harmless. It suddenly came to Calistrope's mind that this was not purely a revenge killing, the insect was to furnish him with spare parts; the Mage stepped to one side and deftly decapitated it. The moth fell to one side, its limbs trembled and then were still.

The vile odors of the cave came back to him with renewed force and before the stench made him gag, Calistrope folded the wings back and pulled the dead insect out into the open. Then, breathing through his mouth, he returned and cut down the carcasses and ensured every one was dead before he finally left the cave.

Calistrope dragged the moth nearer to his campsite and began work immediately. With the benefit of hindsight, the job went swiftly, even to working in changes as he went.

One improvement which became obvious as he worked on the new version was the piloting arrangement. Rather than swinging from the shoulders so his body would act as a pendulum, Calistrope now added a seat of woven wicker suspended beneath the moth's body. Two poles fashioned from naturally bent branches became levers bound to the wing struts which he could push or pull to alter the attitude of his new machine.

The fact, too, that the female was significantly larger than the male allowed Calistrope to increase the reinforcement of wings and body. As a last late addition, he included a small tail plane to the rear segment which he hoped would improve stability.

Finally, there was testing which proved so successful that Calistrope was tempted to fly straight out over the rift. Common sense prevailed and the impulse was conquered; Calistrope landed, collected his cooking equipment, wrapped his cloak about him and doused the fire's last glowing coals.

Then, he flew.

Chapter 12

The new craft was responsive to his every move, he gained a little height with every warm updraft from below and shot out of the hanging valley like the plug from a bottle of over-fermented wine. This was exhilarating, intoxicating. The rift valley laid out on either side of him like a hugely detailed map with the river, a chalk mark scrawled by an unsteady hand along its length. Calistrope banked and headed eastward.

There was no possibility of his seeing Ponderos and Roli from this altitude and in fact, this was his only real anxiety. How far must he fly before descending to a height where he might see them without compromising his range? Calistrope was tempted to take out his map but one false move and not only would it be gone forever, so might his life as well. Its loss was too much to hazard so he compared the terrain below with his memory of the map and gauged distances between landmarks.

He would descend, he decided in five or six hours. Meanwhile, he could settle to enjoying this new experience.

The five or six hours came and went. Despite the slipstream which made his eyes water and chilled him to the marrow, Calistrope's speed over the ground was not as great as he had estimated. Now, rather than enjoying the flight, he began to wonder if he could survive the cold long enough to catch up with his friends.

Another half hour passed, another six or seven leagues. Ice, he noticed suddenly, was beginning to build up on his muffled hands and on his face. Sadly, Calistrope decided he would have to descend, losing what flying time he had left and the only real chance of catching up.

While he still dithered, Calistrope saw a possible compromise a league or so ahead of him. A great spur of rock jutted from the northern wall, its crown was green with bushes or moss and inclined at a slight angle. If he could land there, then he would recuperate and fly on having lost perhaps a half league or a little more in the way of altitude. There was a continuous cross-breeze from south to north, it had been there since he had joined the greater valley and he had been angling into it in order to fly along the rift's center line. Now, he let it drift him towards the north wall and with a feeling of gratitude, the Mage watched the upland come closer. He lost some height, turned around into the wind and prepared to land. Calistrope knew he was too cold and that his legs were too numb to take the landing at a run. With equal parts of self-confidence, practice and good fortune, he raised the nose of his machine and killed the speed.

It was almost perfect; his feet touched the ground and his legs, numbed and stiff, collapsed. The fall brought the front of the craft sharply downward and the wind pressed it down into the ground until Calistrope could crawl forward and secure it with a pair of large stones.

Movement after being immobile for so long came as a glorious pain. Calistrope hobbled into the lee of some rocks and lost no time in building a fire from whatever twigs he could reach. Then he sat and shivered and grimaced at the aches and pains of returning circulation. As his temperature rose, so too, did Calistrope's spirits. The sheer elation of gliding more than a league up in the sky was difficult to contain. With a grin pasted to his face, the Mage went to find water for tea and to boil a strip of the iron rations he had brought with him from distant Sachavesku.

When he was warmed and rested, Calistrope wandered about the plateau, working his arms and legs until they were supple once more and responsive. A shadow came between him and the sun and alert now, he jumped to one side and rolled into the relative shelter of a large boulder before looking up. The shadow, black and menacing as it was, was not threatening him directly. Rather, it was making a tight circle above Calistrope's flying machine—clearly taking it for some intruder.

The creature was a bird!

Here was another surprise, birds were thought to have been extinct for millennia yet obviously, in the high passes and desolate places of the world, they still lived. Killing the creature seemed iniquitous yet Calistrope had to fight it off, for his own survival depended on it. He rushed forward, pulling his sword from its scabbard as he went to threaten the bird. It was remarkably like the only other bird he knew of—a *roc* which he had grown in his own experimental vats. Both had the same cruel beak, the supercilious eye and both were clothed in the same black and pale gold plumage. This one however, was injured, blood from a deep wound staining its breast feathers a rusty red.

Despite its injury, the bird half-spread its wings and leapt at him. The belligerence took Calistrope by surprise and he was forced to defend himself. Deft as he was, the creature evaded his blade time and again, scratching at Calistrope with its taloned feet and ripping at him with the hooked beak. Calistrope backed away several times but the bird pursued him single-mindedly until the Mage was bleeding from a half dozen wounds. Tiring rapidly, Calistrope started a long series of feints and finally inflicted a deep wound close to the one it had already received.

The shock of the second injury slowed the bird and Calistrope managed another telling blow to the side of the neck. His assailant backed off then and sidled warily to the edge of the plateau. Calistrope ran at it, threatening it with his sword and the bird took off, circling the upland for several minutes and then dropping below the edge to glide away and down to the distant valley floor.

Breathing heavily, Calistrope stumbled unsteadily back to his temporary camp.

He sat down next to the ashes of his fire and set out salves and bandages from his ditty bag. Most of the lacerations were superficial despite the pain they gave him but one or two—across the back of his left hand and a cut which had opened his right forearm from elbow to wrist—were deep and would have benefited from needle and thread.

Calistrope had needle and thread but doubted his ability to do even a makeshift job with one hand and his teeth. In the end, he bound both wounds tightly and left it to his own healing abilities to mend.

His stay on the mesa was far longer than he had intended it to be: more than a day before he felt able to launch himself into space once again.

The wind took him close to the great northern cliffs before he straightened out and to his astonishment, he found himself rising in a powerful updraft. Circling above the plateau he gained altitude steadily and within minutes he was soaring above the rift, able to see the endless snow and ice fields which covered the continental plains. Seconds later, he was wafted into the damp embrace of a line of clouds which hung along the northern rim.

Panicking a little, Calistrope turned away towards the center of the valley into clear air and descended. *Why was there such an updraft?* He wondered. A few minutes' rumination supplied the answer. The northern side of the valley was bathed in sunlight while the rock face on the south was forever in shade. The difference in temperature might well be small but the walls were often over a league in height and the air in contact with the warmer rock would heat continuously as it rose. The sheet of air rising along the north wall would draw air across the rift which, on rising, would condense to form the line of clouds he had been lifted into.

The phenomenon gave Calistrope unlimited range. Provided he did not fall too low, below the beginning of this effect, he could regain as much altitude as he wished, whenever he wished.

Laughing at such good luck, Calistrope sent his machine sliding down a series of invisible switch backs until he could see the white water of rapids in the river and faults in the rock like giant steps across the valley. It was difficult, he found, to gauge the height of tall features. Foreshortened as they were, pillars and rock buttresses seemed suddenly to leap up at him as they sped by and Calistrope kept as close to the center of the rift as was possible.

Twice, Calistrope cautiously approached the north wall to gain height before continuing on. He swung round an immense column of rock which had succeeded in staying upright although quite separated from the valley sides; then, back on course again, he spied Ponderos and Roli for surely, there was no one else trudging along this interminable valley.

He circled around again, flying up the valley and shouting as loudly as he could. They neither saw nor heard him. Again, he circled, dropping lower and lower, shouting for all he was worth. Eventually he saw Ponderos look around and then up.

Calistrope waved. Ponderos jumped up and down and waved back. Roli threw his bag into the air and caught it again. The Mage overtook them and looked for a safe landing place. The terrain below was littered with rocks of all sizes, all looking very sharp and jagged. A clearer space appeared just ahead and Calistrope lifted the front to reduce his speed still further.

There was a ridge ahead, an obstacle he hadn't noticed until he was level with it. Urgently, Calistrope thrust forward on the struts, raising the nose still further until only momentum was taking the craft onward. Calistrope cleared the ridge, his boots actually clipping some of the stones at the top.

A crash was inevitable. *Just a little further*, he willed and brought the nose down again. The craft glided onward just a bit more and Calistrope saw the pool just where he needed it to be—a softer landing than the boulder strewn hillside. Perhaps he even found a minuscule trickle of magic that enabled him to reach it. Still an ell above the surface, forward motion ceased and Calistrope and machine dropped like a stone.

There was no splash, no welcoming watery embrace. *A mirage?* He had time to think and then with an excess of creaks and snaps and cracks, Calistrope's flying machine settled about him in a ruin of broken spars and streamers of torn membrane, jagged fragments of chitin.

"Shades," he said aloud and fainted beneath the pile of debris.

"Shades," echoed a small voice. "Hello?"

Ponderos and Roli trotted after the flying machine, up the incline and when they reached the top and saw the crash, they ran. Calistrope was lying a little to one side of the heap of wreckage, stretched out. He had crawled thus far and collapsed, they surmised.

Ponderos reached him first and put an anxious ear against the Mage's chest. "There's no heartbeat," he said and reached to check for a pulse. "No pulse. Oh my poor friend," Ponderos kneeled back and tears began to fall. "My friend."

"He's breathing now," said Roli joining Ponderos on his knees. "Look."

Ponderos lifted the wrist again and touched a finger to the pressure point. "And a pulse," he said doubtfully.

"Simple mistake," Said Roli laconically. "Heat of the moment."

"I don't make mistakes like that. Even in the heat of the moment."

Roli shrugged. "I guess just once in a while is allowed. Shall I get some water to bathe his face, bring him round?"

At that moment, Calistrope opened his eyes and looked from one to the other. "Shades," he said. "Hello? Calistrope?"

"Shock," Ponderos said. "We must make him comfortable and let him rest."

"Tea is good for shock."

"Certainly," Ponderos agreed. "Make a fire and make the tea hot and strong and sweet. Calistrope..."

Ponderos turned back to the Mage and gasped in horror. Calistrope had half melted into a silvery looking liquid. When Roli touched it with the toe of his boot, it recoiled, lifting up and away—a miniature wave, breaking in reverse. "What is it?" asked Roli, revolted by the thing.

There was the sound of debris being pushed aside. They looked round to see another Calistrope standing up in the middle of the wrecked flying machine. "I thought you might have looked for me," he said, sounding a little forlorn. "You might have given me a hand."

Ponderos' eyes switched from the new Calistrope back to the rapidly disappearing version and then back to the one which was laboriously picking his way out of the debris.

"But..."

"We thought..."

Neither one nor the other seemed capable of coherent speech. "Whatever is the matter?" Calistrope asked and then noticed the almost vanished body on the ground and the odd appearance of water.

"Is the poor fellow drowned?"

The substance which seemed from a distance to be water, was an illusion. It reflected rocks at its edge, the valley sides beyond and the sky. The surface even trembled like wind driven ripples. Calistrope recalled the pool he had attempted to land in.

"Hmm," Calistrope touched the toe of his boot to the edge and watched in fascination as it curled up and away. He touched a finger to the surface and was rewarded by an almost instant reaction.

The head, almost all that was left of the body which had lain there, opened its eyes and looked at him. "Hello," said the mouth. "Calistrope?" The eyes moved to Ponderos and to Roli. "Roli, Ponderos. My friends."

The head lifted a little. The surrounding pseudo-liquid humped up into the vague suggestion of a body though it still retained its reflective properties. The body gained definition; limbs separated, flexed and the last of the "pool' of responsive material gathered itself together. Where the substance had rested, the rock was—dusty, dull, denatured in some way.

A quicksilver figure rose to its feet; a half-size copy of Calistrope which quickly darkened and assumed more natural colors. The face wore a slightly perplexed expression as it lifted its hands and spread the fingers. It moved the arms carefully, then the legs, taking several tentative steps which left real, solid impressions in the sandy ground.

"How... very... marvelous," it said, trying out words as if each was a piece of jewelry to be picked to fit with the others. Then, pausing often: "Thoughts, perceptions, movement, volition." The expression changed to amazement. "I." Then came delight. "Others. Not alone."

The humans watched as this metamorphic creature walked to and fro, waved its arms, turned about and began a jig of delight. This was too much, the lower legs became tangled, lost cohesion and dissolved into a shining pool, as though the creature was standing knee-deep in the stuff.

"Too... complicated." And it gave them a grin, rose as the legs reformed. "Do I seem right to you?"

Ponderos nodded.

"Right as nine coppers in a row," said Roli.

"And is that *very* right?"

"Certainly."

"I'd prefer it if you looked less like me," said Calistrope.

"Ah, yes. Differentiation." The visage filled out a little, the axe-blade nose broadened, the complexion turned lighter, the hair—fairer. "This is better?"

"Thank you."

"Um," said Roli, his head to one side. "The clothes look as though they're a part of him—it."

"So they are," replied the creature. "Perhaps..." Some sort of rearrangement occurred and the garments which had had the appearance of being painted on, seemed now to be made from a thin layer of colored clay. "It will get better."

The creature looked at each of the others, silvery eyes shining brightly. "This is all most exciting. To *think*, to *reason*. To converse with others. It has never happened before."

"Where have you come from?" asked Calistrope.

"I don't know. I am just... here."

"*What* are you, then?" Ponderos asked.

"I can't answer that either," it replied. "Oh, I know I have existed—there is a sense of time having passed. I woke before, a little time ago and then I stopped again. Not for long. I woke once more, I am here. It is all I know."

"So—no name?" asked Roli.

"Name? Identification? None was needed before now."

"Let us call you *Polymorph*," Calistrope suggested. "Many shaped."

Polymorph was happy with his new name. Indeed, he was happy with everything. They went on slowly enough for it to practice walking and very soon had mastered the art. The creature's speech lost its hesitancy; even its clothes looked less and less artificial.

"How do you know how to speak?" asked Ponderos during one of the rare gaps in Polymorph's chatter.

"I think it soaks into me from your minds. I am gaining a lot of information all the time, sometimes it makes no sense to me and I have to forget it; otherwise I would be overcome."

"Calistrope, you have not told us what happened to you," Ponderos complained.

"Well, that's so," he replied. "But meeting our new acquaintance here, has made my adventure seem a little inconsequential."

"Nonsense, Calistrope. Polymorph will be as interested as we are," Ponderos seemed curiously eager to hear about the other's adventures.

"Indeed I will," said their new friend.

"Well. It's time we stopped for a rest anyway. I have just escaped with my life from a crash landing, a pause would do me good."

The four of them found a sheltered spot to sit. Polymorph seemed to melt into the rocks slightly. When he shifted, the rock had crumbled to a powder; it seemed this was how the creature drew its sustenance. Calistrope talked about his experiences, explained the principles of flight which he had discovered and how the ground looked like an intricate map when viewed from so far above.

"Very interesting, my friend. I had no idea you were going to recount things in such detail." There was a slight tone of remonstration in Ponderos' voice.

"Ponderos, I have trod on tender toes, I can tell. I thought you were interested. Aha, I know. You have something to tell me too."

"No, no. Nothing of any consequence at all. Shall we go on?"

"Ponderos. Tell me, before you burst."

"Well, it was nothing, really. Roli and I encountered a small village back there. We were delayed, in fact. But for that, we would have been several leagues further along."

Ponderos fell silent. Calistrope refused to use any more cajolery. Polymorph waited patiently. Roli looked from one to the other in frustration."

"We found this village," said Roli into the silence. "It was huddled under a great overhang at a bend in the river. The rock was like a tall column, still attached to the cliffs but jutting out like... like a..."

"Like a buttress, Roli," Ponderos took up the thread again. "The houses, there were about twenty, were built from driftwood and water worn slates for roofs. We didn't see the place at first, we found this bed of river oysters..." And Ponderos recounted their adventure.

"Look at these, Roli! Oysters! Now these are good eating—good enough to eat raw. Ponderos picked up a handful and with his knife prized one open, scooped out the meat and popped it in his mouth He swallowed and quickly followed the first with two more. "Excellent. Try one."

Roli turned the corners of his mouth downward. "They're alive, Ponderos. Drop them in boiling water for a minute and I might try them then but not raw, not *alive*."

"I tell you Roli, there's nothing finer. Some black pepper, a dash of sour wine as well; truly a dish from the gods."

"When they're cooked. Let's collect enough for a good meal and then eat."

Ponderos shrugged and bent to help his companion. When they straightened up again, each with an armful of silver white shells, they found five or six men regarding them from the shore.

"You'd best put them back," said one. "Then we needn't add thievery to trespass."

"Thievery! Collecting shellfish from the river? Come now, let's be sensible."

Three crossbows appeared as if by magic. Their silent argument was effective.

"Well, let's be reasonable about this," Ponderos bent and laid the oysters back in the water. "I mean how were we to know this was a, er, a farm? Is there a sign?"

"A crime isn't cancelled by ignorance, young man. Come along now." The spokesman waved the point of his crossbow to indicate they should come out of the river. "This way and we'll see what First has to say."

Ponderos and Roli were persuaded to walk along the shore until a few hundred paces further on they suddenly saw what had been there all the time: a small village built of driftwood. The ancient timber, bleached as grey as the weather-worn granite, was virtually invisible until the eye knew it was there. Doorways were built from rounded river stones and roofs laid with split slates from the river bed. Even the grey smoke from the grey chimney stacks was largely invisible against the valley wall.

The column halted in front of a particularly ancient house, so tumble-down that it seemed more like a heap of storm tossed branches than a dwelling.

"Ho there, First. We have a pair of filchers here for you to judge."

Nothing happened for several seconds, then planks were pushed aside and a head appeared, it was almost bald on top with a straggly beard beneath. "What?" he asked. "What they been after?"

"Pilfering our best oysters. That's what they've been after."

"Oysters, eh?" First grinned a wide but gap-toothed grin, the teeth which were left were interesting shades of yellow and green. He climbed all the way out of his ramshackle home, a tall emaciated figure wrapped in course grey cloth and strode across into the space enclosed by the houses. "Filchers, eh? Tie their hands."

"People!" He shouted. "Everyone. Young girls, go to where such things grow and gather onions and leeks, potatoes and sour cabbage and crisp water lettuce. Women, gather oysters. Men, go to the brew house and broach a barrel of sweet ale. Young boys, gather enough wood for a fire to burn half a day. Old women, bring back the great fish we set out today and take out its guts, stuff it with herbs. Old men, cover it in clay so we can bake it in the fire pit."

"Well, whatever problems we caused seem to have been forgotten," Ponderos said in a low voice. "The old man has put everyone in mood for celebration."

"What do you think they're celebrating?"

"Us, I'd say. A lot of primitive communities celebrate the arrival of strangers," Ponderos sat down on a convenient stone. "Perhaps they'll untie our hands now."

One of the men who had brought them to the village noticed that Ponderos was sitting down. He came over and pulled the Mage up. "You do nothing First has not said to do. Do you hear me?"

Ponderos did not want to cause trouble. "Of course," he stood up again. "Whatever er, First says."

First stood at the foot of a tall pole, a long straight piece of driftwood at the top of which a crosspiece had been fastened. There was a small platform just below the crosspiece and on the platform was a huge fish with a great under slung jaw and a wide fan-shaped tail. Presumably this was the one First had mentioned. Three old women were manipulating ropes and lowering the fish to the ground. Now it was possible to judge the fish's actual size—as long as a man and much rounder than even the fattest person.

"Second," said First. "Take Fifth and Sixth, they are both good with crossbows, and Tenth too. Take our larceners and offer them to God."

"Did I hear what I thought I heard?" asked Ponderos of Roli.

"Offer us to God?"

"That's what I thought. I don't like the sound of that."

Ponderos began to wrestle with his bonds but too late. Three crossbows were aimed at them, they had a remarkable calming on Ponderos. They were marched to the base of the pole from which the big fish had been taken and there, their hands were untied.

"Climb," Second told them.

"Up there?" Ponderos looked up to the top of the pole twenty ells above their heads.

"To the top."

"What for?"

"Just climb."

With the sharp tips of crossbow bolts making themselves felt, Ponderos, followed by Roli began to climb up the pole using notches which had been cut into each side. Well out of reach, Ponderos stopped and looked down.

"They've left us our swords and knives. That's not so clever." A crossbow bolt *thunked* into the pole below Roli's feet.

"And what good are swords and knives up here? Climb before they do us injury with those crossbows." Urged on by more bolts biting the wood just below them, Ponderos and Roli climbed all the way to the top.

"They have surprising skill with those things," Ponderos said, kneeling on the platform among fish bones and feathers and stinking pieces of flesh. He looked over the edge, below them, preparations were going on apace for the party which First had ordained.

"What do you think it's all about?" asked Roli.

"This is a guess," Ponderos answered. "I think we have taken the fish's place as an offering to their God. No doubt they feed their God the best and today, fish is only second best."

"You mean *we're* the God's breakfast?"

"And loath to waste a really good meal, they are going to have a feast of baked fish." Ponderos concluded.

"What sort of God likes fish or human beings served at the top of a pole?" Roli pressed. Ponderos didn't answer. "I imagine we'll find out anyway," Roli continued.

They did, eventually. Several hours later, after the great fish had been successfully baked and cut into juicy pieces and garnished with savory potatoes and much beer had been drunk, the God came.

There was an almost inaudible sigh in the wind above Ponderos' and Roli's heads. Simultaneously, both looked up. The shape was unfamiliar yet archetypal, a predator out of the Earth's youth which still spoke to some basal principal within. The two blades whispered free of their sheaths. The huge eagle cupped its wings, breaking its plunge with a thunderous double clap of trapped air. Two great clawed feet grasped the crosspiece, a large black eye moved from Ponderos to Roli, back to Ponderos. The hooked beak thrust forward, open, about to rend but Ponderos' sword met the beak and fended it off.

The bird pulled back, unused to hostile offerings. Ponderos threatened it again but this time, the bird was ready, snapping at the milky glass blade and dislodging it from the mage's fist. It bounced off the platform's edge, Men and bird watched it fall, heard it clatter—long seconds later—on the stones below, among the crowd of revelers who were still now, every face turned skyward.

The God lifted its beaked head and looked again at the two humans. It reached forward toward Ponderos, its beak open. Roli's sword caught it across the breast, opening a wound that bled rust red across the pale gold feathers. The eagle rocked back and lost its balance, it half fell, half leapt into the sky and spreading its wings to glide and then slowly pulling itself upward, upward, until it was lost to sight.

A vast groan came from the mass of villagers below.

"Thank you, Roli."

Roli looked down at the villagers. "I think we shall be safer if we stay here awhile." Ponderos agreed and they sat on the platform, back to back, until the God returned.

There wasn't even a hint of sound to alert them this second time. One moment, they were alone, the next, the eagle was alighting on the cross piece and furling its wings. Two wounds on its breast and a gash across its neck were oozing thick blood.

Ponderos and Roli backed across the platform as far as they could; Roli took hold of his sword, Ponderos took out his knife. The eagle seemed content to sit there and watch them.

"Why doesn't it do something?" asked Roli.

Ponderos watched it for some time. "I think it's dead," he said eventually. Look at its eyes."

Slowly, Roli reached out and touched it with point of his sword; there was no reaction. He leaned forward and pushed with his hand; the eagle fell back, tumbling down, a sad bundle of blood stained feathers. Down below, there was hurried movement as people rushed to get out of the way of their falling God. When Ponderos turned round and looked down, the open space was empty.

"Now, I think we can go." They climbed down, unthreatened. The village seemed deserted. Ponderos stopped long enough to find his sword and to carve himself several thick fish steaks.

"Well?" asked Roli as they left the village—which was surely wishing it had showered the two of them with oysters and sent them on their way.

"Well? Well, what?"

"You've not said anything about that animal," Roli pressed.

"It was a bird. Very rare."

"But how did it come by those extra wounds? It must have died from the slash on its neck."

The story had reached its conclusion. Calistrope had been trying to hide a grin for some time with increasing lack of success. Now he spluttered and laughed. Finally, he explained about his own confrontation with the bird.

They walked on. Polymorph learned to match their pace and continued to ask questions, determined to understand everything there was to understand about the world it had suddenly become aware of.

"I wonder if you were made or just evolved," Calistrope mused at one point.

Polymorph turned his grin on the Mage. "Does it matter a lot?"

"No," he said. "Not much. Not at all, in fact."

"What are you doing?" asked Polymorph in turn.

"Nothing," said Calistrope.

"Is that possible?" asked Polymorph.

"I see what you mean. I'm walking, I have a task to complete. It is something we three have to do."

Polymorph prompted for more and they tried to explain the purpose of their journey. It was doubtful whether it could comprehend the working of the solar system and its fate at this stage of its development. There were lulls in the barrage of questions, the humans accepted them gratefully, Polymorph with impatience. The pauses seemed necessary for Polymorph, or *Morph* as he came to be called, to digest the great banquets of knowledge it absorbed.

During one such pause, Calistrope stopped abruptly. "I can smell magic," he said.

"Magic?" Polymorph promptly became speechless as mental osmosis squeezed a whole new concept into the small skull.

Ponderos took a great breath, savoring the false odor that his brain had tricked him into sensing. "Ah, yes. Nearby. I wonder why?"

"Why?"

"Why? It is just *here*. But *what* has brought it here?" Calistrope mused.

They walked on, the sensation came and went as the etheric currents coiled and whirled. They crossed a small tributary stream on stones so conveniently placed as to seem deliberately positioned. On the farther side, Roli stopped and stared up the slope. There had been a significant amount of erosion in this area, a gentler slope backed up towards the higher cliffs. There were patches of green and, here and there, splashes of intense colors which had caught Roli's attention. "What do you suppose those are?" he asked, pointing.

Calistrope looked up. "Flowers?"

"Flowers? Well, I suppose they could well be."

Nearer, the stream had cut a broad depression into the sloping valley wall and a cluster of stone-built dwellings could just be seen against the background. "There's a village up there, too."

"Hmm," said Calistrope and marched on.

"A village," said Morph, sorting through its newly acquired knowledge and filling in the gaps as it went. "A place where people live together. Can we go? Can we see it?"

Calistrope gazed up the hill for several moments, tapping his front tooth with a fingernail.

"Is there any reason why we should not?" asked Ponderos.

"Well, we have lost some time at that village," Calistrope stopped to consider. "No," he said at last, "I don't suppose there's any reason we should not. None at all."

CHAPTER 13

They began to climb the hill alongside the tumbling stream with Polymorph trailing behind as he continued to sort through the mounting abundance of new information and impressions.

The village was built from local stone, small square houses with timber doors and glazed windows set back from the long flight of steps which served as the main street. Between the steps and each house was a terraced plot of red earth. The ground was planted with squash or beans, onions flowered in the corners and one variety or another of a nut tree grew against each wall and blossomed and bore fruit at the same time.

Children crawled between the legs of adults to watch, thumbs-in-mouth, as the strangers passed by. The villagers were silent, blank faced. Some, hoeing a crop or painting a door, ignored the newcomers completely.

Morph pressed his hands to each side of his head. "No," he said as if in pain. "They know less than me, nothing. They are slowly sucking out everything I know."

Calistrope looked at their new companion with concern. "You are losing what you know?"

"No. I don't think so. Copying, I think. Like I did with you."

"I think it's your mind, my friend. Soaks things up, lets things leak out."

Calistrope smiled at one of the villagers who was standing in his way. The villager smiled like a reflection. Ponderos greeted another and the greeting came back like an echo. Both smile and greeting were taken up by others, the expression and words repeated exactly up and down the street until they had run their course and died away like an expanding ripple on a pond.

Roli grinned lasciviously at a pair of young girls. They grinned back, mimicking the precise degree of mischief in the original. One girl passed the grin onto the other; the other gave it to a neighbor and *that* gesture, too, went up and down the village steps.

"They seem mute in a way," puzzled Calistrope. "They appear to just copy what we say or do but there is no understanding there."

"No thoughts there," Polymorph agreed. "Nothing more than a fleeting curiosity. What they took from my mind—which I had taken from yours, of course—has vanished.

"Water passing through sand," Ponderos remarked.

"The picture is an apt one," Polymorph returned.

"It's a very peculiar community," Calistrope looked up and down the street. "If there's a headman or a mayor or some such, I don't see him."

"There's his house, anyway," nodded Ponderos. "It's bigger and grander than the rest."

It was but only a little bigger and a little grander. The house stood a little apart and was surrounded by a garden composed of stones and rounded cushions of moss. A small copse of ash trees grew in terra-cotta pots and a stream ran in through an archway in the wall along the farther boundary and out again through an arch in the nearer wall. The place reeked of magic, not strong magic but a lot of it: many small applications.

There was a closed garden gate in the wall. The travelers entered here and Roli turned back to close it. Beyond the wall, a few villagers stood and watched them. Roli dropped the latch and the villagers and the village vanished.

They were in a different place.

Two griffins stood either side of the gate which was now an impressive affair of black iron and curlicues. The house, still modest but rather larger than the version which obtruded into the village outside, had six windows in the front wall with a central door which itself, had a central door knob. Flower beds lined the pathway to the door, the pot-grown trees were now the nearer fringe of a great forest with the stream become a placid river reflecting a sky which had never shone over the Earth.

Calistrope looked at the griffins. "What do you see here, Roli?"

Roli looked from one to the other. Two carved stone animals, they seem a little indistinct, er..."

"Yes?"

"They're like your gargoyle, aren't they? Set here to guard this manse."

"Well, yes and no," Calistrope smiled. "Well done Roli, your extra senses are quickening. The haze you noticed is the result of mismatching the personalities to the carving, it's only slight, not noticeable by the ordinary man. However, the gargoyle at my manse is a complete personality, it is real. These are not real. Concoctions."

Calistrope held up a warning finger. "Don't touch them Roli, you are not able to deal with these things yet. Nor you Morph, they may be dangerous to you. Now..."

Calistrope left the others and went to bang on the door with the brass knocker, also in the form of a griffin. The sound boomed hollowly and a score of unseen things looked out through the windows at Calistrope. He pushed lightly at the door, it opened a hand's breadth, welcoming almost.

The Mage stood back and the door swung shut again. He returned and patted one of the griffins on the head. "Tell him that Calistrope came to see him," he said. "Tell him I knocked and no one answered."

"Maybe he—or she—won't be long," said Roli. "We could wait if you want."

"Oh, we'll wait," Calistrope decided. "And it is a *he*."

Calistrope indicated the several flagged pathways which led off across the garden. One led to another gate in a wall which faded out of existence an ell from either gate post. Others led over bridges into the woodland or to iron bound doors which stood by themselves where the garden merged with meadowland. One ended only a pace or two from them, at a solid timber trapdoor weighted down by a huge millstone.

"There are many places he may have gone to but my curiosity has been engaged, I'd like to wait and meet with him."

They left the garden. The enigmatic paths, the forest and far-away meadows all vanished. The four of them were back again outside the somewhat larger house of the headman and now, a small crowd of curious villagers watched them close the gate.

"Suppose we eat," proposed Ponderos, always ready with a sensible suggestion about his favorite subject. "We will cook ourselves a meal, make some tea. A surplus of magic lies here, so perhaps a jug of wine, too."

They walked off to one side where there was an open area where they could build a fire. Roli began to select stones for a hearth.

"You remember Phariste, Ponderos?" sighed Calistrope.

Ponderos screwed up his features in thought. "A tall man, broad shoulders."

"A small man, slight of build. He considered meditation to be a useful tool."

"And so it is. It lends idleness respectability. But no, I don't remember Phariste."

"This is all his work, Ponderos. I'm certain of it. He left the College many old years ago, before I last culled my memories else I'd recall him better."

"The manse you mean? Or the village?"

"The villagers."

"The villagers?"

"The whole place smells of Phariste, Ponderos. You know I'm never wrong in these matters," Calistrope laid a long finger against his sharp nose.

Ponderos went to look for firewood without answering.

A little later, Roli came back with six fish from the stream. Morph followed him with a bundle of firewood and Ponderos brought back a canvas bottle of water over which he performed a certain ritual.

Ponderos tested the contents of his bottle. "Adequate," he said. "Not a great wine but then, made in this manner, it is rarely great."

Throughout the meal they had attracted those villagers who had grown curious enough to come and watch. Ponderos let some sip from his wine bottle which, unsurprisingly, never seemed to run out. When several of the villagers brought small cups of blue pottery to him, Ponderos poured with a will.

"Where has Roli gone?" asked Calistrope, suddenly aware that his apprentice had vanished.

"Satisfying mutual curiosities with one or two of the village girls, I imagine," Ponderos poured a little more wine down his throat and got to his feet. "I'd thought of satisfying my own curiosity," he continued, "though in a less abandoned manner."

"Quite," Calistrope replied. "Slake your curiosity by all means but beware the effect of too much slaking. I shall wait here for Phariste."

"As you will. Till later, then," Ponderos took his bottle and ambled away.

Calistrope was perfectly content to wait and to watch the villagers watching him and mimicking the odd action he made.

It's as though there has never been anything novel in their lives, he thought. Their lack of speech was puzzling, too. Calistrope could not remember meeting anyone who could not speak unless actually dumb and even they had the capacity to understand. *Here is yet another subspecies of homo ultimo.*

There were many such. The race had modified and reinvented itself so many times that there were hundreds, if not thousands, of variations on a theme. Some were still close enough to the main genotype to interbreed, others had altered to such an extent that procreation between them and other branches of the species was impossible.

"Morph," he said after watching the behavior of the villagers for some time. "These people have changed since we first came. Do you detect a difference?"

Polymorph was silent for a few seconds. "There is a change. Their minds seem less empty. They wonder who we are, how did we make the new food. I can sense excitement as well somewhere, and pleasure."

"They are learning from us, would you say?"

"It seems likely. However, I believe this is your expected visitor."

Calistrope turned to see where Polymorph was looking, Polymorph had its eyes closed, it had sensed the newcomer by their mental signature. Alerted, Calistrope could sense a current of etheric power coming from behind him.

"Come and sit with us, Phariste."

A figure came into view to his left. "Calistrope? I am afraid I am not this Phariste you expect."

Until she spoke, Calistrope had not realized the newcomer was a woman.

"Certainly you are not." Despite his surprise, Calistrope retained his composure. He got to his feet. "If you are the mage who occupies the manse over yonder, my assumptions have been wrong."

"I am Lelaine," she said. "The manse, the village, these people, they are mine," she gathered a voluminous black cloak of fine silk about her and took a seat across the fire from Calistrope, a faint perfume reached him—a scent of woodland flowers. "And you?" Lelaine drew her knees up and rested her folded arms on them.

Calistrope sat down again. "Calistrope, as you have divined. A traveler, as you must have guessed. On my way to Schune, which perhaps you did *not* know."

"And the Halfling?"

"Is Polymorph. A companion, a friend."

Polymorph's figure became a little more upright, swelled a little with gratification.

"Not human."

"*Absolutely* not."

"This Phariste you mentioned. Why might I be she?"

"He, Madam. Phariste was someone I knew once, a mage as it chances. The nature of the villagers, they reminded me of certain theories Phariste had formulated."

Lelaine had a narrow oval face; she had dark hair, an ivory-pale complexion and eyes like lilac-colored almonds. Expression was conveyed by her eyebrows; all other parts of her visage seemed a mask, her lips moving only enough to form words, her jaw only sufficient to enunciate.

"Tell me Phariste's theories," she demanded.

Calistrope eased himself. "Phariste believed in the power of meditation to cure many ills—both of the mind and of the body. Meditation purged the mind of conflicts, he told me. Thought, he believed—at least, if taken to extremes—overtaxed the body's resources."

Lelaine's eyebrows rose questioningly.

"I don't recall his attempting to put this into practice but he was wont to say that if thought were entirely banished, then the body might continue to function forever."

The eyebrows descended, drew together, formed a straight line. Lelaine considered Calistrope's recollections. "Your friend merely skirted the fundamental truths, Calistrope. Skulked around the heart of the matter like a burglar unexpectedly finding the householder at home."

"I see."

"Indeed. You should not be surprised. Did you say your friend was male?"

Calistrope nodded.

"A woman would have been more exacting in her analysis; men are given to prejudgment.

Calistrope had to admit the fact, if only to himself, that there had been occasions—rare ones—when even *he* had been less than rigorous. Still...

"Well now," he said. In Calistrope's experience, there was rarely anything to choose between the two sexes. Both were equally likely to be affected by prejudice, both prone to prevarication, both would attempt to fit observation to the theory. "There may be something in what you say," Calistrope opted for diplomacy.

"You may depend upon it," Lelaine was firm. "Your friend failed to take his arguments to their logical conclusion. You see, it is the thought which affects the person, not the act of thinking. Thoughts are demons, debilitating, degrading and extremely contagious."

"This seems highly unorthodox."

"Ah! If you were a mage."

"Perhaps I am. What is there to say that I am not?"

Lelaine smiled. The first time her lips had been used to express an emotion—sadly it was disdain. "Would a mage have left his name with my griffins?"

"Your griffins? How can this be?"

"The stone griffins at my gate are guardian spirits. If you were a mage, they would not have let you pass—and they heard what you said and related it to me."

"Well now. Perhaps if I were a mage..."

"*If* you were a mage, trained to assess—better yet, a woman with her faculties unclouded by the hormones which rage through men's bodies—in that case, I could explain all of it to you."

Calistrope shook his head, sighed. "If I were *only* a mage."

"And female."

"Alas."

"You see, ideas are the curse of the human race."

"But surely, thought is what makes us what we are. Thought elevates us."

"Every thought you believe to be good, or useful, or uplifting has its counterpart, driving mankind lower than the beasts. The thoughts themselves pass from one to another of us, shaping our brains to their own ends."

"You make it sound as though thoughts are independent, entities in their own right."

"And so they are Calistrope. They are demons, I tell you. Their sole purpose is to multiply, to be stored in our brains and to be passed on to infect others."

"Mage or not, I simply cannot see this."

"Because there is no *I*, no *you*. Self consciousness is a trick of the thoughts which inhabit your brain."

"We are no more than the vehicle by which thoughts propagate themselves, then," Calistrope recalled the moth that had tried to lay her eggs in his body. "Hatching grounds for new thoughts."

"My villagers are incapable of pursuing a thought for more than a minute or two, incapable of linking two thoughts together."

"Is this not degrading?"

"Is happiness degrading? They know nothing that is ignoble or hurtful."

"They know nothing ennobling or inspiring either."

"The simple things of life. That is what they have, all that is necessary."

Lelaine had been frowning in concentration, now her eyebrows rose as high as could be: astonishment, amazement, disbelief; her eyebrows conveyed all this in one movement.

Two villagers, an old man and a younger woman grappled unsteadily with a pitcher which first one held and then the other. Occasionally, whichever was in temporary possession would remember to drink from it.

"What are they doing?" Lelaine's brows bunched together, conveying perplexity.

"I would hazard a guess," Calistrope answered. "Squabbling over a jug of wine."

"Yes, yes. I see that but what does it imply? Don't you see? They are fighting for ownership. Fighting presupposes purpose, purpose demands constructive thought and that is not possible."

"Interesting."

"It is impossible! And where did they get wine? Did *you* bring it? *You* have done this, haven't you?" The black brows drew down, close together, accusatory.

"Me? Certainly not! I swear it." Truth, yet truth shaded with deceit, for it was obvious where the wine had come from.

Roli chose that moment to return. He looked tired; in fact, *exhausted* was the word which sprang to Calistrope's male and prejudiced mind. There was a reasonable amount of happiness in Roli's expression, too; contentment, perhaps. To Calistrope's male and limited imagination, it suggested *satiety*.

"My apprentice," he introduced as Lelaine inspected the boy and her eyebrows signaled disapproval. Lelaine admired neither slovenliness nor disarray.

For a moment, Calistrope thought she was going to quiz the youngster but she was interrupted by an older woman assaulting two grinning young men a little older than Roli. If Lelaine had not just explained how it was men's veins which were brimming with hormones and that women were the detached sex, Calistrope might have believed that the woman was tearing at the young men's clothing.

"What *are* they doing?" Lelaine asked, shocked rather than ignorant.

Roli was equally shocked. "Yes, what *is* she doing? She must be three times their age."

"Twice their age perhaps—though age hardly matters, surely. I'd say she had been watching you make sport with some of your new friends." Calistrope replied wryly.

"Watching me?" Roli was aghast at the idea.

"You have given her certain ideas, now she obviously wants to try things out herself."

Roli began to see the humor. "But she *is* quite old."

"You seem to have a problem with age, young man. Lovemaking is not just the prerogative of apprentices you know," Calistrope observed.

Roli giggled. "Well, perhaps not. It's just that we're better at it."

"Not even that. *I* can assure you."

Meanwhile, Lelaine had risen and was trying to part the *ménage a trois* and inevitably one of the men had become interested in her as well.

"What *do* you think you're doing?" asked Lelaine sharply as she attempted to resist when he pulled her cloak from her shoulders and laid it on the ground.

"Now stop it," she admonished. "Stop it or I'll... Oh, er..." Somehow, he had persuaded Lelaine to lie upon the cloak with him.

"Now this is not the time, not the place... ouch! Oh I..."

Otherwise occupied, Lelaine did not notice the departure of Calistrope, Roli and Morph. They left quietly, not wishing to disturb the sorceress who they could not help but notice was rather a handsome creature.

"Lelaine may well discover some enhancements to add to her hypotheses," said Calistrope to Morph.

CHAPTER 14

The four of them climbed the eastern slope rather than backtrack through the village, which they could hear, was in an uproar. When they reached the ridge line, the land could be seen to slant gradually downward towards the floor of the rift. They continued on along the gentler gradient.

Dense thickets of tangled oak and dwarf spruce grew all across this upland and forced their path to wander. Each of the larger clearings were dotted with barrel-stemmed plants surmounted by bright flower heads nodding in unison, a phenomenon which implied that the group grew from the same plant. Fireflies, sparkling like stray reflections of sunlight from a shower of sequins, hovered in the shade cast by the many-colored flowers.

"These are the colors we saw from beside the river," said Roli. "You said they might be flowers."

"So I did," Calistrope grinned, pleased at the accuracy of his earlier guess.

It was the first time in Morph's short sentient life that it had seen such vivid colors—reds and blues, yellows, dark purples—a single color to each glade. Morph investigated each new crop of blooms with a child's wonder.

They passed a group of chrome yellow blossoms. Morph poked at the nearest and with an audible *snap*, it closed and withdrew into the ribbed green trunk. The attendant fireflies blinked out. A little nonplussed at the sudden reaction, it went to another and—careful to avoid touching it, the creature gazed raptly at the tossing flower.

"Are they alive?" he asked after some time, hurrying after the others.

"Oh yes," Calistrope thought a moment or two. "You may be related to them more than to us. I remember that when you were in your... *quiescent* phase, you seemed to draw something from the rock beneath you."

"I believe that's so," agreed Morph. "And do these do the same?"

"They extract minerals and certain nutrients from the soil."

At the next clearing, Morph went to stand next to a perfectly white blossom. "I cannot detect any thought at all."

"Ah, no. Plants—which is the term we give to this type of life—are not sentient. At least, not on Earth and not as far as I know. You will note too, that they are rooted in the ground, they do not move from place to place."

Again they walked on and again Morph scurried to catch up, only to stop at the next group of plants. "This exudes a considerable odor," he said of the orange bloom. "I would classify it as similar to decaying meat, I doubt you would care for it."

Morph stood on tiptoes to look into the centre of the flower. "There's a hole at the middle," he said. His changeable body stretched up a little more. "What are these? Ulp!"

Calistrope, Ponderos and Roli had passed the clearing and it was several seconds before they realized their friend was no longer with them. "Morph?" called Calistrope. "Where are you?" Then, to the others: "We had better go back, we don't want the fellow getting lost."

They returned to the last clearing. There were eleven of the big orange flowers and one where the long fleshy petals were folded in.

"This is the right place, isn't it?" Ponderos asked.

Calistrope nodded. "Orange ones. Yes."

"You don't suppose it's fallen in, do you?" Roli swallowed.

"Into one of the flowers?" Calistrope rubbed his chin. "Morph was saying something about a hole inside, but falling in…"

Ponderos picked up a long twig and waved it over one of the flowers. "Just wondered," he explained a little sheepishly. "You hear these tales of carnivorous plants, don't—"

The stick was whisked from Ponderos' hand and an instant later, his hand and forearm were enfolded by a ring of muscular petals. "It's going numb," he gasped. "Can't feel it."

Slowly, Ponderos' arm was being pulled into the flower. Calistrope and Roli caught hold of him and pulled against the plant and slowly, Ponderos' arm came out. There was a squelchy, sucking sound and suddenly, he was free; they tumbled backwards, laughing with relief until Calistrope thought of Polymorph.

"Morph must be already inside one of these!" Calistrope shouted.

"That one," said Roli. "The one that's closed up."

Ponderos' arm would not work properly but Calistrope and Roli attacked the plant with their swords, carefully slicing the stringy stem open. The stem was quite hollow, with downward pointing thorns growing in the internal space. When they had completely cut it away, the tubular stem carried on below ground level to unknown depths. They rolled a stone down the tube and it vanished out of sight without a sound, a cut sapling longer than Calistrope reached no barrier.

"I'm afraid that Morph is gone, my friends. Beyond our reach."

Roli and Ponderos nodded, the latter rubbing his right arm in an attempt to restore some feeling. Calistrope noticed and was instantly remorseful. "Ponderos, I am so sorry. I quite forgot that it had hold of you."

He looked at Ponderos' hand and arm. The skin was covered with myriad scratches and was slick with a film of blood. "We must have absorbed quite a lot of power in Lelaine's village—can you make it heal?"

"Of course. I've grown so used to doing without magic that I'd forgotten." Over a space of twenty seconds, the skin healed and feeling returned to his arm and fingers. The blood dried and fell away in flakes as Ponderos rubbed his other hand over it.

"Good," Calistrope nodded. "I'm as forgetful as you, too. If we both use our power, we can tear this plant out by the roots. Morph may still be alive."

The two mages concentrated. The broken stem came up out of the ground as though an invisible giant was tugging at it. Ell after ell of green tube was extruded, broken side vessels showed where it had been connected to the other flowers. The flowers nearby shuddered and wilted as each junction was broken.

Soon there was a huge pile of split plant stems. Rings of brown vegetable muscle clustered around many of the sections; these would be a part of the plant's digestive organs. Of Morph, there was no sign, however.

"I think we have to admit it," Ponderos said gently. "Our friend is gone."

They recommenced their journey, a sad and silent group of travelers. Despite the short time that Polymorph had been a part of the company, all three of them had come to regard the little creature as their friend. Nature had given Morph an exuberant character; the fresh point of view from which it saw everything made the mundane new again, its enthusiasms were contagious.

Now that it had all gone, the travelers felt Morph's absence more keenly. There were times when each of them preferred to keep his own company and would walk apart from his companions. Calistrope in particular would stand at the edge of the upland and gaze in silence into the depths below while the other two walked on.

Time improved their dispositions gradually, but it was not until they reached the continental edge and the awesome plunge to the ancient seabed that they were able to put the tragedy behind them.

CHAPTER 15

The ground dropped away steeply, a breathtaking fall of almost a league—the eastward side of the continental massif through and across which they had journeyed. The river, a very respectable torrent by now, cascaded over the lip of hard rock and plunged downward over a series of slides and falls. Long before it reached the marshes which bordered the great river below, much of it had broken into spray and mist, drifting down as a constant rain.

Far off to the southeast—perspective had changed over the past few days—was the sugar-loaf mountain rooted in the nearer waters of the Last Ocean. This was where the single word Schune was situated on their maps. Before them and beyond the shadow of the continental height, the Long River sprawled along the wide alluvial valley.

Their descent was by means of an ancient trail, once the final stage of an ages-old trade route. At some time in the long ago past, steps had been cut into the granite, what had once been a huge and imposing stairway was now a worn and crumbling path overgrown with slippery mosses and algae nurtured by the ever present vapor from the plunging water. There were signs that handrails had once been fastened into the rock along the edges of the steps but these had long since collapsed and rotted away to stumps.

Everywhere was wet and slippery and treacherous, slick with slime and decaying matter. The shadow of the continental massif stretched out several leagues across the marshlands towards the river, the steps had been dark and gloomy since the world had stopped turning. Rest stops were out of the question, the continual rain drove them on to the finish. It seemed like climbing down the edge of the world—three hours to descend to the confusion of fallen boulders and unsteady slopes of scree which covered the lowest levels. Aching and more exhausted than any of them could have believed possible, they negotiated the final obstacles and made a rough and ready camp at the very edge of the Long River flood plain.

Here, on the banks of one of the many streams which took the falling waters to the Long River, the air was filled with water droplets and vapor. It was an uncomfortable place to be for long. Wood would not burn without the continual urge of magical power to keep the chemical processes going, clothing was never dry, fish and larvae from the nearby pools tasted too foul to eat.

"I'm still tired," said Ponderos after half an old day. "But I cannot sleep, the food is unappetizing, I feel as though I'm rotting from the feet up. I believe we should move on as soon as possible; get out of this constant rain."

"Here," said Calistrope to Roli, "is a man who speaks in euphemisms. Frogs croak without cease, no one can sit down without getting one's bottom wet, fish taste like mud and the hornets are as big as my thumb and the most vicious I have come across—thank the fates nobody thought to improve their gene base."

"Someone improved the wasps," Roli pointed out.

"Just so, perhaps there are hornets as big as me. Let us go before they come to torment us."

They went. Striding out across the soggy marshland, jumping sluggish streams, wading through turbid ponds and black mudflats, testing the perfidious surface for quicksand beneath its emerald covering of moss and weed.

The companions reached the bank of the Long River, it had taken them more than a day to cross what, on Calistrope's map, were a few finely drawn flood lines. They made a more agreeable camp at the side of a rare shingle beach beyond the reach of the continental shadow. Here, out in the sunshine at last, they could wait days or weeks for one of the occasional trading flotillas which were the only means of bypassing the marsh and swamp flanking the Long River's course all the way to the sea.

Time passed and the three relaxed while keeping watch up river. They talked of this and that; about the journey, the way magic faded in and out, what might be at Schune.

"What is magic?" asked Roli as though Calistrope and he had never discussed the matter before.

"I've told you—the remnants of old... Ah," Calistrope realized the question was different. "A sort of broadcast power," he said. "Those with the proper training can trap it and make use of it. It can be channeled into pure energy, or physical movement, action at a distance... This is not what you asked, is it?"

Roli shook his head.

"The answer then, is that I don't know. Perhaps I used to but not anymore."

"The ether that you talk about, what is that?"

Calistrope sat and thought about the question. "The ether is the interface between reality and nothingness," he said slowly. "At this level, the smallest particles of materiality spring spontaneously into being then, more often than not, they vanish again. The power we call magic seems to be an imbalance between certain of the most minor particles of reality."

"And human beings alone can extract this power?"

"As far as is known. Ponderos? Do you know more than this?"

Ponderos shook his head. "I have not heard of another creature that can do this."

"Perhaps people are magical," Roli suggested. "Perhaps all life is magical by nature."

Calistrope shrugged. "Perhaps so." And smiled at Roli's enthusiasm.

Three days and a part of a fourth passed by. Ponderos, whose eyes were the keenest and who watched upriver with a set of magnifying lenses noted a speck on the surface of the brown and turgid water. He waited an hour and looked again and nodded. "A raft," he told the others. He looked again. "And another and more. There are houses on each one."

The caravan numbered seventeen rafts. Most were in line astern although there were also two pairs where the craft were secured side by side. More hours passed by slowly and eventually the leading raft came abreast of their camp. Fifty ells long with two huts on it and a long pile of boxes and rolled-up skins secured between them.

Calistrope signaled with a mirror and a skiff was detached from a half dozen along the side of the raft and rowed towards them.

There were two men in the boat, one manning the oars and another dressed rather grandly in dark maroon with gold frogging to the sleeves and hip-high water boots of white and grey lizard skin. This second individual stood in the stern in a studied pose, peering ahead over the top of the man who rowed the craft.

"I am the caravan's Purser," he said, introducing himself. "You wish for transportation?" he asked. "To what destination?"

Calistrope explained their ultimate destination.

"Shune," he nodded. "You will have to go to Jesm and arrange passage there to cross the delta." The travelers were appalled at the price he stipulated.

Calistrope shook his head. "We don't have that much copper."

The Purser shrugged and ordered the oarsman to pull away.

"Wait," said Ponderos. "Surely there is work to be done on one of those rafts. We are strong, resourceful. Can we not work our passage?"

"There is always the possibility," agreed the Purser readily. "Food and passage. No more. Let me think," he frowned for a moment. "We have seven prisoners on board, some of them are desperate men and only two guards to spare if river pirates inflict themselves upon us. I see you wear swords—even the boy."

Calistrope nodded. "We have traveled a hundred leagues and used them well and truly thus far."

"But have you killed men? Hmm?" asked the other. "One man's life is worth a dozen snapdragons."

"What you say is true but we, too, are desperate men. Be they escapees or pirates, our blades will carve one as well as the other."

The Purser nodded and made a show of looking them over. "Very good," he decided. "Step aboard and lively. Every instant, our raft drifts further away."

They scrambled on board and the oarsman leaned into his oars, building up his speed to overtake the rafts which had been sliding by while they talked.

"I will take you to see Karkadee who is master of the caravan. He it is who must decide whether you stay or must swim for the shore."

Calistrope raised his eyebrows and the others also expressed shock and surprise.

"I shall recommend you to him. Master Karkadee has seventeen rafts under his authority and three hundred men and women but Karkadee rarely goes against my advice."

The oarsman coughed and spat into the river's muddy water.

"You were about to say something?" The Purser asked him.

"I?" Said the oarsman. "I have work to do with these oars. I have no breath to spare for conversations."

"Hmm," said the Purser.

"Even if I ventured an opinion, who is there would take note?"

The oarsman's question went unanswered and after a little while, he decided the situation should be remedied.

These three fine gentlemen? They will have nothing to say on any matter that *I* might speak of," he sucked in his lips and bent to his oars for four, five strokes. "And you Rem Alcudea? It is well known that..."He was cut short.

"Kindly do not address me by name when either of us is on duty. It is proper to use my rank." The Purser, stood in the stern, tiller in hand and stared with stiff formality over the head of the oarsman.

A further five or six strokes sent them skimming over the water. "The *Purser*," Rem began again with emphasis and sucked his teeth for a few seconds. "The Purser and I do not converse together and if we did, well, my advice would be ignored. If we were the last two left unfrozen at the End, he would not take my advice. No." The oarsman shook his head and pulled strongly again. "I would not waste my breath."

"Quite so," agreed the Purser. "Best to save all the breath you have to pull with."

"I will."

"Hmm."

Their introduction to Karkadee, Master of the caravan and *de-facto* commander of every soul on board, was an anticlimax after meeting his Purser. Karkadee was short and stout and nondescript where Alcudea was tall and elegantly dressed; Karkadee was worn down with weighty matters of polity while Alcudea's mind was free to concentrate on the only conceivable item of interest—Rem Alcudea.

The Purser bent to speak briefly in the Master's ear. Karkadee nodded and turned back to the instruments before him.

The Purser gestured them away from Karkadee's presence and took them aft where he had words with another officer.

"The carcery?" he inquired, raising his eyebrows.

"Just so," Alcudea confirmed.

The Purser had brought them to the leading raft which, despite its cargo, was master Karkadee's command and navigation post. From here, the master calculated the position of the ever-shifting deep-water channel. Behind, the other rafts followed, keeping to the same course and speed.

The Purser left them with the officer.

"Minallo," he introduced himself. "By chance I had come to see the victualler and I find that my command is increased by three."

Minallo pointed to a small boat made fast to the starboard quarter. "We shall be turning a point or two to westward very shortly. Wait by the skiff there until I have seen the victualler once again."

The officer left them and was back again a few minutes later. "Right, gentlemen. Into the skiff with you and we will fall back to your new home."

Once into the skiff. Minallo, undogged a winch; the rope from the winch was fastened to a mooring post on the side of the raft. He let the winch unwind freely and they found themselves drifting back down the line of rafts until they came to the fifth in line. Here Minallo slowed the winch, stopped it and allowed the skiff to float sedately up to the side of the raft. The timbers below the deck level were laid with a space between every third and fourth stringer, making a sort of ladder. Following their new acquaintance, they climbed up the side to the deck which was an ell or so above them.

Here Minallo stopped them. "I am Minallo, first officer of the carcery." Minallo made the boat fast. "As Karkadee is the absolute master of the caravan so am I the absolute ruler of this one raft—responsible only to the Master. Do I make myself clear?"

"Absolutely," Calistrope nodded.

"Perfectly so," said Ponderos.

Roli looked around the raft with interest.

"Young man." Minallo looked pointedly at Roli. "Do *you* understand?"

"Oh yes Sir. I do," Roli vigorously made amends.

"Very good. When I left here an hour ago, there were five of us here to guard seven prisoners. Now there is one of us to each prisoner and one to spare. Do you think the Purser has a plan which he has failed to mention to me?"

"The Purser mentioned river pirates," Calistrope ventured. "He said that only two guards would be left if we were called upon to repel river pirates."

"Well, that's as true as may be." Minallo wagged his head and blew out his cheeks. "But river pirates are a dying breed in these parts. I will tell you how it is." And he lowered his voice to a conspiratorial rumble. "The more men and women Rem Alcudea commands, the better he seems when he applies for a new berth. It was I who controlled thirty and four under Master Felwith and a hundred and twenty when I sailed under Master Jalem." And Master Karkadee was very impressed—as were we all." Minallo waved his hands about. "Next time of course he will push out his chest and swagger, "three hundred men and women and a boy when I sailed with Master Karkadee' but will he tell you fifty and more are make weights? Hmm?"

"It seems doubtful Sir. Is there no work for us then?"

"We have two river pirates incarcerated here and they are the whole population of such miscreants between Istanfa and Jesm. I will post double guards so there's no question of escape. Neither for them nor for any of the others. Why should I worry so long as I am dealt my proper purse when the caravan breaks up? Come this way."

There were indeed seven people in the carcery: a passenger who had been found rifling a fellow passenger's strong box, a factor who had tried to sell the Purser a case of corked wine, a religious fanatic who had impugned the Pursers' good name. These three were the three most ordinary.

Less commonplace were the two river pirates to which Minallo had referred. They had been caught during a raid on an earlier caravan and were now being transported to Jesm for sentence to be carried out.

There was a third man who made a point of speaking to no one; he was well-to-do—judging by his dress and his jewels—but whatever he was guilty of or suspected of doing, was a secret known to Mater Karkadee alone.

The seventh prisoner was the most unusual and as mysterious. A woman, wealthy according to Minallo, who had hoisted her strongbox and been rewarded for his trouble. She was also going to Jesm; in fact, she was being returned there by the man she had contracted to wed. Minallo hinted she had fallen short of expectation in some way though it was clear the officer added surmise to the few facts that were available.

Roli was taken into the power house and shown the engines. His job was to add water to the boiler and charcoal to the furnace when either was in danger of running low. Calistrope and Ponderos were added to the guard rota and paired with experienced men during the first few watches.

"There are three hundred people on the caravan," Roli said to Calistrope as soon as he came off-duty.

"Yes. I remember Captain Minallo saying so."

"Do you sense any magic?"

"Magic?" Calistrope tipped his head back and smelled the air. "No. A faint trace perhaps, no more than that. Unusable. Why do you ask?"

Roli shook his head. "A thought, nothing more."

Ponderos also returned in an indignant frame of mind and determined to hold forth. "Do you know, Calistrope," he said at once, "whatever that woman has done, it does not warrant her being treated in this manner."

"What sort of treatment?" asked Calistrope.

"Transporting her like a criminal."

"Well, that is what she is, I presume. Even so, her cell is twice or three times the size of the others, she has privacy, her food is prepared specially. She seems to be treated uncommonly well. Does she complain?"

"Not a word Calistrope. She is a model of self-restraint. But her imprisonment, Calistrope, it is degrading."

"Her affianced husband has repudiated her, by all accounts. I suppose she must be returning home in disgrace."

"Her husband is a fool. At the very least, he has overreacted at some imagined slight."

"How do we know all this?"

Ponderos explained. He explained certain concepts of behavior in a civilized society. He broke his explanations down into details of conduct and the details of conduct into standards and expectations. It was all very clear.

Calistrope gathered that the woman was very beautiful. When he mentioned this as a possibility, Ponderos expounded on her beauty at even greater length.

Several watches went by, both men were paired with a variety of partners in the complicated roster devised by Minallo.

Ponderos divided his spare time between sitting outside the mysterious woman's cell and wearying his friends with continuing acclamations of her beauty. On duty, Ponderos contrived to spend a substantial part of each watch in guarding the mysterious woman and eventually, she disclosed her name to him. She was called Shamaz, a fact which she had refrained from telling anyone else.

"You see, Calistrope," he explained, "It shows how she is beginning to care for me. A great pity that Polymorph perished, its talents would have been useful. We have to think of some way of releasing her."

"Well now; *we*, did you say?"

As much as any of the other guards, Calistrope was grateful for the respite from Ponderos' paeans of praise granted by duty periods and like them, often reported early for work.

The prisoners' accommodations were not large—except for those of the Lady Shamaz, who occupied a specially built enclosure with windows larger than the regulation slits and a private area for ablutions and sleeping. The other cells were strongly built of thick timber and free-standing—so they could be craned on and off whenever a prisoner had to be transshipped or put ashore.

The alleyways left between the cells were narrow and gloomy and it was these which had to be checked carefully for here, miscreants bent on freeing a prisoner or even meting out personal justice, would hide.

Calistrope began his first inspection and shortly was certain that he had heard a soft footfall from around a corner.

Calistrope armed himself with his sword and drew a long bladed knife which he held left-handed. He crept to the corner, listened, nodded. There it was again, a stealthy sound, a boot sole on the rough timber decking, furtive.

The Mage leapt around the corner, his weapons ready. A shadowy figure moved as he moved, they feinted, thrust. There was a clash of hardened glass, back and forth went the blades... two, three times. Both of them froze. A sword was touching Calistrope's throat, pricking it; the most minute of movements would pierce an artery. Calistrope was most careful to make not the slightest movement.

"I am disadvantaged," he said after some moments, shock making his voice hoarse with emotion. "I am defeated," he dropped his sword to the deck with a dull thud, the knife followed, clattering against the sword.

"I had supposed..." began the other and administered Calistrope's second shock. The miscreant who had defeated him so easily was female. *Were there such creatures as female river pirates?* He wondered, coming back to the present to hear her continue. "... that the talk of river pirates was so much drivel. But no. Here we have just such a specimen."

The woman swaggered. *A decidedly unfeminine female*, Calistrope decided. The sword point dropped to his breast and urged him back to an intersection where more light was available.

"Lady," he said and was ignored. *The woman's voice had been husky,* Calistrope thought. *Attractive.* Then quickly qualified the thought, *in a way,* he added.

"More presentable than I had expected," she said. "Raffish perhaps but well dressed for a pirate."

"Madam," Calistrope tried again. "I am no pirate," he swept an arm about. "I am here to guard these criminals."

"Clever, too—and plausible. But you see, that is why *I* am here. Come, I must take you before the Captain of the Guard. This way." And she put pressure on the sword point until he backed out to the carcery's perimeter area.

Now, for the first time, Calistrope saw his captor properly. He blinked in surprise as he recognized the woman for what she was, one of the Komori, a female order of knights proficient in martial skills and dedicated to recording the histories of Earth's diverse peoples. "Madam, I do believe you but I really am a guard," *she is very beautiful,* thought Calistrope.

She looked closely at him. "I don't recognize you and I have been on this caravan since it left Twinmis. Besides, Lawfock is paired with me on this duty. Come along now, we should not keep the Captain waiting."

"I am new. We—my colleague and I came aboard a day or so ago. My name is Calistrope."

"And mine is Anas. It proves nothing."

So Calistrope was prodded along to the small office—hardly distinguishable from the prisoners' cells—where his superior worked out his schedules and tallied the hours spent.

"Now, now. What's this then? Hmm?" he looked up at Calistrope. "Have you been upsetting this young lady."

"I found him sneaking round the cells," Anas told the Captain of the Guard. "Just behind the big one, the woman's."

"Sneaking a look at her, was he? Like his companion?"

"His companion? No, he was skulking, up to no good."

Calistrope found a chink between words to make himself heard. "I was carrying out my duties," he said between his teeth. "I was on guard duty when this..." Calistrope looked at the woman again, her sultry features, the cap of hair like spun silver, her shining eyes... Calistrope was lost. "When Anas mistook me for a criminal."

"Duties!" Minallo's eyebrows rose. "Today?" he looked at the roster tacked to the wall of his cabin and shook his head. "Not until the thirteenth hour."

"I am too early," groaned Calistrope. "I suppose I misread the time. I was over-anxious to escape my friend's prating about the wonders of this woman."

"A mistake we might all make in the circumstances," allowed Minallo. "I am quite tired of his eulogies. Still," he tried to look stern but the grin was glued to his face and would not budge. "We must strive," the grin became a chuckle. "Strive to..." the chuckle hatched a laugh, "be professional at all times. Ha ha ha. Take our duties at the proper hour. Ha ha."

"Anas," said Calistrope sometime later, relating his encounter to Ponderos. "One of the Komori, you know of them?"

Ponderos nodded. "I think Shamaz's people must have come from Amzonea," he said looking far off along the river where the mountain loomed ever closer, its plume of vapor grey against the nightside sky beyond. "They are the only society I know of where women have such magnificent physiques."

"A little over-endow..." Calistrope bit his tongue, the remark might be misconstrued and anyway, Ponderos' predilections were none of his business. "The Komori extol vitality in both mind and body. Anas is very athletic."

"A trifle on the lean side," Ponderos nodded, his mind disengaged from his tongue. "Somewhat meager about the chest. A somewhat boyish figure, perhaps," he smiled. "Shamaz though, a fine example. Bosoms fit to suckle an army."

Calistrope found the metaphor unappealing. "Intelligent and beautiful," he said, gazing back the way they had come but seeing Anas in his mind's eye.

"Oh yes, indeed," Ponderos heaved a sigh.

"As knowledgeable in her field as I am in mine. Did I say she defeated me with her sword?"

"Her demeanor is regal of course, rightly so. Yet she..." Ponderos smiled at his own thoughts.

"Proud, but as you say, rightly so. She has masteries to be proud of."

"How do you know?" asked Ponderos, suddenly disquieted. "Have you been disturbing her?"

"Me? Disturbing her? Anas?"

"Shamaz. We were discussing Shamaz."

"*I* was discussing Anas."

At this point, Roli, who had been sitting in a corner with a bowl of soup, climbed to his feet and left. *Two men,* he thought, *old enough to be my great, great grandsires at least and each of them so besotted with a woman they can think of nothing else.* Roli shook his head and returned to his duty at the propulsion unit. It was just a little unwholesome that men of such an age should act like rutting youths.

Roli dipped a bucket of water from the boxed-in hole through the hull and topped up the header tank. Water percolated down through the fine pipes over the charcoal bed, it boiled, steam issued from vents at the rear, the raft drove forward.

There were no women of an age to interest Roli, not here, on this raft. He considered it outrageous that others should find ardor when he, himself, was deprived of the opportunity.

Above, out on the deck, Calistrope and Ponderos continued their oblique debate.

"Skin as dusky as the eastern sky, Ponderos. That is why I failed to see her straight away. She moves like a shadow."

"She does not let her admiration show when others are near," Ponderos murmured. "It would not be fair. I have told her our intentions. She nods. We cannot discuss the matter openly."

"Those eyes," Calistrope stretched and sat back again, "gladly would I drown my soul in their depths. *Our* intentions?"

"Exactly. Timing must be exact."

"Timing! If only we had met earlier. So little time."

Ponderos was on watch, Hafool walked the perimeter. Ponderos stood to one side of Shamaz's window.

"It is all arranged," he told her.

"All arranged?" Shamaz's voice was contralto, her enunciation firm, clear. "What is all arranged?"

"What we were talking about. We agreed that being confined like this was bad for your health."

"Ah that. You have spoken with Minallo about guards?"

"No, no. Not Minallo. Quiet now, Hafool is passing," they paused, Hafool passed by. "All right. You need not worry about the guards, I and my friend will keep you safe."

"I do need the exercise, you are quite right. Spending all my time in here is not healthy."

"I will let you know as soon as it is time. Goodbye."

"Goodbye... and Ponderos..."

Ponderos turned back.

"Thank you for your concern."

"More than concern, Shamaz."

The time came for Ponderos' arrangements to begin. Calistrope stood just to the side of the window to Shamaz's rather opulent prison cell. "Shamaz," he called and tapped lightly against the window frame.

A few moments later, the curtain was twitched a little to one side. "Ponderos. Ah! It is not Ponderos, who are you and how is it you know my name?" her tone was a frosty one.

"I am Ponderos' friend," Calistrope explained. "He has a scheme which he wants me to help with. Ponderos tells me you want to leave here and..."

"That is quite true." Shamaz's voice was warmer, the curtain opened a little further. "Ponderos had persuaded me that staying in here is not good for my health and he is right. A daily walk around the raft will improve my constitution remarkably."

"Ha! I see. Exercise. Now, I see. I see I have misconstrued the situation. I thought... well, never mind what I thought. My friend has excellent judgment, I shall see you in due course. Goodbye," Calistrope bowed and returned to his guard duty before anyone had a chance to see him fraternizing with the prisoners.

Ponderos had scheduled his operation for when both he and Calistrope were on guard duty together. Ponderos took the perimeter watch while Calistrope paced along the inter-cell alleyways. A quarter hour later, when Ponderos was convinced there was no one watching the watchers, he went directly to the cell which held Shamaz. He broke the bumanda-wood lock, drew the locking bar out and opened the door. Beyond the brief sound of wood splintering, there was nothing to draw attention to the break in.

"Shamaz?"

"I am coming."

Calistrope? Are you there?"

"Right here, Ponderos. What do wish me to do?"

"Take Shamaz to the perimeter walk on the starboard side."

Shamaz came to the door, pulling a cloak around herself. As Ponderos had hinted, she was—broadly speaking—very well developed. The lady was also very tall; a hand's breadth taller than Calistrope who was taller than Ponderos by a similar margin. In fact, in proportion to her height, Shamaz was perfectly proportioned, even a little on the slim side.

Calistrope noticed Ponderos' eyebrows rise as he saw Shamaz outside her cabin for the first time. "The starboard... that side?" Calistrope, pointed off to the western side.

For an instant, Ponderos was shaken. He had only ever seen Shamaz seated and her height was a little startling. "Just so," he said, regaining his composure. "While you do that, I'll get Roli."

"Roli? Is that really necessary?"

Ponderos looked at his friend strangely. "Of course, naturally. We three are comrades, are we not?"

"Well, yes," Calistrope was doubtful. "By all means, if that is your wish."

Ponderos ran towards the rear end of the raft and ducked under the low roof which covered the sunken engine room. "Roli?"

Ponderos eyes accustomed themselves to the gloom and he saw Roli pull the bucket from the well and pour its contents into the tank. He traced the pipes through which the water must trickle, saw the valve which was controlled by a cable from the steering point in the bows. An idea came to him.

"Roli, it is time to go. You will find Calistrope on the starboard walkway."

"Go? Are we leaving already?"

"We certainly are my boy. Now make haste," he pointed to the valve he had seen. "Is that the valve which controls the flow of water to the boiler."

Roli, pulling on his jacket, nodded.

"Very good. Be off with you now."

Ponderos reached for the valve, he turned it fully on and twisted a loop of the control cable around a nearby bracket. The water ran unchecked to the boiler where it flashed into steam. The gentle pop-pop-pop sound of water boiling changed to a continuous hiss. Gradually, the speed of the raft would increase and hopefully sow confusion among the regular crew.

Ponderos hurried to reach his friends.

He came to the place where he had secured the skiff ready for their escape but where were the others? The walkway ahead was deserted. Ponderos looked behind him and there he saw them, walking slowly towards the stern. Not daring to call, Ponderos ran after them.

They turned when they heard his footsteps.

"This way," he said. "I have a small boat ready for us."

"I'm sure the Lady Shamaz does not wish for a cruise, Ponderos. A refreshing walk is quite sufficient. Shamaz was just saying how invigorated she feels."

Ponderos clenched his teeth. *Was every word he uttered to be questioned?* "The boat is for our escape, Calistrope. Have you no imagination? Quickly before we are discovered."

Shamaz took hold of the railing for support. "Escape? Ponderos, what are you talking about. I have no need to escape, Protection is what I require. Surely your friends are here to protect, not to abduct."

Thoughts flitted through Shamaz's mind, her surmise became certainty. Perfidy!

"Help me!" She shouted with considerable force. Her brief walk had evidently achieved excellent results, Shamaz grasped the railing tightly with both hands and resisted Ponderos' quite gentle efforts to disentangle her fingers. "I am being carried off. Help."

And help was at hand. Minallo came hurrying from the forward part of the raft, Hafool and Anas from aft and several more from other directions. Swords were much in evidence, Minallo and Anas both had bows and arrows tipped with wicked glass barbs pointed at them. Ponderos and Calistrope raised their hands to signify surrender.

Calistrope noted the knowing smirk on Anas' lips and some of the joy which, earlier, he had taken from her presence, leaked away. "This is all a mistake," he said, attempting to mix dignity and mild outrage at the possibility that anything else might be suspected.

"Absolutely. I agree with you," Minallo replied. "Now place your arms on the deck and come up here one at a time. You first Ponderos. Where is the strong box which you have doubtless taken from Shamaz's residence?"

"We have taken nothing," Ponderos was outraged.

"If that is the case then you must be as inept at piracy as you are at guarding. Prest, run and take a look in the lady's accommodation and see if her belongings are still there. Terny, go and watch Prest to be certain he leaves everything as he finds it."

At that point, with the pilot's attention on what was taking place amidships, the prison raft caught up with the raft in front of it. The shock of collision, knocked most of them off their feet.

Roli's mind turned immediately to thoughts of escape. As nimble as if he had been running along the roof ridge of a house, he took three steps along the walkway, vaulted the railing and slashed at the cord which held the skiff to the side of the raft. "Calistrope, Ponderos, quickly."

However, nimble and fast as Roli was, there was one faster still and more nimble. There was the *twang* of a bow string released, there was a tug at Roli's sleeve and an arrow with scarlet fletchings pinned him to the skiff's gunwale. Above him on the raft, both bows were drawn taught with arrows aimed at him, the arrow held in Anas' fingers had scarlet fletches.

Master Karkadee stood stiffly and listened to the story without comment. Calistrope suspected there were times when the Master would have laughed, had the occasion been less grave. The Purser's demeanor gave no such impression, Rem Alcudea saw his prestige and repute in great danger; anger and an overwhelming desire for retribution were written plainly in his expression.

"Every day I see intelligent men whose reason is suddenly replaced by hormonal urges," Karkadee told Ponderos. Calistrope remembered how Lelaine had said something rather similar. "However," the master continued, "I have rarely seen this process taken to such extremes."

He turned to Calistrope. "And you, who I presume, are a reasonably intelligent person under other circumstances, should have dissuaded your friend rather than joined him in this escapade. It is a farce of such proportions that it will be told up and down the river for a score of generations."

Karkadee's twitching lips stilled, his next words were severe.

"Which brings us to the matter of the collision you engineered. I am unable to express my feelings on this. It is certain that Purser Alcudea's reputation will suffer and deservedly so. Just as certain is the damage inflicted on my own renown; doubtless, that too is deserved.

"Purser. Lock them in the cells until we come to Jesm. Shackle the boy in the engine room to work double duty and ensure that he is watched every minute of the day. They will be given over to dry land jurisprudence at Jesm."

Calistrope and Ponderos were locked together in the same tiny cell for an old week, Roli worked two watches out of the four every day. When, at last, they were taken outside, Calistrope and Ponderos could hardly walk and shuffled like old men. Roli was so used to gloom and smoke he had to screw his eyes up against the orange sunlight.

The five days had wrought big changes in the scenery, too. They had left behind the high cliffs and long shadows of the continental massif. The banks spread out on both sides, flat expanses of mud covered in brilliant green and red slimes; ahead, the horizon was flat, the Last Ocean glittering with orange highlights out to where it met the sable sky of nightside. Near enough to dominate the East was the great bulbous mountain with the huge plume of vapor erupting from its higher flanks.

As they boarded the skiff which would ferry them across to Jesm, Shamaz came onto the deck. Towering above the slight figure of Anas, she gave a forlorn wave of the hand to Ponderos. Ponderos gave her a slight bow in return and climbed down into the boat.

CHAPTER 16

Jesm lay along the edge of a bay on the south western shore of the Long River. It was separated from the water by a strip of noisome mud and to a large extent, it was itself built upon mud. When they docked, Calistrope saw the quays and the streets beyond were built of tarred timbers laid over box-form floats resting on the surface of the mud. Behind the roadway, shops and warehouses were built on foundations of identical design. Two story buildings were rare, and where there was an upper floor, it was small compared to the ground floor to prevent it overbalancing on the floats.

The air was filled with the odors of decay, a fact which went unnoticed by the populace and quite probably disregarded by regular visitors. Calistrope, Ponderos and Roli were marched along the boardwalk street. A mud lizard basked in the heat from a baker's window; a pair of insects with great fan-shaped feet hopped out of their way and went flap-flapping across the mud beneath the walkway.

They came to a more robust building than most. A civic hall, Calistrope supposed, for inside was a maze of corridors painted mud-green and mud-brown and through which they were conducted to the *Enforcer's* office. There was much discussion in heated whispers between the Enforcer and the Purser while the travelers watched long slim-winged insects hovering around the light globe and crawling across the ceiling.

At length the Purser left, his expression a mixture of disappointment and satisfaction. They were to be accommodated in spare rooms at the house of one of the town's lawyers. A pair of constables conducted them along the main street and back to the more elegant part of town where the wealthier citizens lived. In fact, two of the lawyer's three daughters were moved to share a single bedroom to make space for Roli. The situation surprised the three travelers and they discussed it with their host.

"Jail?" asked Linel the Advocate. "No, no, we have no jail. I am responsible for you until the trial has run its course."

"And what if we escape?" asked Ponderos. "After all, this is all a mistake and will be corrected in due course but we might be desperate men."

"Escape?" he asked, amazement loud in his tone. "Where to? Jesm is bordered on three sides by salt marshes where your lives are not worth the flick of my little finger." Linel the Advocate made a complicated gesture—at the end of which his little finger clicked satisfactorily. "The river awaits you on the fourth side but it runs through those same salt marshes. Escape by all means. You deprive me of my fee but what of that? I am wealthy enough."

"Then suppose we take your wife and children as hostages?"

"Goodness me!" exclaimed the Advocate. "As close as we are to the final freeze and you expect me to believe that such unruly behavior is possible here in Jesm? The militia would bring you down with three crossbow bolts in each of you before you left my gate." Linel took out a large handkerchief and wiped his brow. "Sir, your conversation is quite disturbing."

Calistrope sought to calm their host. "My friend was merely interested in local custom. Please compose yourself, there are times when he exceeds propriety."

Linel's wife and daughters served the travelers with good, wholesome food. The wife and children—including a babe in arms—sat and ate at the other end of the room. Afterwards, Linel asked the travelers to sign a requisition for the food which he would tender to the town's governors.

After the meal they discussed the case in detail until Linel leaned back in his chair, his chest heaving with great guffaws. "I cannot present this as a serious defense of your actions."

"But it happens to be so, what is the matter with it?" Calistrope could not understand.

"The Lady Shamaz is traveling back to her home town of Jesney, along the coast. She had contracted to marry a certain merchant of the hinterland who, she found, was a coarse fellow of low breeding and interested largely in her dowry."

Linel opened a bottle of wine and handed round glasses. He filled them, added a figure to the bill they had already signed.

"She is a woman of considerable wealth. The Lady refused the contract—she had that right—and had been accommodated in the carcery at her own request and expense—and for her own safety."

Linel tasted the wine. "The very best vintage, you will agree if asked?"

Calistrope found the wine to be rather ordinary but readily agreed since it would not affect *his* purse. In any case, tastes differed from region to region, his own partialities were hardly commonplace and if Linel made a copper flake or two, well...

"She supposed her erstwhile betrothed might pursue her and take the dowry which he maintained was his whether she married him or not." Linel held out his hand and rocked it from side to side, "The law is not clear on the matter, but in any case, this is all beside the point. Misleading the Lady Shamaz is nothing, a minor affair. What should concern you is the matter of interfering with the governance of the raft. This could well be a capital offence."

"There was no damage Sir, no injury."

"Principle is all in such things." Linel opened a wall case and consulted a chronometer inside. "Besides, it is sleep time. We must do our duty and then sleep will refresh us. A gong will sound when the first meal is ready, you may return to this room to break your fast."

Calistrope took advantage of his civilized surroundings and drew himself a bath of steaming hot—if slightly brackish—water. He disrobed and stepped into the tub and settled down to enjoy the warmth.

It was sometime later, aroused from a state of somnolence by loud voices, that Calistrope discovered how cold the water had become. He dried himself vigorously and dressed again while he listened to muffled shrieks mingled with the lower and increasingly vexed tones of Ponderos.

Calistrope went out into the corridor and listened at the door to the adjacent room. Ponderos seemed to be thoroughly exasperated, what little patience he still possessed was fast running out. Calistrope opened the door and went in. One of Ponderos' discarded boots almost tripped him up, the other lay on the windowsill and his great coat had been tossed in a heap in one corner, apart from these, there was no immediate sign of Ponderos' presence. What he saw was a pair of naked girls, plump and nicely rounded, bouncing up and down on a pile of bedclothes.

"Calistrope," said the pile of bedclothes in the voice of Ponderos. "Thank the Graces, save me."

Calistrope raised an eyebrow and looked more closely. A hand poked from under the blankets and waved feebly.

"Help me," called Ponderos. "Get them off me."

Calistrope bent and put an arm around each plump waist and heaved. He cheated a little, applying a minim of magical power and lifted the two buxom girls off the couch. Ponderos' face looked up at him with evident relief.

His burden was kicking and screaming theatrically with an occasional giggle. Calistrope carried them to the door, lifted the latch, opened it with mind power and set them down on their feet outside. He administered a sharp slap to each pair of buttocks to send them on their way. The girls ran off, jiggling and bouncing along the hall.

Calistrope closed the door. "Ponderos?"

Ponderos shrugged. "Neither would take 'no' for an answer," he said. "I told them to go and bother Roli, that he was more their age. They wouldn't listen to me."

"Clearly you have something which appealed to them. Why didn't you use magic?"

Ponderos sat up and clutched the blankets to himself. "I…" He looked around the room. "I, er, that is, I was concerned that I might hurt them." His shoulders slumped, he gave Calistrope a sheepish look and shook his head. "In truth, I never thought of it… magic," Ponderos sighed and pushed the blanket away.

He was partly naked. His boots and hose were gone. His shirt hung in strips from his shoulders. His breeches, minus several buttons, were down around his thighs.

"I wish I had a bright, incisive mind like yours, Calistrope. Magic!" The ribbons of his shirt rewove themselves together. Buttons flew back like golden bugs and sewed themselves back in the right places. Socks, boots, coat, kerchief, pocket contents; all flew back from various parts of the room and fitted themselves to Ponderos' person or folded themselves up in a neat and tidy pile. "Never gave it a thought."

"Well, I'll leave you to rest. You seem to have straightened up well enough."

"Thank you, Calistrope."

Calistrope laughed. "Rest easy. I'll see you when they call us for the meal," Calistrope left and returned to his room.

The curtains, which he was certain had been open when he left, were now drawn. There was a faint but unmistakable scent of woodland flowers in the air. Someone sat on the edge of the couch, hair falling in a long cascade over one shoulder, a sheer gown of silk hinting at a slim figure and long, charmingly proportioned legs. Even in the gloom however, Calistrope could see that the woman was less than charmed to see him.

Silence, he decided, was the most propitious approach.

"Well," she said when the silence had stretched out long and thin. "Do not think you will come to me now."

The remark was puzzling. She was angry—this was obvious. Very angry, and her voice identified her as the wife of their host. "Come to you?" his considered course of action was forgotten in an instant.

"Certainly not!" There was considerable venom in her tone. "You keep me waiting like a common hireling while you and your gross friend play with my daughters for half an hour. Now you come back expecting me to still be waiting, dewy eyed and breathless."

Calistrope held up his hands as though to fend off the tirade. "Madam, I assure you that neither I nor Ponderos *played* with your daughters.

The woman stood up and smoothed her gown down over her hips and thighs. "I am going. If that is discourtesy in my husband's house, then so be it. Even if I were content to be treated in this way, I daresay it would be time wasted after all the efforts I heard you making with the girls."

"I don't understand you," Calistrope spoke loudly, trying to make her listen to him. "I did nothing with your daughters. Nothing. And nor did Ponderos."

"And now you compound the insult. Stand aside and let me go."

"At once, Madam," Calistrope stood aside and she swept past him. The door slammed behind her. Calistrope lay down and put his hands behind his head. He attempted to make sense of the bizarre argument. After a while, he dozed a little then woke and puzzled some more until the gong sounded for the meal. This signaled breakfast, the meal taken by ephemerals after sleeping away a third of their arbitrary day.

Calistrope, Ponderos and Roli met in the same room where they had taken their previous meal. Breakfast turned out to be a somber affair and a brief one. The Advocate's wife brought in two trays of toasted breads and two pitchers of ice cold spring water; one was placed in front of the travelers, the other on a table at the far end of the room where she was joined by her offspring—two of which cast surly glances at Ponderos and giggled whenever they caught Roli's eye. The Advocate came in then and as silently as the others, placed another receipt on the table and laid a pen beside it. He went to join his family.

The travelers began to eat. "That's very queer," said Roli. "I smiled at the Advocate and his wife and they ignored me."

"I believe I've made sense of the situation," Calistrope spoke through a mouthful of crisp bread.

"The situation?" asked Roli. "This lack of courtesy?"

"And?" asked Ponderos.

"How many people are there here? In Jesm."

Ponderos shrugged. "Six thousand? Seven?"

"There is magic here too, isn't that so?" Roli asked. "I heard you mention it, I'm certain."

"Seven thousand at the outside, I would guess. And the same for other villages along the river. Each one self-contained, a tiny pool of inheritable traits," he turned to Roli. "Yes Roli, a certain amount."

"Small communities but the river links them all. *Aha,*" Ponderos saw the shape of Calistrope's hypothesis. "Without new genetic material being accepted at every opportunity, these villages would become terribly inbred."

"It is tempting to imagine each one becoming a separate subspecies over the course of generations."

"Will someone explain what we're talking about?" said Roli. "Please?"

"Miscegenation is a necessity," Ponderos continued. "Welcomed."

"By the younger ones, Ponderos. I cannot vouch for the older generation."

"Oh yes," Roli nodded. "The younger ones go for miscegenation in quite a big way."

Roli's companions stopped eating and looked at him. "Is this the case?" Calistrope asked, and then signed the receipt with a flourish.

Linel the Advocate was right when he had expressed his doubts about their defense. The judge, a small man—barely able to see over the bench let alone visualize the truths of the matter—was plainly unimpressed by the case before him.

"Abduction? Yes?"

"As you say, Sir Arbiter." The prosecuting lawyer nodded.

"A vile business. And you allege the injury, Sir Phelan? Correct?"

"I do."

"Onward then Sir Phelan. I am eager to hear the arguments."

"The Lady Shamaz was traveling back to her family home in Jesney. Her accommodations were broken into by these despicable men, intent on making off with the Lady's strongbox..."

Linel the Advocate stood up, raised his hand."

"Sir Linel?" asked the Arbiter.

"At last," whispered Calistrope. "He will end these calumnies."

"All this is quite unnecessary, Sir Arbiter. We acknowledge the verities of this case and crave your indulgence. We admit to grave errors of judgment."

Calistrope and Ponderos gaped. Calistrope was about to protest but the Arbiter intervened.

"For the record, Sir Linel, just for the record. I am as anxious as you to say judgment and get this tiresome business over with but the forms must be observed. They really must."

Sir Linel covered a yawn and nodded. He sat and became intensely interested in a law book.

"Sir Phelan, proceed if you will."

"The miscreants went so far as to attempt to abduct the Lady with what odious and abhorrent ends in mind it is best not to enquire." Sir Phelan shuddered with great dramatic effect and the Arbiter shook his head at such a tale of misdeeds and perversions.

"Only the vigilance of the brave caravan guards and of Captain Minallo in particular saved the Lady and her wealth."

Sir Phelan bowed. "And there you have it. A sorry tale, Sir. We beseech you to spare no punishment, to set an example in your judgments that will echo up and down the Long River. Strike fear into the hearts of any who might consider such base deeds as we have lain before you."

"Excellent, Sir Phelan. Clear, concise, telling. A pleasure to listen to such eloquence." The Arbiter turned to Sir Linel who had taken his nose out of the book and was standing, waiting for recognition. "Now, Sir Linel, to your trade. Do your best. The prognostications may not seem good but do not stint on the well-turned phrase, the grand gesture. Let us hear what you can do."

Sir Linel bowed to the Arbiter, to Sir Phelan. He cleared his throat, ordered his notes. "Sir Arbiter, my distinguished adversary, gentlemen. All that Sir Phelan has said is undoubtedly—aye, incontestably—true.

Calistrope raised his hand. "A parody..."

Sir Linel spoke more loudly, ignored the attempted interruption. "Yet these, er, these travelers are from a far-off land. Refined customs are not understood by them, the pleasures of gentle company are lost on them. Let us not mince words, these provincials are uncouth, unused to the niceties of civilized life. No doubt they share their houses with domestic animals and consider wrestling to be the height of cultural activity. In short, these rude, ill-mannered, barbarians know no better."

"Sir Arbiter, we entreat the forbearance for which you are so well known."

"Oh splendid, splendid. Most enjoyable Sir Linel. And so, judgment." The Arbiter closed his eyes for several moments, deep in thought or perhaps, he was overcome by the emotional appeal of Sir Linel's oration.

The eyes opened, he peered down into the holding pit. "Gentlemen. I am decided; let no one call me a harsh man. My judgment is to set you free. Go and from this moment on, lead a blameless life. Is this agreed?" he beamed down at the three men. "Well?"

"Assuredly," said an astonished Calistrope. "Every one of us."

"Good, good."

"Now. What is next? Why, Sir Phelan, are you still here?"

"A matter of nefarious intervention with sundry navigation mechanisms, Sir Arbiter."

"Ah yes, of course. And who is alleged to be responsible for the mischief?"

"The three whom you see before you, Sir."

The Arbiter expressed disbelief. "Are these not the same three I have just implored to be upright and moral?"

"The very same, Sir Arbiter."

"What can you say to this, Sir Linel? Hmm? Have you powers of rhetoric which will convince me of their innocence a second time?"

"I confess, Sir Arbiter. I have not."

The Arbiter shook his head in sorrow.

"I placed trust in these three and it is thrown back at me. Truly, duty is a grievous burden. What else is there? Hmm? Expulsion. They are not fit to be a part of our society."

The Arbiter held his hands up to block them from his sight. "Take them away."

Later, after they had been taken by the constables, Linel came to see them. "Well now, there it is. Despite my exercising my skills to the utmost, your crimes were too monstrous to be ignored. Still, what is expulsion?" Linel shrugged his shoulders. "You did not wish to stay in Jesm and now you will be escorted on your way. These gentlemen, "he indicated the two heavily muscled constables, "will conduct you to a barge which I am given to understand will sail within the hour. Farewell."

Linel bowed and watched them go. His face bore a curious expression. Relief? Satisfaction?

"Well. We seem to have been lucky," observed Calistrope as they walked along the boarded street. "I am not proud of this escapade; let us forget it as quickly as possible. Ponderos nodded curtly. Roli, blameless in the affair, walked ahead, pointedly ignoring the exchange.

The barge which waited for them was already more than half full of men and women. A few were obviously highborn, many had the shifty look of the professional embezzler or the dainty step of a cat burglar. However, by far the greater number appeared ordinary and commonplace.

"Quickly now," said the steersman. "The gates will have opened, we dare not be late."

Without exception, all but Calistrope, Ponderos and Roli seemed unhappy with their circumstances.

"Evidently, none of our fellow travelers care to leave Jesm."

"I expect they all have lives which they are loath to leave, Calistrope. I remember you were depressed on leaving Sachavesku."

Calistrope nodded. "Correct, Ponderos, absolutely correct. It is our good fortune that we are on our way again."

At that moment, the pilot came aboard and the gangplank was withdrawn. A great circular cage at the centre of the craft began to turn as a heavy centipede was urged into motion by hanging a large piece of putrescent meat in front of it. The moorings were slipped and the barge moved away into the faster offshore river currents.

The craft straightened its course and headed down river towards the sea. An hour or so later, they entered the labyrinthine channels of the delta and floated between islands of tall tufted grasses. Strange insects, with breathing tubes at the tops of their heads, basked on the mud in the red sunlight and watched them pass. Finally, out onto the Last Ocean itself.

Such a great expanse of water unenclosed by the usual league high walls of rock affected every person on board except for the crew. Most coped with the incipient ago-raphobia by ignoring what was beyond the guard rails around the deck. Calistrope fixed his attention on the great vapor-plumed mountain ahead of them and therefore realized before his friends that the barge was actually taking them to their destination.

"I expected to have to cajole someone into bringing us out here from a village along the coast," he said. "But here we are. Our misfortunes on the river have worked out far better than we could have hoped."

"Calistrope, you have a deplorable habit of always looking on the bright side," Ponderos was determinedly morose. "Things do *not* work out better than we expect. If things work out even within jumping distance of what we expect, it is entirely due to our own efforts."

Calistrope dropped the subject and strained his eyes to see some mark of habitation on the mountain's steep flanks. There were none visible, even when he borrowed Ponderos' magnifying glasses and scrutinized the rocky slopes a second time.

As they approached the mountain, all they could see were granite cliffs with white waves crashing about their bases. Closer still, the stinking haunch of meat was taken from the centipede's cage and they slowed. Four crewmen deployed long sweeps and rowed them carefully along the coast.

Openings appeared in the rock, a line of black cavern mouths almost half a league in length. They passed these by at a respectable distance and it was possible to see that sea water poured into the openings. Onward and more openings appeared, torrents of water flooding through at such a rate that the pilot had to steer an oblique course to cross the currents safely.

Calistrope looked from the huge water intakes to the outpouring vapors above them. He wondered at the connection until cries of dismay brought him back to the here and now.

The cage had been disconnected from the driving propellers and dogged to other gears below the decks. The boards beneath them heaved up, guard rails along the port side collapsed and one by one, then in threes, sixes, dozens, the people on board slipped down the increasing slope into the water. Those who hung grimly on to ropes or bollards had their fingers rapped with belaying pins wielded by grinning crewmen. They followed the others in to the freezing water.

CHAPTER 17

At once, they were seized by the current and sucked towards the dark mouths of the water intakes. Here was the final conclusion to the process of justice.

Calistrope, Ponderos and Roli slid down the green rush of water into darkness; Roli screamed himself hoarse. The fall seemed endless but might have been only seconds before they were swept into a great swirling pond with an ominous vortex at the center.

As with their fellow deportees, the fall plunged them beneath the surface and when they came up again, it was to find themselves circling a great round cavern with smooth unscalable walls. Inexorably, the circle became a spiral which ended in the central funnel; it sucked them downward through twisting pipes and dropped them into a river which surged away down tunnels dimly lit by fronds of luminescent moss or fungus.

Again, the sides were smooth, devoid of anything which could be used to climb above the torrent. Even if such were possible, the roof curved over and down again on the far side; there was nowhere to escape to.

Around a huge bend and downward swirled the water, with its flotsam of exhausted men and women. Suddenly, Calistrope was spread-eagled against a web strung across the watercourse. All of them who had made it this far were caught against the barrier and where possible, they began to crawl to one side or the other. Roli was there but seemed paralyzed by fear until Calistrope slapped his cheeks hard enough to secure his attention.

"We are safe," he told the boy. "Safe."

Some were too far gone and fell beneath the flood before others could help them. Calistrope supported an old man to the side and then turned back again to help until eventually, there were none left clinging to the smooth strands of plaited silk.

Those who had survived and scrambled along the web to the side found a dimly visible border of white sand to either side. Beyond the web, the river plummeted into black depths beneath a footbridge joining both banks of the river. On the left bank, they found a metallic track leading off towards a low archway some distance from the racing waters.

Calistrope, Ponderos and Roli, together with the rest, followed this silver ribbon buried in the sand and crowded through the arch. Phosphorescent fungi gave sufficient illumination to follow the tunnel beyond, the roof was low enough to cause both Calistrope and Ponderos to duck in places but it rose again further on. There was more space around them, more places for vegetation to take root and grow and thus provide a brighter light.

The brighter light showed only too clearly what fate had in store for them. There were cries of horror; many of their fellow convicts tried to turn back or merely fell to their knees to wait in abject fear.

Great golden armored ants reared above them—both ahead and behind. Huge glittering orbs stared down from the trapezoidal skulls. Mandibles reached down and tugged the collapsed to their feet, urged them on again towards the far side of the cavern where they were herded on to a ramp spiraling down and down into the ground, into the very roots of the mountain which stood above them.

Roli asked, with a distinct tremor in his voice, "What do you think is in store for us?"

"It is difficult to imagine," said Calistrope. "Whatever it is, we should be marginally better off than these others. There was a certain amount of magic in the ether streams at Jesm. Ponderos and I have a modicum of power available to us; we may be able to use it to advantage."

"Will they eat us?"

"The ants at Sachavesku ate only vegetable matter," said Calistrope.

"It is not a universal attribute," Ponderos pointed out.

"Well, no. But there is no point in dwelling on the more disagreeable aspects unless we have to."

Ponderos remained silent and the subject was dropped as they continued to descend. At length, when the temperature had risen high enough to dry their clothing and the air had become humid and over-rich, the way leveled out and they passed into a reception area.

The large golden ants took up stations around the perimeter and the humans gravitated towards long tables set with bowls of assorted fruit, various fungi and hot broths and vegetable soups. Clay pitchers of clear water and fruit juice stood at the back of the table next to earthenware beakers.

The three travelers ate their fill. The food was good, it was fresh, the juices newly pressed from the fruit.

Calistrope looked at the empty plate he had been eating from. "Hand made," he said. "Turned upon a wheel. These were not made by ants," he took up a spoon carved from wood and brandished it at the other two. "Not made by ants. Humans. There are human beings down here, there must be."

Ponderos took the spoon from Calistrope and looked at it, nodded. "Nor were they made under duress, this is good work. If it was forced, it would be hasty, rough."

After eating, they found a place with running water and cleansing agents to use. The convicts washed away the grime of travel and tidied themselves. The simple acts of eating and bathing restored spirits, people told each other that this was not so bad; they rediscovered hope; apathy was washed away.

Roli attempted a grin and asked, "Better than we expected? Eh?"

"Perhaps. Or perhaps our psychology is better understood than theirs," Ponderos' mood was still grim.

"They've not fed us meat," said Calistrope.

"No," Ponderos smiled for the first time since sliding into the water. "No, there you are right my friend. Better than we... than I expected."

After that, there were lines of cots and most of them slept. Calistrope and Ponderos rested and watched the ants march to and fro.

Later, several hours later, they were roused and led off through a long passage. It seemed to be an ancient rift in the rock, sharp corners above them and no upper limit visible; below, the floor and the first two ells were worn smooth by the passage of bodies over tremendous lengths of time.

Further on, the narrow passage narrowed still further so the score or so of men and women were forced into single file. One of the large golden ants took a place in the column after every six or seven persons, they were given a wide berth. They came to a gateway guarded by two of the insects who scrutinized every individual who came through. Some sort of selection was in progress; every now and then a person was thrust towards an opening at the right while most others were sent straight on. A few paces ahead, the process was repeated and in both cases, Ponderos, Calistrope and Roli remained together.

A third selection was made and a stricken Roli was tugged gently from the line and sent towards an opening in the tunnel wall while his comrades were pushed onwards.

"No," Ponderos and Calistrope shouted in unison and resisted, bringing the line to a halt.

The two ants who had made the selection urged them on, to no avail. When the great mandibles came towards Ponderos, he grasped one in each hand and held them apart. With obvious difficulty, the ant forced the appendages slowly together. Before they met and perhaps, severed Ponderos' fingers, he pushed the creature back several paces and let go.

Both of them expected the creature to come forward and either force them onward or to merely dispose of them. They drew swords and stood ready to fight. However, the expected did not happen. The ant that Ponderos had treated in so cavalier a manner shook its head several times and turned, touched an antenna to its fellow.

Movement stopped. Calistrope and Ponderos stood watchfully; the two ants reared back onto their four rear legs and froze, waiting for something. A few minutes later another insect arrived. As golden and as shining as the imposing creatures they had already met, this one was smaller, standing no higher than Calistrope's chest.

"You ressisst," it stated, vibrating its antennae to simulate human speech.

"Our friend has been taken away," Calistrope said loudly.

The ant backed away a little, perhaps as the result of the volume Calistrope had employed. It turned and conferred with its fellow by more touches. It turned back to Calistrope. "The individual wass a young humann."

"That is so."

"Young and old are ssegregated. They are taught differen' proficienciess."

"Not this one," Calistrope insisted. "The young human is taught by me."

"You are teaching?"

"I am teaching."

The creature was silent for some time. It stared at Calistrope then at Ponderos. It looked at the guards. It reached out and touched one antenna to that of a guard and went away. Calistrope and Ponderos were gestured away from the waiting line to a corner of the small enclosure.

The line behind them resumed its motion and while they waited, two more of the younger convicts were selected and marched off through the narrow portal where Roli had gone. A few minutes later, trailed by the smaller ant who had spoken to them, Roli came back suddenly grinning at the sight of his comrades. This time the ant remained silent, it waited for one of the guards to move them all back into line and then itself took up a position in the file behind them as they started away.

They passed several more of the selection points and although the accompanying ant communicated with the others, all three humans were scrutinized as carefully as before. It seemed however, they were to be treated as a group.

Eventually, the line of human beings in front had diminished to six or seven, behind them there were only three; the dozen or so were taken to tables where puzzles were laid out to be completed. There were tests of dexterity—shape matching, assembly; there was color selection, tests of geometric recognition and even simple evaluation of arithmetical knowledge.

When these were done, the small ant drew Calistrope, Ponderos and Roli to one side and flanked by a pair of the large guardian ants, she gave them her assessment.

"It iss clear that you are not the ussual type of human that iss ssent uss."

Calistrope nodded to himself. *It was obvious that there is a regular supply of unwanted humans.*

"The majority are malcontentss and criminalss," it continued.

"So are we, according to the Arbiter at Jesm."

"Our tests tell you are different. Most are suitable for general dutiess, for cleaning and repairing. Many create things or manufacture what otherss have created. A few, like yourselves, are useful in abstract projects."

Ponderos asked, "Abstract?"

"We cannot stay here," Calistrope said forcefully. "We are already engaged on important business."

"Here," the ant told them, "importance is decided by the Nest," it stalked away leaving the guards to hustle the three of them off through labyrinthine passages to a suite of hemispherical rooms occupied already by several human beings.

The guards departed and two men and a woman came out of adjacent doorways to look at them.

"Hello," said Ponderos, smiling.

The others looked at him blankly, then at each other. "What are you here for?" asked one of the two men, a short, somewhat overweight individual with a piercing stare. All three wore a long shift of silky material, their feet were bare; the men were unshaven with long grey wispy beards.

Both Ponderos and Calistrope shrugged. "Whatever the ants have in store for us for the moment. We intend to escape as soon as possible; we have urgent concerns elsewhere."

"You will learn that your concerns have little relevance down here. Joon, Melli, we have work to do. Come." Joon, Melli and their spokesman retreated to a large room where they sat down on wooden stools and continued some debate that had been interrupted.

The newcomers explored their quarters, choosing three of the domed cells as far as possible from those in use and then convened in the center one of the three.

"Ponderos," Calistrope asked. "Well? Abstract pursuits? I heard your surprise."

"Philosophy?" Ponderos suggested with a grin.

"Planning nest expansion," said Roli. "That way we can find our way out."

"Now, that is practical," said Calistrope, nodding. "Perhaps we could suggest something like that if the opportunity occurs. What do you suppose our earnest companions are doing?"

"Eavesdropping should be quite easy."

"Roli, you still think as a thief!"

"I have spent far longer as a thief than as apprentice to a sorcerer," Roli's response was a little sharper than he had intended.

"It was not criticism, Roli. It is an immensely useful trait, especially in our present occupation."

As Roli had surmised, eavesdropping was not difficult.

"...it needs more pressure." The woman was speaking

That is obvious, Joon. The point of my observation is where does it come from?"

"A larger boiler is where it comes from, Pol. A larger boiler will have to be requisitioned."

"Can't we improve the existing one? After all, we're supposed to think about these things."

"Think away. So long as they feed me and provide me with suitable company in the glad room, I prefer to let others think."

Meli raised his eyebrows and winked at her.

"Suppose," said Pol, "that the outlet was made colder. In fact, suppose we built a condenser at the outlet."

"Suppose," replied Joon, uninterested in cooling and condensation.

"It would increase the pressure difference." Meli was suddenly intrigued. "It would make it more efficient. I'll go to the library later on."

Although they listened for some time, apart from Joon's proclivities becoming ever more clear, the subject of conversation remained obscure and they returned to Ponderos' room.

"That did not tell us much."

"No, Roli, not a great deal. Engineering, it was to do with engineering," Calistrope thought about what he had heard. "It reminds me of something, *condensation*, something. It will come to me."

Their own conversation lapsed into occasional comments.

"We ought to start looking around while we are left alone."

" How deep into the earth are we?"

"Steam! That's what is being condensed."

"*Abstract*, is what the ant said. You remarked on it. Something which exists as a concept but not in reality."

"Steam is hardly abstract. So?"

"I can hear insects coming."

It was the small ant again but this time, accompanied not by a guard but by a rather larger creature than itself; an ant which suggested a disturbing and un-antlike quality. Calistrope frowned, unable to decide what it was. The insect possessed the same golden colored chitin, the same gleaming black faceted eyes; its carapace, its head, was of an odd shape. Larger in proportion to its body than the others, the skull bulged with what Calistrope suspected was intelligence.

"Come," it told them.

"Follow uss," Added the smaller companion.

They were led from their new domicile along corridors. Up ramps, over viaducts, through arched tunnels and came at last to a huge cavern where the ubiquitous growths of fungus shed a far brighter than usual light.

At one end, close to the archway through which they had entered a great black beam pivoted about its center. Each end in turn rose three ells or more before descending to the accompaniment of gargantuan gasps and wheezes.

Calistrope stood rooted to the spot for a minute as the others continued on, he had to hurry to catch up, whispering to himself: *steam, a steam engine, I was right, steam...* When he had caught up he addressed the ants. "What *is* this place? And what is a steam engine doing in an ants' nest?"

His questions were ignored. The insects went on until they came to two large barrel-shaped objects. One was built of green and brown glass reinforced with carbon filaments, the other was constructed from gleaming segments of brass and copper and...

"*Iron?*" Calistrope breathed the word with disbelief. "Iron? I had no idea there was so much in the world."

"More than enough," said the larger ant. "The Nest smelts as much as it needs."

Followed by Ponderos and Roli, Calistrope walked around the two objects—each one as high as himself. They were secured to the floor of the cavern with steel bolts as thick as Ponderos' thumb, a shaft of shining steel connected the two cylindrical machines together, steel pipes rose from conduits in the floor and connected to the ceramic machine.

Calistrope frowned and asked the larger ant, "What are they?"

"The Nest has a great deal of knowledge," it started without preamble. "But knowledge is not enough. The Nest requires also, understanding."

Calistrope and Ponderos nodded in unison.

"This is a generator of galvanic energy. The Nest requires you to formulate several projects which will make use of this power so its practicalities can be assessed, so its limits may be probed."

"It is true that I have conducted experiments with certain galvanic fluxes," said Calistrope thoughtfully, a hand to his chin. He paced forward and back as he thought. "Hmm. The project is of interest," he walked two more paces and stopped, looking up into the faceted black ocular organs of the great golden ant. He smelled the faintly acidic air which was expelled from the creature's bellows; as well as improving its breathing capacity the mechanism helped to cool the body—so much larger than nature had originally intended.

"Still, it cannot be done," Calistrope turned and looked at the generator.

"I don't follow your reasoning," said the big ant. "Why can the task not be done?"

"Ah. Let me rephrase my statement. More accurately, it can be done. An interesting task indeed. However it cannot be done by me, by us. "I and my companions already have a job which is of the utmost urgency."

"There is nothing you have to do except that which the Nest decides."

"You are wrong."

Calistrope's contradiction caused the insect noticeable difficulty. It conferred with the smaller creature.

The smaller ant replicated speech, "How can the Nest be wrong?" although the words were almost without inflection, the humans' imaginations supplied tones of amazement.

"The Nest may not be in possession of all the facts."

This suggestion, though presumably far-fetched, was within the bounds of ant-reason. "Of what facts may the Nest not be aware?"

"The fact that the sun is dying and the world will freeze eventually. Even the air will freeze solid."

"That iss known. It doess not concern us."

"The Nest is content to die?"

"The world will surfife for many queenss yet." Continued the smaller ant while the larger simply watched the humans. "Long before, we shall understand the nature of the cossmoss and will trafel to another world."

"We delay," broke in the larger insect. "You have seen our experimental generator. Return to your accommodation and consider projects to help our understanding."

"It would help," said Ponderos, "if we could visit the library. We are not wholly familiar with the sort of energy you are proposing to use."

The small ant looked at its companion. There was the merest suggestion of movement in the antennae. "It iss permitted." And the large ant left them to be taken to the library.

More passages, bridges, tunnels and a low-ceilinged cavern as large in area as the previous one. The atmosphere was hot and the humidity high. Everywhere they looked were racks of pigeon holes extending from floor to ceiling; low tables were set in alcoves around the periphery. Ants and here and there, a human being, stood around many of the tables consulting rolls of grey papery material. Their guide took them to an empty table.

"What is it you wish to see?"

Calistrope shrugged, looked at Ponderos who frowned in a moment's thought. "Um," he said.

"Alarm systems," said Roli into the silence. "Signaling at a distance. Security, locks. All of these when referenced to er..."

"Galvanism," supplied Calistrope looking at Roli with admiration. "More thievery?"

Roli grinned and looked away.

The ant nodded and manipulated studs which protruded from a square plate at the table's center.

"What is that?" asked Calistrope, nodding towards the control.

"It alerts the clerks at the proper storage racks. They will extract what documentss there are and send them here."

"This is already signaling at a distance," Calistrope pointed out.

"The system ussess steam," replied the ant. It indicated a number of pipes which ran up the adjacent wall and across the roof. "Wherever possible the Nest choossess learning schemess which are of practical falue."

They waited. The ant began to groom itself, folding its legs up one by one and running the fine copper colored bristles on its mandibles along the limbs. Calistrope and Ponderos were happy to wait, watching the busy insects at other tables, examining the steam pipes which—now they had been pointed out—were visible everywhere. Small puffs of escaping steam and damp patches on the floor below showed where pipes were imperfectly joined. There were also wires strung tightly between the pipes and running in all directions.

"Perhaps the documents are difficult to trace," Ponderos suggested when the insect had finished its toilet.

"A fault may have occurred in the system," it replied and issued some sort of call for assistance. The signal went unheard by the humans but was obviously sensed by all the insects in the library, almost all of them looked up from their work for a moment.

A minute later, an ant—far smaller than their guide and with a red-gold integument hurried up to them. It stood, lifting first one foot and then another—the very picture of impatience.

There was a swift exchange of information via antennae, the messenger was on the point of leaving when Ponderos spoke quickly.

"Also, diagrams of the steam generating site. So we can assess the capacity."

"What capacity?" asked the ant.

"The power generator is driven by steam, is it not?"

Another touch and swirl of antennae and the attendant worker was off, skittering between tables and record racks. They waited a further ten minutes and then, with a *whoosh* and a snap of springs, a bundle of scrolls came to a stop at the end of one of the tightly strung overhead wires. "Pleasse detach them," said the ant.

Calistrope did as he was asked and spread the papers out across the table. He stood up in amazement. "These are written in human's script."

"Naturally. Iss there any point in re-infenting an alphabet and written language?"

"No. No, I suppose not. I suppose human beings do the writing anyway?"

"For the time being. At some time we shall usse genetics to create suitably equipped clerical workerss. For now other thingss are more important."

The humans bent over the table to look at the reports and records. Roli fingered the thick grey paper. "This is damp," he said and turned to the ant. "The air in here is not very suitable for a library of papers."

"No. The recordss must be copied often."

"If we replaced your steam pipes with er..." Roli waved his hands at Calistrope inquiringly.

"Galvanic conductors."

"With galvanic conductors, the air would be drier. The papers would last longer."

The ant was taken aback to find that a useful enterprise had been suggested so quickly. "Is this possible?"

"Quite," Calistrope grinned and pointed to where several pipes bent and curved around one another. Water escaped with a steady drip, steam jetted with a subdued hiss. "Much tidier, too."

The conversation was punctuated by a second set of documents arriving on the overhead wire system. Calistrope took them down and opened out a series of diagrams showing square oven-like boxes with the depiction of flames underneath.

"This is your steam generator?"

"Yess."

"You heat water with fire?"

"The heat actually comess from the rocks. Further down from here, the rocks are very hot. The boilerss are attached to the rock."

"And this one is your steam engine?" he asked pointing at a drawing. "The one we passed on the way?"

"Iss so. Yess."

Calistrope contrived a fierce expression of cogitation. "It seems to me," he said, remembering the conversation he had overheard, "that the engine would be far more efficient with a, um, a condenser," Calistrope looked closely at the diagram. The depiction of a pipe with steam flowing from it caught his eye. "Here," he said. "At the outlet."

"Why would that be more efficient?" asked the ant.

"Pressure," Calistrope answered. "The pressure difference would be greater."

"I see the possibility. It will be conveyed."

They stayed a little longer, examining diagrams and written records. Ponderos took particular note of the location of the steam boilers. "I think it essential that we visit the boilers," he said. "Absolutely essential."

"It will be conveyed." But the ant was quite preoccupied.

Calistrope folded up the papers and rolled up the scrolls and attached them to the overhead clips. A handle on the end of a cord almost asked to be pulled. Calistrope pulled the handle, let it go. *Twang* went a coiled spring, *whoosh* went the papers and they disappeared along the wire.

Calistrope grinned. "Morph would be in his element here, don't you think?"

"He would never stop asking questions," Ponderos smiled. "Not a minute's peace."

Later, after food had been brought to them at their rooms and paper and writing tools provided at their request, they started on two projects. Calistrope began to design an electric signaling device, Ponderos and Roli made a drawing of what they could remember of site plans for the steam generators.

Their neighbors came by as they were working.

"You told the ants to add a condenser to the steam engine," accused Pol, his brows pulled together in a dark frown, disapprobation loud in each syllable.

"It was something we mentioned in passing," Calistrope replied. "Of no real importance but it seemed a good idea at the time."

"The steam engine is our responsibility. You keep to your own work, we will keep to ours. Is this understood?"

"Of course," Calistrope agreed. "No one wants to gather leeks where another has planted."

"Just so." And Pol, followed by his colleagues, stalked off to his own room.

Hour followed hour, mealtime followed mealtime until an ant—either the larger one or another of identical caste came to see them.

"We are informed that you provided several insights of a practical nature."

"I believe that to be so," Calistrope nodded and sketched in one or two lines.

"With remarkable dispatch."

Calistrope leaned back against the wall. "We, that is the three of us, spend our time in intellectual effort. It is what we have trained ourselves to do, our vocation."

"The Nest recalls that you had another mission, to do with the cooling Earth."

"That is so. But on reflection, it will do later just as well as now."

"You will certainly die before leaving the Nest's service."

"I doubt it."

The ant was silent for some considerable time.

"You expect to outlive the Nest?"

"By a considerable margin."

"How did you expect to affect the freezing of the Earth?"

"Near here is a community called Schune. There are people there who can control the engines which move the Earth. We have to tell them to start the engines, to move nearer to the sun as it shrinks."

"The Nest knows of the place you name but be assured, there are no persons there. It is deserted. It has been deserted since before the Nest was established and there have been more than eight hundred queens. Where did you come by this information?"

"From cousins of yours. A nest near Sachavesku. Engineers, though they shape living creatures rather than hard machinery."

"They are not known to us. Sachavesku? The name is not familiar. Doubtless there are many subspecies of ant across the world, it is only to be expected that they explore areas of obscure and minor interest."

"Not all nests have the foresight of this one?"

"It is unlikely. As to your objective, I suggest you put this from your minds; you will not be leaving the Nest so your hypothesis cannot be tested

Calistrope shrugged. "Well, it is of no importance. What is important is the matter which my friend Ponderos raised. We need to see the steam generators with our own eyes."

The ant left without further conversation. It returned later with a guardian and its smaller companion. "Suqe will take your friend to see the steam generators."

"We should all go."

"That is not necessary."

"Take the young one, then. He is still learning our profession."

"Very well. You will stay here; the guardian will watch you."

"I will stay. I need information in any case, so perhaps you will stay here as well."

"What information?"

"About resources. I have completed a design for the library, I have to discuss feasibilities with you."

"Very well."

Ponderos and Roli were conducted away by Suqe. Both carried writing tablets and styli with them.

The ant waited as Calistrope continued to make notes and draw diagrams. "You wished to talk about resources," it stated eventually.

"Indeed," said Calistrope putting down his stylus. "Resources."

He sat back and folded his arms. "What do you know of galvanism?"

"A force is induced in a conductor when it moves within a magnetic field."

"And the force, what is it?"

"*I* do not know. Others do."

"A conductor is made of many kinds of particle. Some of these can be made to move along the conductor, this movement is termed a flux. The conductor needs to be covered with a sheath which prevents these tiny particles from escaping and dissipating the flux.

"You can draw metal out into fine wires—I saw this in the library. Metals are conductors..."

Calistrope explained the concept of insulation, the bundling of conductors together to carry galvanic signals and the interpretation of the signals. By the time his friends returned, he had established the availability of copper and of its being drawn into fine wires. The ant went away intrigued by what Calistrope had taught it.

"Well?" asked Calistrope. "What do you think?"

"I took several opportunities to scout around while our guide was engaged with Ponderos," Roli said. "Almost certainly we can escape that way."

"Possibly, we can escape that way," said Ponderos.

"Can you find the way again?"

"In the dark," said Roli.

"Probably," Ponderos said.

"Was it hot?"

"Certainly it was hot. Very hot."

"And how did Suqe fare—in the heat?"

"Hmm. She seemed jittery to me. Jittery and her speech was quite bad."

"I thought it might be the case. A consequence of their growing bigger, they don't handle the heat so well. Affects their brains and nervous system. So the sooner we go, the better," Calistrope suggested.

"Now," Roli was eager.

"After our next meal," Ponderos was more cautious. "What will the ants do to us if we are recaptured?"

"I have made us seem as indispensable as possible. We might convince them we had gone to see the boilers again."

"And got lost," Roli added.

Chapter 18

Roli, who had gained a much better sense of their path than Ponderos, took them quickly down through half a dozen levels. He took them along a passageway which seemed to his companions to be no different than several they had already passed. They met a number of worker ants—the small ruddy-golden variety—and were ignored. At the top of the next spiral ramp, they were confronted by a pair of guardians but these also ignored them as they strode purposefully to the entrance and started down.

"I think they might report our passage when they are relieved," Ponderos murmured.

"You're probably right," Calistrope nodded. "All the more reason to make haste."

They descended once more, continuing down through level after level. The temperature rose and the light emitting fungus became dimmer as the heat increased.

Roli consulted his notes. "Here," he said.

"This was not the one we came along," Ponderos protested.

"No but it's the one where we came back. The layout here and the one below are identical. If they trail our scent, this is the better route, don't you remember the pool of hot water?"

Ponderos nodded and they left the spiral, stumbling along the darkened tunnel until they reached a chamber which echoed and re-echoed their steps.

"To the right here," said Roli. "The water is hot so do not wade in too deeply."

They paddled through the margins of a pool of steaming water for a thousand paces until they could step up onto a high shelf of stone which Roli had spied on his earlier visit.

"Quiet now," he said in a whisper. "They are coming."

Alarmed and almost giving voice to a startled cry, Ponderos crowded back into the shadows where the shelf met the ceiling. Calistrope did likewise and as the sound of insect feet scraping on the rock floor became distinct, so did Roli.

A minute later, a glow became evident. Two of the six guardians carried bowls of the luminescent fungus aloft—a mistake on their part for the brightness so close to their eyes made it difficult to probe the shadows. They passed the humans without pausing.

"They will be following our earlier scent," Roli said. "I expect they will go on down to the steam generators before turning back, so now is our best chance."

The three of them descended into the hot water and followed the group of ants, leaving a path of wet foot marks on the rocky floor. They crossed the gloomy chamber and found themselves on a tiny landing where a narrow arch led onto a closely spiraling ramp.

"There," said Roli, apparently pleased with himself. "I wasn't able to check on this level but I guessed it must be the same as the one below, the one we used earlier. I think it's an emergency way."

"How do we know it goes all the way up?" Ponderos, as ever played cautiously.

"Feel the draft. The wind is going somewhere, there must be an exit up there don't you think?"

"As good a reason as any, Ponderos. You have to admit Roli's instincts in this sort of a situation are better than ours."

They started up. Roli set a brisk pace but after three or four levels the three began to separate—Roli at the head, Ponderos several paces behind and behind Ponderos, Calistrope who soon began to complain about the ache in his calves.

"Quiet," commanded Roli after several more levels. "I can hear something ahead."

They closed ranks and listened. The something that Roli had heard approached: the clicks and scrapes of insect feet on hard rock, a dim light reflected fitfully round the bend ahead.

They turned and started downward. Calistrope was at first grateful that the way was now downward but soon complained as much as before about the effects on his leg muscles. They passed the entrance they had arrived through, lights could be seen in the distance; they passed on. They arrived at the next level, where the boilers were situated more lights coming towards them; they continued on.

Down and down. Behind came what sounded like a gathering army of ants.

Down and down. The air grew steadily hotter, drier and soon they were gasping.

"Listen," panted Roli. "They've stopped."

"Not surprised," puffed Calistrope. "Too hot... for them. Addle their brains. Boil them. Let's... try... through... here."

Calistrope led the way out onto a balcony, a ledge which wound off into the distance around an immense shaft, so immense that it was hard to make sense of what they were seeing. At length, they grasped perspective, a space furlongs in diameter and leagues deep. They leaned on the balustrade and gaped at the sight— surely the archetype of all steam engines.

Calistrope experienced a strange feeling of déjà vu but try as he might could not expand on the whats or the whys. He resisted an overwhelming urge to stay and examine the workings of this phenomenal machine.

"Shades," whispered Roli.

Far below were what seemed to be flames, league-long flames leaping and smoking from the mythical inferno, from the very throat of Hell.

Many, many leagues below them were the glowing levels of rock which lay relatively close to the last remnants of the planet's molten core. Water—hundreds of tons a minute—fell in a continuous roar from higher up. The water spread out, heated by the fierce updraft of energy and much of it was vaporized; even so, a proportion reached the incandescent rocks and in a perpetual explosion, flashed into superheated steam to climb back up the long funnel. The wavering sheets of steam and air refracted the savage light from below, creating the flame and smoke effects.

Equally high above them the vapor with air injected from liquid reservoirs, spewed out through unseen fissures to create the conspicuous plume of steam which marked the mountain.

The noise was deafening, indescribable. The air was almost un-breathable, scorching lungs and skin, drying their eyes and mouths in seconds. They retreated back to the emergency ramp and began to climb slowly back up again. They met no opposition, whatever force had pursued them had melted away as the growing heat became impossible for the insects to cope with.

Their ascent was slow. The three of them were in poor condition after their chase and the effects of the heat. They expended every last erg of magical power they had and still, it was hardly enough.

When they estimated that they had climbed well past the level at which they had entered the spiral, Roli slipped away to find water and provisions. Again his talents as a thief stood him in good stead and he returned with an armful of bottles and a sack of fruit from the ants' subterranean farm.

They drank thirstily and ate what they could and then Roli said: "Now for the bad news."

"What?" asked Calistrope as he took another long swallow of water.

"I am almost certain they are still searching for us."

"Oh no, did you see guards?"

"No. I overheard some people talking about us. Farm workers. They had been questioned."

"Then let us be off," said Calistrope. He took three paces and groaned. "It's no use, I can't climb another ell. My muscles have stiffened up."

Dismally, the three sat down with their backs against the wall, too weary to think, too tired to talk until Roli suddenly sat upright. "Magic."

"We have none," Calistrope pointed out wearily.

"Where have we found magic, in the past?"

"At Jesm, at Lelaine's village—a little, at the village near the wasps' nest, at home."

"Exactly. Where there are people! At Jesm there were seven thousand, at Lelaine's village maybe a thousand, at the wasps' nest—several thousand, don't you see?"

"It depends on what I am expected to see."

"People must make magic. There is something in the human body which makes it, like tears or digestive juices. Perhaps most people make a little too much and it accumulates in the ether around the community."

Both Calistrope and Ponderos were silent as they considered this. Eventually Calistrope nodded. "It makes a great deal of sense. However, is there relevance to our present situation?"

"Magic would help us a lot."

"It would repair our exhausted bodies, we could refresh our muscles."

"It could be used to bewilder the ants if they seek us out."

"Well, yes. Go on, I'm sure this is not just a *what-if* exercise."

"Do you remember the dormitories, where the farming people sleep? We could join them, pretend to be the same. Even work in the farm for a time."

"Aha! Accumulate magic," Ponderos frowned as he thought about it. "It would be a slow business, assuming your theory is correct."

"It doesn't matter if his theory is wrong," said Calistrope. "We can hide there in plain sight, now that the ants have actually searched there. Can you imagine them searching in the same place twice? No. We can wait until we are recovered and the hue and cry has died down. Then we leave in a dignified manner, when we are ready."

And so it was. They waited until the current shift was finishing and quietly joined the column of workers returning to the dormitory. Roli filched some of the coarse drab clothes from a laundry and later, after he and the other workers had slept, they shared breakfast and filed out to the plantations of marrows and mushrooms where they copied their new comrades in caring for the plants.

Roli and the mages stayed for eight work shifts. As Roli had suggested, there was a weak energy reservoir in the surrounding ether and as Calistrope had pointed out, if there was still a search going on, it did not return to the farm. When the time was ripe, they simply walked away.

The overseer worker ants seemed to enter a sort of coma state when they were not shepherding the humans. Calistrope, Ponderos and Roli left part way through a sleep period, ignoring the immobile ants and once again, used the emergency ramp to escape. On this occasion, they had had the foresight to take water and provisions with them and they climbed steadily, stopping at intervals to eat and drink.

They climbed for most of a day before stopping for an extended period of rest. Supplies were running low and Roli, once again a thief, left them to find provisions. The boy returned almost at once, running, agitated.

"They have seen me and recognized me, I'm sure. We must go on at once."

The other two, got to their feet and at a fast pace, set off up the ramp again.

"What caste of ant saw you?" asked Ponderos as they went.

"Some of the smallish type. Like Suqe. When one saw me, they all turned and stared."

"We may have a good lead on them then. I think they will organize guards to do the chasing."

They went on, conserving their energies but losing no time either.

"Thank the fates," called Ponderos who was a little in the lead. "This is the top, I think."

Certainly the ramp came to an end and a narrow doorway led through into a dark cavern. Water raced along in front of them and from their right came the sound of a mighty waterfall, in the dull light, the water was a leaden expanse, its velocity disguised by the smooth monochrome surface.

Ponderos, who had Voss' light globe, held it up high.

"How far across do you think it is?" asked Calistrope.

"Impossible to say. I cannot discern the far side, the light goes nowhere."

Calistrope stretched out his arms, strained as if he were pushing against a solid wall. A sheet of white light erupted from his fingers and arched away across the water, reflecting from the surface and shining on the rough stone of the cavern roof. "I think that's the last of my magic."

"A league, at least," answered Ponderos.

Calistrope shook his head. The waterfall we hear must be where it goes into the recycling shaft. We would be swept over before we could swim across."

"If we could all swim that far," added Ponderos gloomily. "Come, we shall have to go upstream, see what we find."

They hurried on and behind them, a furlong distant, there was the suggestion of light. Guardian ants, they surmised, carrying the glowing fungi to light the way. They increased their pace until forced to stop by another watercourse, smaller than the mighty river to their right, a tributary in fact.

"Marvelous," Ponderos grinned. "We can swim across here and it will stop them following us. We shall be safe."

Roli paled as he saw the water. "I cannot swim so far. Not halfway, not a quarter. You must go on without me."

Ponderos looked at Calistrope. Instant understanding passed between them. Ponderos took hold of Roli's right arm; Calistrope, the left. Without allowing time for Roli to realize what was happening, they plunged into the water and swam strongly into the current. Roli twisted and struggled, swallowed water and screamed again and again until abruptly, it was born in upon him that he was not drowning; that in fact, the far shore was coming closer and he could feel the river bed beneath his feet.

They climbed ashore and looked back. The guardians were standing in a row on the farther shore. As they watched, one ant trod carefully into the water—just the front legs. A second climbed on top of the first and climbed over it until it was floating with the first insect holding its back pair of legs firmly in its mandibles. A third ant repeated the exercise, a fourth, a fifth...

Calistrope, Ponderos and Roli were already running by the time the ant bridge had reached their side and the first ant was clambering over the backs of the others to dry land. The humans could probably outdistance the ants while they had the energy to run but insects are notoriously persistent and in the long run, the humans knew they were doomed to failure unless they found an escape route.

Calistrope skidded to a stop on the water worn rocks before he consciously realized what his eyes had seen. "There," he shouted, breathless. "Is that a doorway?"

It was. By good fortune, the Mage had noticed it even in the dimness, a huge arched doorway let into the side of the cavern. Now they had stopped, it was obviously artificial, cut smooth and vertical into the worn and chipped rock wall. There was every possibility that the entrance would lead them from the cooking pot to the dinner plate but there was no time to debate the possibility. They rushed through and were even more thankful to find on the inside a pair of stout doors opened flat against the interior wall.

They pushed them shut. They were made of metal and incredibly heavy, they closed with a great clang, giving the three of them a sudden feeling of safety.

"Is there a locking bar?" asked Calistrope looking wildly at the inside of the doors.

"No," said Ponderos. "Find some stones to hold them closed."

There was very little light. Stones of any size were few and far between but they found a half dozen or so and piled them up against the doors and used smaller ones as wedges, driving them tightly under the lower edge.

"Thank Destiny," gasped Roli, his back to the door.

Bang! They started and then realized that it had been an echo of the doors' closing reflected from some far distant part of the space they had entered. A moment or so later there came a whole regiment of echoes. Bang! Bang! Bangangng!

Like every place they had seen within the mountain so far, this was huge. Ponderos turned away from the doors and looked around the gloomy place. Lit dimly by the glow from strings and curtains of the same moss and lichen which illumined the ants' catacombs, it was just possible to guess at a cathedral-high roof far above them.

"The ants aren't going to get through those, surely?" Roli asked in disbelief.

"They surely will. Nothing is more certain. Pressure of numbers will push them open and if not, they will chew away at the stone to either side or underneath," Calistrope looked this way and that but the floor was unnaturally flat and bare. "Any more stones?" he asked. "Anyone see any more?" Their feet kicked up a fine dust in little puffs but beyond an occasional pebble or a collapsed skeleton, there was nothing.

"Bones?" Said Calistrope to himself. *Bones?* "Bones," he shouted. "There are bones here and there, find the strongest you can, we'll brace the doors as well."

But even as he said it, there was a groan of tired hinges and one of the door panels swung open by a hand's breadth. Ponderos heard the sound and whirled about to slam the door shut again. "Go on," he shouted. "Get away from here, I'll hold them closed as long as possible then follow you."

Ponderos leaned against the doors and felt the insistent pushing of the guardian ants on the other side. After a second's pause, Calistrope nodded and he and Roli set off at a run. A minute passed, another, a third and the pressure behind the doors began to build up. Ponderos' muscles bulged.

As the others ran into the gloom, there came a rushing sound above them, a flutter. Not the steady hum of dragon flies nor the dipping darting whine of mosquitoes, this was a ragged, flapping; a thousand scraps of parchment racing through the air just above their heads.

Back at the doors, Ponderos could feel the panels pressing against his hands and arms, pushing him slowly across the floor. A dozen pairs of unblinking bright eyes looked through the widening gap. He drew in a huge breath and heaved the doors shut once more then turned and bolted after the others, following the dimly visible footprints in the dust.

Close above him, he also heard the uneven beating of thin wings and turning as he ran, saw a cloud of black scraps silhouetted against the bright opening between the double doors. As their erratic flight took them closer, Ponderos saw the doors begin to close once more and just before the bright bar of light vanished completely, he saw a half dozen of the flying creatures dart between them.

"Something seems to worry the ants," said Calistrope, catching and steadying Ponderos who was still trotting with his head turned back towards the now vanished opening.

"Certainly does," rejoined Ponderos. "I wonder what they are."

"Bats," said Roli.

Calistrope asked, "Mm? Bats? And what are bats?"

"Flying animals. Tiny, size of your thumb."

"Animals," Calistrope was hardly convinced. The only animals around Sachavesku were those which he had grown in his vats over the years. There was a small herd of unicorns and four pairs of very small elephants, one or two others which he had seen in old books and had taken a fancy to. "They exist in the wild? Are you sure?"

Roli nodded. "I saw them around the Raftman's Ease while you were sick. When the air was thick. After rain, sometimes. Jiss showed me their roosting places.

"Well, well. Still, those weren't the size of my thumb," he nodded in the direction of the doors.

"Perhaps they're better fed."

Calistrope did not find it an amusing remark.

"Ponderos. How about a light?"

"I don't know Calistrope. We're almost certain that it needs a large number of people to generate a field of power, and there aren't many here," Ponderos held up his hand and a tiny flame grew from the tip of his index finger. "You see?"

"I know all that. But we do have a certain globe of light tucked away in your coat pocket. No?"

"In my... Aha. Well yes, of course." Ponderos reached into first one pocket then another and finally, the last pocket, the pocket which held the globe.

"You'd forgotten it I suppose?"

"For a moment only," he felt around. "Just for a moment. Ah!" Ponderos brought out the globe and tapped its surface, a pearly luminescence shone forth and holding it aloft, it shed a circle of soft white light around them.

They looked around them. The dusty floor was a light grey. Above, a suggestion of a rocky ceiling could just be made out but around them, to right and left, behind and before, not a single glimpse of a supporting wall could be seen.

"Let me," suggested Calistrope, "I am a little taller." He held the globe higher.

"This is a stupendous place," said Ponderos in a stage whisper. "Gigantic. Will the light attract these flying animals, do you think?"

"Probably so," said Calistrope. "Roli?"

Roli shook his head. "They are practically blind I believe."

"Well then. Blind, Ponderos. Roli's bats are blind."

The three of them continued on. Now that *Roli's bats* had frightened the ants into closing the doors—or so they supposed—they walked at an easy pace.

Calistrope stopped and pointed to several piles of small bones which they were about to pass. "This shows there are indeed animals here, insect remains are quite different," he indicated other debris. "You see, broken chitin plates, hollow tubes of the stuff."

There were other marks in the dust, smudged tracks from something that must drag its feet, long grooves as though some bony snake had writhed its way between the debris.

"Bones, yes but flying animals? That's quite a leap of imagination," Ponderos stopped and scratched his head, he was not convinced that Roli was right.

"These bones are quite light though. Look," Calistrope broke a long slender bone in half to see its cross section. "Triangular and they're hollow, too. Look at that, it weighs practically nothing."

"At least they're..."

"There are a lot of them here," Roli's voice came from further on where he had been investigating more remains. "These are broken and... and I think they've been chewed."

"I was about to say small. There must be something here bigger than bats, then."

"It wouldn't need to be very much big..."

"We're about to find out, I think," said Roli and drew his sword from its scabbard.

Roli was looking at a pile of stones almost as tall as himself.

Ponderos approached and asked, "Do you see something?" Roli pointed with his sword. "There. Big, I think. Very big."

"Yes. Take care."

A pile of broken rock had been dragged together to make a protective lair. From one end a large triangular head like a ploughshare rose to stare at them. It moved slowly from side to side, warty green hide covered the angular skull and bulges at either side had the appearance of eyes. The jaws gaped, a bulbous grey tongue bulged behind a ragged fringe of yellow teeth.

"I think it must be blind," said Calistrope. "Like Roli's bats. Perhaps it locates us by the sounds we make. And it seems to move slowly, if we go around it quietly..."

The creature moved out into the open and the light illuminated it more clearly. A fat body set on four splayed legs which worked in diagonally opposed pairs; the belly was gross, a distended bag brushing the ground as it moved—a long spiny tail dragged a groove into the dust. From nose to the start of its tail was the length of a man, the tail was easily as long again.

It looked sick and weak. Beside the laggard movement and probable blindness, the forlorn crest which ran from the head along its back was limp and drooped to one side.

"It really is an animal," gasped Roli. "I never dreamed they could grow so big."

"If that is an animal in the wild, give me insects," said Calistrope. "At least they cull the terminally sick and the healthy look after the others. Anyway, whatever it is, let us edge around to the right. Quietly, maybe it's harmless..."

There was the merest flicker of movement between its jaws and something long and nauseatingly smelly flashed past Calistrope. The tongue which had been fat and swollen had suddenly become a long rope, dripping with sticky fluid and firmly wound around Roli's' arm. It started to retract, pulling the boy, struggling and shrieking with terror, towards it.

The two men, for long moments petrified with shock, rallied and dashed towards the creature's head with swords upraised. Closer to the animal, they saw that there were eyes behind the green swellings, each one shining behind a tiny aperture and moving independently, one watching the struggling, screaming boy, the other swiveling to keep Calistrope and Ponderos in focus.

Calistrope brought his blade down to slice the tongue in two but to no avail. It was made of some marvelously resilient fiber and showed no sign of harm at all as the glass blade rebounded. Ponderos attacked the gross abdomen but with similar lack of success. Try as they might, neither weapon inflicted more than minimal damage.

From somewhere Roli drew on reserves of courage. He ceased struggling, exchanging panic for icy calm. With teeth clenched viselike, he pulled a long thin-bladed knife from his belt then turning, letting the loathsome tongue pull him closer, he plunged the knife down through the tiny opening at the center of the armored turret into the creature's left eye.

The tongue let go, retracted and let Roli go free. He fell to the ground, panting and gasping with reaction now the danger had gone, he crawled away. Calistrope and Ponderos stood watchfully as the obscene creature backed into its pile of stones, shaking its head where the hilt of the knife still protruded from its eye.

"Is he all right?" asked Calistrope.

"Roli?" asked Ponderos turning back to the boy.

"Yes. Yes I'm all right. Let's just get out of this place. Lizards, ugh!"

"Let's go by all means," Calistrope replied. "But where to? I'm not sure which way we were going?"

Ponderos held the light high and there, thrown into shadowed relief were their foot prints trailing off into the darkness. He pointed in the other direction. "That way."

They walked on, light held high and eyes open for further attack. As time passed and nothing came to trouble them, they relaxed a little. Now and then, in low tones, they discussed the obnoxious animal.

"Lizard," said Calistrope suddenly. "Roli, you called it a lizard. Do they also roam around the Raftman's Ease?

"No. I don't think so. I heard the hunters there though. They talked about the things they hunted. One showed me some hide, it looked like the skin on that thing."

Calistrope nodded. "I met a lizard in the high valley, where the moth took me but it was the length of my hand, we became friends. I fear my education has been neglected."

"Or forgotten," suggested Ponderos.

"Perhaps. I really ought to review my memory vault when we return."

They came at last to what must have been the far side of the cavern. To either side of them, the walls had closed in until now, they were only a few ells apart. The roof had lowered low enough to see that it was natural rock cracked and fissured and stained white with guano. A faint odor of ammonia had been evident for some time and had grown in strength as they approached; heaps and drifts of bat droppings lay along the walls.

The wall ahead boxed them in. A wall that was not rough rock; here, the stone had obviously been dressed.

"We're blocked in here," said Calistrope and even as he said it, the sound of unevenly flapping wings reached them from above, like a hundred scraps of parchment fluttering down on their heads.

Down they came again, tiny eyes gleaming in the lamp light, like black ink blots suspended on brown dried-up leaves. Into and out of the sphere of light, closer and closer to their heads, brushing their hair, tapping their faces with wing tips, claws scratching at skin like tiny thorns.

They waved their arms and shouted to no avail. The scratches became bites, some of the animals clung on and began to feed on the living flesh, to lap at the blood flowing from wounds.

"Shades," Roli wailed. "Here come those lizards again," he pulled out his sword and sent it scything through the bats before taking up a guard against the reptiles.

Two lizards lumbered towards them like giant geriatric frogs. Their turreted eyes were never still, swiveling and darting as the creatures looked first at the humans then up into the clouds of bats.

They bunched together, Calistrope trying to keep the flying animals at bay while the other two watched the lizards, ready for attack. The expected never happened though. The bats—formidable as a flock and obviously panicking the ants—held no terrors for the chameleons. The long sticky tongues shot upward, picking bats out of the air with uncanny accuracy.

The flock was enormous, though; too large for the lizard's feeding frenzy to make a substantial reduction in numbers. However, once the creatures realized they were also the hunted as well as hunters, they took more care in their approach, slowing their attack to a point where the humans had time to do more than defend themselves.

"Look," shouted Ponderos battering his way from a cloud of the things with two or three clinging to his shoulder and neck. "There's a way out; another door there, in the wall."

"Lead the way," returned Calistrope. "Can you open it?"

There was more than one doorway, all but one of them closed. The three crowded through and the bats stayed outside, disliking the confined space within. Calistrope was covered in bats clutching at the shoulders of his coat though only one had managed to find anywhere to bite into—just beneath his ear.

Roli—perhaps due to his smaller stature—had largely escaped notice and helped to work the animals free from the other's flesh. Ponderos had suffered most, blood ran in half a dozen streams from bites and lacerations.

Free at last, they looked around the tiny cell into which they had rushed. It was square, small enough for Ponderos to touch opposing walls with outstretched arms, and the roof was low enough for him to touch. The interior was smooth and grey, featureless.

When they had dressed their wounds, they ventured outside to examine the other doors reasoning that one or other of them should lead into a passage away from the cave. The closed panels, like the interior of the cubicle, were smooth; there were neither keyholes nor handles. Apart from a dark grey circle on the lighter grey panel, they were blank. They pushed and thumped and tried to slide the panels without success and it was not until Calistrope accidentally placed his palm against the dark grey circle that the door at the other end suddenly opened. It opened onto a dark pit for a fraction of a second and then was closed again.

They tried the other doors but Calistrope's hand seemed to be the only one with whatever quality caused the doors to open. There were four doors in all, the permanently open one, the two central inoperable doors and the other end one which opened fleetingly on to the pit where the light that Ponderos held could not reach the bottom.

They experimented with the functioning door which, they found, neither swung in nor out, nor slid to one side. It seemed simply that it ceased to exist.

Above them they could still hear the restless movement of bats in flight. Roli's call was a considerable relief. "Here's another way out," he had walked farther along the wall and found another door, a narrow panel let into the rock face. There was no magic grey circle; he pushed, it swung inwards with a creak. "Like a regular door," he laughed and from inside, there're steps here."

CHAPTER 19

The steps spiraled upward, upward, upward, turning in a broad circle, gritty with dust, and small gravel and rock fragments which had fallen from the ceiling onto them. They continued to climb the steps, the tall risers making climbing a strenuous business. At length they reached a small landing where another door opened to one side before the steps carried on. There was dust and debris here as well, which had been disturbed by small clawed feet that had crossed and recrossed the floor space, leaving tracks.

Ponderos pointed the tracks out to Calistrope who nodded. "Yes. Both animal and insect, I think. I wonder if it's the proximity of the atmosphere plant, the air is thicker here than we're used to."

"And warmer, too," added Roli. "I'm just going to look through that door there."

He was back a moment later.

"Like down below. Four more doorways although I can't open any of them, do you want to try, Calistrope?"

The Mage's hand opened each one in turn. The two outer doors opened only for an instant onto gaping shafts, the two central ones were inactive. They returned to the stairs and began to climb again. Signs of animal and insect activity decreased as they went and soon there were only occasional tracks, a very rare pile of bones or a dried up insect casing.

Everything they saw attested to the great age of the structure. The stairs were blocked here and there by roof falls and these they had to file around or squeeze past or climb over. They reached a second landing identical to the previous with the four doors exactly like those below, they came to a third landing and here they sat on the top steps to eat some of their meager food supply.

"Shall we check the doors outside?" Roli asked when they had finished.

Calistrope pursed his lips. "I suppose we had better, assuming there are some."

There were and they yielded exactly the same result as those on the lower levels. The fourth level though, was different.

One of the central doors opened into a cell similar to the one they had sought refuge within, this one was illuminated by a flat glowing panel in the ceiling. On one of the wall panels was a dimly illuminated rectangle enclosing a ladder-like grid, one line of the grid was illuminated about a quarter of the way from the bottom.

While Ponderos stood in the doorway to keep it open, Calistrope touched a finger to the lower grid marking just below the bright one. An angry buzz sounded from somewhere. Ponderos, step inside would you?"

With the doorway empty, the door materialized and Calistrope repeated the action. For the briefest of moments, there was a sensation of extreme cold. The grid was now illuminated at the line where Calistrope's finger touched it. He nodded, as though some thought had been confirmed. "Roli, would you go to the stairs and tell us what you see there?"

Roli nodded and went outside while Calistrope stood in the doorway and watched him disappear through the access door. He returned, breathless. "It's where we stopped to eat. We've come down a level."

"Just so."

When the door closed, Calistrope put his finger on the top bar. An icy sensation enveloped them leaving them feeling slightly clammy. The door dematerialized and the air pressure fell noticeably. Outside, the walkway and the landing beyond were similar to those below except that the layer of dust on the floor was unbroken; nothing had come this way for decades, perhaps for centuries, longer.

A second difference was the fact that there were no more stairs leading upwards.

"Can you smell something Ponderos? Roli?"

They took deep breaths.

"The air is fresher here. Easier to breathe," decided Ponderos.

"It's thinner," added Roli.

"What you say is true but there's something else, something faint."

Ponderos drew another breath of air. "I don't know what it might be."

"Nor I, though it's familiar," Calistrope looked towards where the landing ended at an arched passageway. "I suppose we go that way."

"Hadn't we better check the other doors first?" asked Roli. "There may be more levels above us."

"Indeed," Calistrope touched the adjacent door panel, it remained inert. The door at the right hand end revealed the shaft below it momentarily. The leftmost door stood open. The shaft which they expected to see was blocked an arm's length below.

A cubicle box-structure was canted to one side, jamming itself tightly against guide rails. From its top, thick heavy rope, twisted from metallic fibers led slackly to a winding drum set further up the shaft.

"A mechanical lifting machine," Calistrope was lost in admiration for long seconds as he took in the great loops of steel cable and the device which somehow passed torque to the huge winding drum "Mechanical. And I'll wager the one at the far end is the same. The two central ones you see," he turned to Roli, his voice assuming a lecturing quality, "alter the spatial co-ordinates directly. Whatever occupies their interior is translated to a new location while the devices at each end haul their cargo from one place to another."

Roli was frowning. "We were moved instantaneously, as when we step from the hallway at your manse to the workshop?"

"Exactly, or so I believe. The workshop is actually some way from my manse, as you remember. Yet it requires no more than a step from the hallway to reach it."

Ponderos asked, "Then why the lifting engines?"

"They were the main method of transport I'd say but they have broken down, no?" Calistrope nodded. "I think we have used the alternative ascending system, the fail-safe system."

"Or vice-versa," suggested Ponderos. The three walked across the landing, leaving footprints in the virgin layer of dust. At the passageway, Ponderos looked back, a slightly puzzled expression on his bronzed face. "Roli, hold the light down near the floor," he pointed to the faintest of indentations running across the landing, it stopped just short of the lifting system. Ponderos wiped a thick layer of dust away. "Do you recognize this Calistrope?"

The Mage nodded. "Down at the subterranean lake, before we were captured."

"Exactly. A track, a metal marker, whatever you wish to call it."

"Should we follow it? The other led us into the ants' nest."

"I hardly think it was a trap, Calistrope. As we thought then, it is likely to lead us to something constructed by men."

"Then let us go."

They marched off, Calistrope in the lead with Roli at his shoulder and Ponderos bringing up the rear. The track, now that it had been discovered, was plain to see; it ran along the center of the passageway as straight as a die. The passage itself was semi-elliptical in section, it had been cut through the rock with the precision of a machine although, like the stairs they had climbed earlier, nature had spoilt the exactitude of the original work with rock falls and cracks.

They traveled in a straight line for almost an hour before the passage turned left through a thirty degree angle and an hour or so later it returned to its original direction with a right turn. Just around this second corner, they came to a region where a great deal of movement had occurred within the mountain's core. They were faced with a pile of broken rock which had fallen from a great rift across the ceiling and had to spend a considerable effort on moving enough of the heavy blocks to allow them to climb over the barrier.

The way beyond this point led up and down and it twisted and turned—all due to movements and tilting of mammoth blocks of living rock. At one point, Calistrope stopped and spoke to Ponderos. "How long ago do you think this passage was cut?"

Ponderos shrugged. "A hundred old years? A thousand? Who can say?"

Calistrope pointed to a curtain of stalactites which hung down and joined with several stalagmites growing upward from the floor. The metallic rail continued under the deposition. "Say ten or twenty thousand, perhaps one or two million". The rock here is quite dry, wherever the water came from to form this structure, it is no longer active."

The stalactites formed a massive barrier and an impassable one until Ponderos retraced their steps to collect a sizeable piece of stone to use as a hammer. They broke through the stalactites and one by one, squeezed through the opening only to find successive walls of natural stone bars erected against their progress. When they finally won free of the obstacles, they sat down and ate the last of their provisions.

"Wherever we are going," said Ponderos, contemplating his last piece of dried meat, "I hope we arrive soon."

Later and further along the twisting passageway they came to a gaping fault in the floor. The metal track had been pulled out like taffy into a thin strip across the ravine. Roli, quick to exhibit the skills of cat burglary, casually walked the tightrope to the far side.

"Now you Calistrope."

The far side of the fault was two steps higher and it was necessary to walk up hill on the metal strip as well as across it. With somewhat less confidence than Roli, Calistrope stepped out. He took three steps and then found that the hard sole of his boots would not grip the smooth metal, he began to slide back, his boot slipped off the track, he fell.

Ponderos reached out to catch at his friend's coat but was far too late. So heightened were their senses that Calistrope seemed almost to float down to an impact on an outcrop a few ells below. Horrified, Ponderos and Roli waited for him to move and look up at them, but he did not. He lay there, belly up, spread-eagled over the spur; they could not even be sure that he was breathing.

Ponderos placed the light on a flat rock at the edge of the chasm and climbed swiftly down. Clinging to the rock wall, he bent over Calistrope, placed a finger against the other's neck and remained in that position for a time before finally straightening up. "He lives," Ponderos announced and Roli, who had forgotten to breathe, suddenly sucked in a lungful of air.

"Thank Fate for that," breathed Roli with relief. "Though we don't know what injuries he might have suffered, there may be spinal injuries."

"I think he'll be all right. A mage rarely dies by accident or even suffers any great injury. Luck, you see. It takes only the tiniest measure of magic to sway chance if the force is applied at the right time. Sorcerers learn to apply that force by intuition."

Ponderos chafed the Mage's wrists. "Of course, it might be the talisman I gave him. It was once efficacious against weapons of bone or stone..."

"All motions are relative," said Roli seriously. "If we consider Calistrope to have remained stationary then the world has struck him a vicious blow. A considerable weapon, your sigil must be a powerful instrument indeed."

Ponderos looked up at Roli and away again He continued to massage the others' hands and slapped his cheeks and was at last rewarded by movement. "Take it carefully old friend. Does anything hurt?"

"Hurt? No I don't think so." His manner was slightly confused. "Strange dream I had."

"You dreamed you were falling? Or perhaps you dreamed of flying? Eh?" Roli laughed though the circumstances were not amusing. Relief made him react a little inappropriately.

"Mm? No, no. About this place." Some memory seemed to come back to Calistrope. "Did I fall?" he looked down into the Stygian depths of the chasm then up to where Roli knelt. "Down there?" he swayed where he was sitting and Ponderos steadied him with an arm around his shoulders.

Ponderos told him what had happened and as Calistrope seemed to sway again with vertigo, distracted him by asking about the dream.

"It was about this place, I think," Calistrope said. "That smell I mentioned? You remember that smell? Magic. Somewhere near here, the ether must be thick with power."

Ponderos concentrated, trying for various magical effects. "I cannot draw any power whatever. Not an iota, which is a shame because we have to get you up there again."

"But the source is nearby. Very strong. And I know we shall soon be out of here, very soon."

"We have to get him up there," Ponderos said slowly and took off his coat. He bent and carefully worked Calistrope's coat free and tied the two together. "Yours now," he said and a moment later was tying Roli's coat to the chain. He let out the impromptu rope and looked at it. "It's not long enough. We'll have to take off shirts—and our breeks if necessary."

In the event, breeks were not necessary and they hauled Calistrope, still unable to fend for himself, up to the edge of the cleft. When Roli had gone once more to the far side, Ponderos took off his boots and put his socks inside before throwing them across; he carried Calistrope across his shoulders, balanced his way across in six long steps.

And once he had recovered enough to walk, Calistrope found his forecast had been perfectly correct. Two hours later, they reached the end of their tunnel, a portal into a huge cathedral-like space which in spite of the damage that had occurred, was still unmistakably *made*. The roof was a single vault completely spanning the width, there were two huge walls at either end which had once been flat and vertical but were now visibly leaning and furrowed with fissures and bulging from uneven pressure behind the surface.

A dim illumination came from long strips of fluorescent material set into the roof and the light reflected off a maze of narrow gleaming tracks running from scores of tunnels which pierced both the end walls.

They entered and across the wide shadowy floor there was an uneasy shuffle of half seen forms, a half heard whisper. Afterwards the lights brightened, status boards shone, colored signals blinked. Now they saw that the movement had been the lifting of the hundreds of flat bedded transports which hovered a hand's breadth above the shining metallic track ways where a knee-high pall of repelled dust still hung in the air. The changes left an air of expectancy behind, a waiting, a readiness.

When the companions walked from the tunnel mouth into the hall, there was an awareness. Waiting cranes shifted as they walked past, transports bobbed, insect-like maintenance machines scurried away from their feet.

"This makes me nervous." Ponderos skirted a low box with a half dozen articulated arms that were making adjustments to a carrier's control box. "Where are we going, anyhow?"

"There," Calistrope pointed. "The far end."

"Why there? There are several portals along the wall over there."

"Because... I don't know. Perhaps I saw it in the dream I had."

"When you fell?"

Rather more dubiously than before, they crossed the track ways.

"Ah! Look at these machines Calistrope. Machines aping life."

Ponderos stopped before a cluster of small hand sized machines on the ground. They did indeed resemble insects with dull grey carapaces and a variety of antennae and jointed limbs.

"And there," said Roli, pointing, "are two real insects among them."

"So there are."

And as they recognized the real among the sham so, it seemed, did the machines. Two of the mechanical contrivances turned on the insects and touched their antennae to the insects' heads, there was a bright spark of power and the two impostors were dead; blackened husks.

"They're dead, Calistrope. Killed by machineries," Ponderos evidently found the concept distasteful. "Quickly. Let us leave this place." Which was easier to say than to do; the far end was several furlongs away.

They continued on but as they approached the far wall, it became clear that it was not what it appeared. It was, in fact, an archway, the lower edge, a half-ellipse as long as the hall was wide. Like the roof above, the lower surface was pocked with cavities left by the fallen masonry which littered the floor.

At the far side of the arch was a drop to a lower level. A gap to one side of the chest high barrier gave onto a spectacular stairway which curved down to the city at its foot.

The City of Schune.

Breathtaking.

Even from this height, a hundred ells, it was obvious the city was a mixture of architectural styles: the tall, needle shaped towers of a millennium past; the crystalline Fortunus vogues; circular fora from the Paddacene; even genuine stone and timber buildings copied from prehistory. Yet, despite the amalgamation, it worked, blended. Placement had been careful so each variation complemented another. Streets radiated from a paved area at the foot of the steps, intersecting with other streets spreading from small parks at opposite corners of a triangle. Streams ran haphazard courses across the city; linking, splitting: a tracery of silver waters crossed by filigree bridges and stepping stones.

"Beautiful," said Calistrope. "What a simply lovely place."

"Dead," said Roli. "Empty."

"There are lights," Ponderos pointed out.

"But no movement."

They descended and as they did so, so the true vastness of this new space became apparent. Beyond the archway, the wall went upward—so far that it was not possible to guess how high. The ground area was not as great as it seemed to begin with, the city was not that large but the surrounding walls curved protectively round it without quite meeting on the far side.

"Are those stars?" Calistrope pointed to the hard points of light in the darkness.

"It is not possible," Ponderos objected. "We are far too high to be open to the sky— we couldn't breathe."

"If that's a simulacrum, it's tremendous. It would have to be a hundred chains across but I suppose a window as large as that would be almost as formidable."

"And as high," said Roli. "But look at that."

What Roli was looking at was a single, slender, shining curve. It sprang from a domed building at the center of the city and leapt up to the roof which it pierced and passed beyond.

Calistrope shook his head. "At least it gives us something to aim for. Whatever it is."

They completed the descent to the plaza at the foot of the steps and chose a street which seemed to take them towards the central area. The three passed by shops and eating houses, dwellings and meeting halls; all of them were brightly lit, all of them empty. Beneath their feet, the pavement was a creamy white stone with a myriad crystals embedded in the surface.

"It feels," Calistrope said, "as though everyone was here just a minute ago, as though every single person just left."

"Hmm, yes. And every one of them expected back in a moment of two," Ponderos looked from side to side. "Do you suppose we are being watched?" his stomach rumbled. "And I'm hungry."

Calistrope asked in return, "Watched by whom? Schune is kept alight and warm by mechanisms, like those we met in the great hall up there. They sweep away the dust and no doubt, they repair the buildings when time wears them out."

"Then that is what is watching us," Roli said. "Mechanisms. Machines with beady glass eyes and long metal fingers," he shivered.

The domed building they were making for was nearer now but the streets which surrounded it were annular, leading nowhere. Narrow paths led from street to circular street and these were blocked by further walls at random intervals. A maze. Was it purpose or fancy that had made it?

"I'm hungry," Ponderos complained. "Have I mentioned it before?"

"Indeed you have. Have you looked in the streams we have crossed? Fish, Ponderos."

Unbidden, Roli ran to the nearest bridge, a high arched affair with delicate scrollwork hand carved from old stone. "Yes, yes. There are fish down here. Plump, every one a good meal."

"Why do I always overlook the obvious, Calistrope?"

"Hunger drives away reason, my friend."

But when they tried to catch the fish, they found them to be contrivances, simulacra made of wires and diaphanous films. Ponderos' hunger remained unsatisfied.

The maze took seven hours to solve but at last they stood before Schune's domed City Hall. Between the pillars were two great doors of a dull brown metal which gleamed like oiled silk. A great hoop of the same metal hung at the center of each door panel.

They tried the doors, they were locked solidly. The circular handles would not turn and not even Calistrope's recently acquired facility with door locks could open them.

"Hmm," said Roli and lifted one of the circular handles which hinged up and down easily enough. He dropped it, banging it with a great brazen clang that echoed back and forth between the buildings.

Slowly, the door swung inwards until it was wide open.

"More thievery?" asked Ponderos.

"Hardly. No thief would announce his presence with a door knocker."

"Unless he were a very clever thief."

"In that case, I'm certain you're right."

Light flooded out of the opening, bathing the steps in brightness. Inside was a circular room with a coiled staircase reaching up into the cciling.

"I don't like the look of this, at all," said Calistrope.

"What is wrong," Ponderos looked around the deserted room. "An ambush?"

"Steps. How many steps do you suppose there are between here and the roof above the city? It's a very long way to climb. But it's the only obvious place to go, you don't find a control room in an empty city."

"Do you find them at the tops of mountains?"

Calistrope shrugged. "I am willing to listen to arguments," Calistrope answered. "Reasonable arguments."

The steps took them to the dome above the building. A glass cage stood there at the base of a single gleaming bar as thick as a man's wrist. The bar sprang upward, disappearing into a circular tube which in turn, vaulted to the cavern roof high above.

There *was* only one thing to do. They entered the cage and waited. An alarm sounded, a high note which fell in pitch over the course of five seconds and then stopped. The cage moved, lifting them gently through the building's roof and up into a transparent cylinder. Gentle pressure against their feet indicated acceleration which cut off as they approached the cavern roof. Progress slowed until the elevator crawled up to and through the vaulted ceiling.

When the capsule came to rest, they stepped into a small lobby, a narrow closed door was the only other exit from the claustrophobic little room. It was grey and a circle of darker grey color was marked at each side of the panel.

Without thinking about it, Calistrope touched the nearer of the two circles. The door panel vanished. Within was a ramp of ribbed, grey material and when all had entered and begun to walk upwards, the surface beneath their feet began to gradually move upward too. So smoothly did it start and accelerate that none of them were initially aware of the motion. When they did realize, however, it was just one more marvel among the many, no one saw fit to remark on it.

The floor leveled out but continued to take them along what was now a long hallway with walls covered in tapestry works, rugs, fur pelts, artistic designs and paintings. The ceiling, several ells above their heads, was a curved, barrel vaulted section built from interlocking blocks of polished granites. Sometimes black and white, sometimes pink or green, it reflected a million glittering points of light from the crystalline lamps which clung to the ceiling every few paces. The lights were activated in turn as they moved along so that before and behind them all was swathed in darkness; *onward* was an unknown quantity.

"You know, my friends," Ponderos' voice was ruminative. "I'm hungry."

"You are always hungry, Ponderos."

"I'm tired," Roli said. "Did your dream tell what we might expect, Calistrope?"

"And you are always tired. No, what lies ahead is a mystery.

They were whisked on their way for what seemed a long time before they sensed that the pace was slowing. A minute later, they were walking. A division of the way ahead appeared, the corridor divided into two—although the right hand passage was blocked by closed doors across its width.

The barrier drew them—perverse curiosity. It was a pair of double doors similar to those they had met before. Calistrope extended his hand to one of the lighter grey circles in order to deactivate them. Nothing happened. Calistrope tried the circle on the other side, again nothing. Puzzled, Ponderos and Roli tried with similar lack of success.

"Well," Calistrope looked at the doors and tapped a front tooth. "The other way then."

They turned about and walked in the other direction. As before, a band of illumination stayed with them until they reached a second set of doors. With a certain lack of expectancy, Calistrope touched a light grey circle.

The door panels vanished. Before them extended a brightly lit hall which was so vast that distances could not be easily reckoned, so wide and so long that the walls were lost in haze. Above, the roof was an immense inverted plain of creamy white. Roli wrinkled his nose, the air carried a mixture of odd smells which defied analysis.

The companions spent little time on the broader scene however. As they crossed the threshold, a cage fashioned from bright bars of green light flicked into being in front and to either side of them. Turning, they found the doors had silently returned to bar their return. The beams of light were stacked well above head high and about a hand span apart.

"Hah!" Roli walked forward, lifted his hands toward the light beams, ready to climb them, they seemed so solid.

"No! Calistrope reached forward and jerked Roli roughly back. "No. Dangerous, look," he picked up a piece of litter from the floor, a stick or some such and tossed it at the light bars. There was a flash, the stick fell through the bars in three pieces. "*Cutting light*. I know about it from somewhere."

Roli gulped and stood with his back to the doors. "Thanks."

Through the bars, beyond them, stood a tall pile of junkyard art in the form of a gangling human form. Whoever had built it had been overgenerous with arms, there were—four, counted Calistrope. He indicated the sculpture and what appeared to be various exhibits behind it.

"An exhibition hall, do you think?"

"Well," Ponderos shrugged, a gesture which rippled all manner of muscles, "I suppose you could well be right Calistrope. But to what purpose?"

Calistrope shrugged as well, utilizing considerably less energy.

"You," said a new voice, like the fall of a rusty bucket down a stony slope... "Are you the director of this party?"

Both Calistrope and Ponderos wheeled about and looked in all directions. "Who addresses us?" Calistrope said, becoming weighty in his speech and tone.

"I do. Up here." Four clanging syllables.

The three of them looked upward and there, atop the sculpture a bright blue eye looked down at them from a battered cylinder which took the place of a head.

"Aha, I have your attention. So you, the one in dark blue, you are the leader, yes?"

"Yes. That is so."

"Good,"—an empty can dropped onto a tin tray, "And now..."

One of the arms stirred, piston muscles flexed, too many elbow joints at different angles bent along its length. A metal clawed hand at its end reached through the light cage, its surface sizzling and suddenly bright where the light impinged. It caught hold of the unsuspecting Calistrope's coat and hauled him aloft, over the wall and swiftly dropped him to the floor.

"Now, we go for examination." Speech like the sound of unoiled hinges.

"Examination?"

"For my exhibition."

"Which exhibition is that?"

The thing of many parts turned partly, a process of squeaks and groans as the upper part revolved on bearings at the waist. "Over there..."

As it rose to point, Calistrope ducked away from the hand which had released him. The creature was not to be fooled, in another instant a second arm, all metal tubing with telescopic sections shot out and caught hold of Calistrope's arm in a gentle but immovable grip. Above him, the cylindrical head tilted and looked down, it turned slowly from side to side—well-oiled bearings, a low hum from a motor.

"That won't do. Not at all. Now come, I wish to copy you."

"Copy?" Calistrope was pulled along, willy-nilly.

"I told you, for my exhibition. I will build a simulacrum, very durable. Not like this," the creature stopped for a long moment and considered its captive, tapped Calistrope on the chest. "Not this sort of thing. This sort of body dies."

"Only when misused."

"It dies," insisted the other.

Calistrope was pulled along, a hairy ape-like arm with rough red hair sprouting along its length held his head close to the thing's ribs. There was a sharp smell of corroding metals and the tang of lubricating oil mixed inextricably with the odor of sweat.

"Here now. My office."

The office was a space between buttresses supporting the wall of the main hall, it had been closed off by sheets of glass. Inside, there was a hard-looking bench and several wheeled trolleys piled with enigmatic equipment. Brighter lights flared as they entered the enclosure, the beams centered upon a dusty couch.

"There," said the creature. Muscles bunched along the length of the great hairy arm, muscles magnificent enough to make Ponderos feel inadequate, a finger the size of a cucumber pointed to the couch.

Somewhat anxious, Calistrope raised his voice. "By what authority do you haul me off and sequester my companions?"

Calistrope's bluster was hardly noticed, the great rumbling, clanging voice, even at its mildest, was sufficiently stentorian to cow the Mage a dozen times over. "I am the curator," announced the creature. "You enter my domain; you place your fate in my hands. Now lie down."

The curator propelled Calistrope with a gentle but irresistible push back on to the couch. Calistrope collapsed onto it. A cloud of dust arose around him, bringing tears to his eyes and a sneeze to his nose.

"I am responsible for all this." The great hand swung to and fro and Calistrope considered making another break for freedom but the hand swept back towards him, two fingers rested upon his midriff. Escape was a fantasy. "I procure new specimens, spruce up the old."

Contriving to keep Calistrope pinioned, the curator reached across the space with his extensible arm and pulled a trolley towards him on squeaking wheels. Outside of Calistrope's view, it made adjustments, pushed switches, plugged plugs. A humming sound began behind Calistrope's head. "Now lie still. Do not move. Have I made this clear?"

Calistrope nodded.

"Don't move, I said."

"Yes," said Calistrope, "Er, no."

A few moments later something appeared at the top of Calistrope's field of vision. It crept over him, an oval pod on the end of a thin rod. The pod moved on—a sensing device, Calistrope assumed as it crept over his torso, down along his legs and stopped at his feet. The hum ceased, a thin whine commenced and the sensor was retracted.

"Ah, well," said Calistrope and sat up. "Interesting. I must be away now..."

The hand reappeared, pushed him back to a semi-reclining position. "Be still. Memorise now." The trolley with squeaky wheels went away, another on silent suspensors was pulled forward to where it hovered in front of his face. A fourth arm, one which Calistrope had only had a glimpse of before, came into use; it supported a hand with long thin digits—each with five or six or more knuckles.

Small verniers were set, toggles snapped back and forth and then power was switched on. The machine flashed and crackled, a smell which Calistrope associated with overheated galvanic machinery, assailed his nostrils.

"Memories?" asked Calistrope, a trifle plaintively.

"Quite painless, I assure you, heh heh." Two sniggers like snare drums. "You will not remember a thing."

Calistrope was suddenly alarmed, very alarmed. "What do you mean? It takes my memories, is that what you mean?"

The curator shrugged—a minor dislocation of tin cans and brass barrels and cast iron pipes. "The equipment is old, unreliable," it told Calistrope sadly. "However, rest assured they will be perfectly preserved in your simulacrum. I shall replay them again and again, it will be like living your life over and over again."

"But I shan't experience them. They're mine, they make me, *me*!" And Calistrope struggled to such effect that he wriggled down and almost out from beneath the curator's great fingers.

"You will begin to accumulate more immediately. It will do you no harm, I may even leave some for you in your brain. Deliberately, the curator tapped a stud and the recording machine began to hum.

Calistrope's last sight was of a dewdrop hanging from an overhead girder. A huge drop of water which stretched out impossibly and then fell to the floor. His vision darkened, his mind lost volition.

A succession of memories paraded before Calistrope's inner sight, memories so old that he could not remember where they had been acquired... a small boy playing on a grassy slope, the sky was blue; sunlight a blinding light overhead... A waterfall against a black sky with stars as hard and as sharp as diamond shards... a woman's face which brought sudden tears to his eyes...

Calistrope opened his eyes, rubbed them and found himself staring at a puddle of clear liquid on the tile floor of the curator's office. The puddle bulged upwards at its center and continued to rise for some seconds. The top swelled out a little, there was the suggestion of a head with features. Shoulders broadened outward, arms separated from the main mass, the lower part bifurcated and became legs.

"Morph!" Calistrope breathed the word in amazement. "Am I remembering you?"

CHAPTER 20

The curator was bending over Calistrope, and one of its long, slim fingers was poised above the activation button. "What was that you said? I must calibrate the equipment, and then we shall begin properly."

As Calistrope watched, the translucent being moved on silent feet to one side, gaining in color and solidity as it moved. It crept up to the curator's side and pulled at the memory recorder, which slid easily on its suspensor field. Momentum carried it out of the curator's immediate reach and it caromed into a row of glass cases, sending them crashing. "What is *this*?" cried the curator, its voice suddenly as thin and as high as a distant shriek of tortured metal. "An alien! I declare it to be an alien!"

The curator danced carefully in the confined space, its huge feet cracking and gouging at the floor tiles. "Centuries?" it mused as it shot out a hand. "No, I am wrong!" The hand had evidently missed its target, for it struck again. "Millennia! It has been seven millennia since I last had an alien life form to prepare for my museum." The curator's arm retracted, and Morph was securely gripped by metal fingers interlocked about the waist.

"Go, Calistrope! Do not fear for me—*go!*" Morph's right eyelid drooped in a slow-motion wink. "Leave this juggernaut to me."

Calistrope sidled around the curator's back as Morph lost some of its rigidity and slid partly through the curator's fingers. "Oops," said the curator in astonishment as it used another hand to hold on to Morph's gradually elongating body. As Calistrope left the doorway, the curator was already employing all four hands to hold onto the lengthening alien. Outside, Calistrope looked left, then right. To the right were scuff marks in the layer of dust that covered the floor of the hall; Calistrope followed them and within ten minutes was back at the entrance where his two comrades were still imprisoned.

"Calistrope! You got away—or perhaps you disabled the grotesque thing?"

"Morph helped me. He distracted the curator while I escaped."

"Morph is dead, Calistrope," Ponderos shook his head, wondering if this was a sign of instability since his friend's accident. "Does your head hurt?"

"My head?" Calistrope put a hand to his head. "No. There's nothing wrong with my head."

"Perhaps you saw another of his kind," Roli suggested.

Calistrope shook his head irritably. "Morph spoke to me. I don't know how he survived but it *was* Morph—there is no doubt of it."

"Well! Let us just be thankful," Ponderos thought it better to let the matter drop. "How can we get out of here?"

Calistrope inspected the walls to either side of the doors where the light beams emanated from a number of small holes. There were no visible switches or knobs, no controls of any kind. "It's only light, when all is said and done. Surely we can block it," Calistrope mused. He looked around and spied a sheet of dark material. "This should do! It will absorb the light."

He picked it up and discovered that it was heavy. "Metal! There is metal everywhere in here—ransom for a thousand grandees!" Callistrope thrust it into the path of the light beams and the metal bagan to sizzle. The coating burned away and three holes appeared—large enough to put a finger through.

"So much for that! A mirror then, a mirror is what we need," he said as he looked around again. "A mirror, or perhaps a bright, shiny piece of metal!" Calistrope bent over and picked up a piece of polished, silvery stuff. Back at the enclosure he tried again, gingerly. The green light beams were deflected upwards and a blackened track appeared on the ceiling material where the light touched it. "Quickly now, this is working."

Ponderos and Roli came through the gap, stepping over the lowest beam that was still functional, and ducking the higher ones above the reach of the deflector. Just as Calistrope was about to pull the metal plate out, he cried out and dropped it. "It's hot," he explained. "It got very hot suddenly."

"We're still on the wrong side of the door," Roli grumbled.

"But free to roam about. There must be other exits," he replied. The hall could have been as much as a league in length, and they had entered through one of the shorter walls—a furlong wide, perhaps. Tall double doors occurred every one or two chains, and each of the first four were closed and refused to open to Calistrope's hand. The next exit, which was the fifth, was also closed and unresponsive to Calistrope's touch.

"Uh-oh," Roli pointed to their left. "The curator!" They had been following an aisle which paralleled the wall; here, its inner side was lined with a row of cabinets depicting the evolution of a tall, dignified biped from a frog-like creature. The development was detailed, the line of cabinets long and some above head-height. Beyond this line, following some avenue nearer the center , the curator's head and shoulders could be seen and occasionally, one or more arms were being brandished in the air.

"What now? Where do we go?"

"These are the last doors along this side," Calistrope said and sniffed the air. "There's that smell again—you remember? Magic?"

Ponderos sniffed as well. "Well..." he sniffed again, harder, longer. "Yes. Yes I *do* smell something now."

"The curator!" Roli was anxious.

"Yes, well—keep low and we'll go on, as far as the end wall. Even if the thing sees us, we can keep well ahead now that we know about it. As a curator, it is not likely to crash its way through the exhibits; we can circle around as long as is necessary."

Ponderos' stomach rumbled loudly, "And how long is that? I'm still hungry—we don't know if the curator even eats."

"For the moment, we must go on," Calistrope prodded. They bent low and scuttled along the aisle until it turned at right angles. Here, they could move in either direction to keep out of the curator's sight.

"There's another door there," Roli pointed. "A small one." The other two looked. Two buttresses had been erected at some time to take the strain imposed by a crack in the rock face which ran jaggedly out across both the floor and the ceiling. Between the two was a doorway closed by a panel displaying the familiar dark grey circle. The smell of magic issuing from the crack was strong enough to make even Roli's nose itch, and he sneezed violently. They crossed to the door.

Calistrope made a face. "Well?"

"Try it," Ponderos shrugged. "There is nothing to lose."

With a dramatic flourish, Calistrope slapped his hand against the circle. The door panel vanished and out rolled a waft of hot dry air accompanied by a smell of overheated copper. The interior was lit by a fitful red glow. Cautiously they entered—Calistrope, Ponderos and finally, Roli.

The room was small, little more than an alcove and the crack which had split the wall outside ran across the floor and appeared as a deep fissure in the inner wall. Calistrope noticed this peripherally as he stepped across the gap in the floor, what took his primary attention was the simple-seeming apparatus at the center.

Two slim cones, each an ell or so in length with their narrow ends fused together formed a venturi. The device rested vertically upright in a stand with the lower end clear of the floor and apparently open. The open ends of seven square-shaped wave guides were arranged around the narrow waist and merged into a single square-sectioned duct which disappeared into a void cut into the chamber's wall. None of the seven pipes actually touched the venturi although they were machined to precisely match its contours.

From the top of the upper cone, a dull red glow suffused the atmosphere. It radiated heat, air was evidently drawn in at the bottom, was heated by whatever process went on inside and exited from the top taking with it some of the energy gathered within the device. Calistrope supposed this to be a side effect of the real process of energy production.

"Magic," said Calistrope at last, gesturing toward the device. "Magic extracted from the ether."

"How though?" Ponderos scratched his gleaming pate. "Roli has demonstrated that magic proceeds from living things, particularly from people. We have found it available only where there are a number of people living in a community."

Roli shook his head. "Ponderos is right. There has been no usable magic in the ether until now. The machine apes whatever is inside a person, it manufactures magic. The magic you are using must be a leakage from the machine."

Both Calistrope and Ponderos looked blankly at the younger man for quite some time. This was a new concept—the debating of advanced theories with an apprentice of scarcely an old year's standing.

"The major part is collected by these... these things," Roli pointed to the square tubes which girdled the mechanism.

Calistrope nodded slowly. "Well, the proposition has merit," he said.

"It covers the known facts," allowed Ponderos. "But what is the magic manufactured from?"

"That is a different question."

"You have a bright student there, my friend."

"Hmm," Calistrope felt a certain envy. Had he been as quick, as discerning in his youth? The question was academic, the answer buried in his archive and Voss had the memory vault. Even if he cared to search out his early memories, the means were not to hand.

He stirred himself from his reverie. "You are right of course, Ponderos. However, while there is magic to be used, let us use it," Calistrope grinned, uncharacteristically jolly. "Didn't I say that I could smell magic, way back?"

"You did, back when you had fallen down that cleft..."

"And you thought me befuddled?" Calistrope chuckled.

"Befuddled? A good word," Ponderos chuckled as well and admitted it. "I do... I did think that, yes."

All three seemed to shine now, with excess energy. Their flesh was firm, muscles solid; their step was springy, paces long and assertive. Even their clothes were renewed: the many tears and catches were gone, the faded colors now brilliant and fresh. For Roli, the feeling was new, heady; his face shone with good health and the boundless energy of more than just youth.

Calistrope opened the door and stepped backward almost at once. Before the panel materialized, all had seen the figure of the curator standing outside.

Calistrope replied to Ponderos' and Roli's unspoken question. "We have a great deal of power to wield, far more than we should need or even use. Roli, you are inexperienced, you must stay behind us and observe—no more. Ponderos, we must synchronize our efforts."

A few moments later, Calistrope deactivated the door panel and almost at once, two of the curator's arms stretched out towards them, the hands flexing eagerly.

The two Mages flung a barrier field at the curator. The field lifted the being and swept it back into a diorama opposite the door. The curator's limbs swung around wildly, dismembering the model of a mantis and destroying several small mountains in the background. Bits and pieces flew off the curator, an arm, chest plates, nuts, bolts... A steel-clawed hand came to rest at Calistrope's feet.

When the thing came to rest, it moved feebly for a minute or two and then became still. Only the incongruously blue eyes swiveled this way and that until it focused on the three humans. "Now what have you done to me?"... A slow roll of kettle drums.

"We defended ourselves. That is all."

"Go. Leave me. Leave my museum."... Empty brass vessels falling down stairs. "Go."

"We go."

At the doorway out of the curator's exhibition hall, Ponderos and Roli took cover while Calistrope readied his armament. He formed his will, a tall cylinder of energy hung before the door, Calistrope triggered it. The cylinder imploded into a narrow streak of incandescence and then exploded with a resounded concussion.

Several showcases to either side of the doorway disintegrated into matchwood, those further along were swept away. Stone and metalwork around the door was chipped or twisted.

"Care. Take care." The stentorian roar somehow conveyed anguish, distress. "Oh no." This was in a much quieter tone, almost resigned. "Not you, too?"

The door panel itself stood there unscathed, untouched, pristine. Calistrope took a pace forward and touched it. As firm, as immovable as before.

"I think," he said after a moment or two, "this is an energy field and cannot be broken by projecting energy against it. Indeed, it may even be augmented by my attempt."

"We should therefore think sideways."

"Another insight, Roli?"

"Not me," declared Roli, "I said nothing," he looked around, "Well now, it *is* our friend Morph."

Calistrope looked where Roli was pointing. "Morph? You got away from the curator?"

"As you see."

Ponderos grinned. The creature's apparent death had saddened them and its sudden reappearance delighted them all the more.

Ponderos, thought back to the plant which had swallowed Morph. He queried, "How did you get away?"

"From that overgrown dandelion?" the small figure asked—perhaps lifting the idea from Ponderos' head.

"More to the point," Roli interrupted. "How do we get out of here before the curator recovers himself?"

"We use the curator's hand," replied Morph, holding up the steel claw that had come loose when the two Mages attacked it.

"Well, thank you," Calistrope took the metal claw and crossed to the doorway. He pressed it against the dark colored circle on the door and the door vanished. "Excellent, Morph! What made you bring it?"

"I had observed the comings and goings of the artificial creature earlier, while I waited for you. He merely had to touch the doors and they opened." The doors reappeared behind them, sealing them out of the curator's hall. They were in the same corridor as before or one which seemed identical.

"You were waiting for us? Here?"

"Oh yes. I made that carnivorous plant belch me out by kicking at the stomach walls until it was sick. Then I followed after you. I have been here quite a long time."

"But you didn't catch up to us before?"

Morph shook its head. "The river slowed my progress. I found I could not swim, and moving underwater was too slow. So I followed along the bank—I was just in time to see you embark from the village, but too slow to join you."

"I think this may be a dead end," said Ponderos, pointing. Ahead of them, the corridor led into a long low empty hall.

"We had better look at the place anyway," Calistrope said. "There may well be doors opening from it. But go on, Morph. You were left behind at the town of Jesm when we were deported..."

"I reasoned that others would be going your way. I simply waited until your craft returned and slithered up the rope which tied it to the quay before it left the next time. I reached this mountain you had expressed interest in and made my way up it—not in this form, of course. I had abandoned *that* before I reached the village."

"And you found a way in and waited for us?"

Morph nodded. "I could hear your thoughts faintly. It took you a long time to get up to this level. What were you doing?"

"That is a tale on its own, Morph. I'll tell you when we stop to rest."

"I could do with stopping to rest now," said Roli.

"I'm hungry," complained Ponderos. "Where are we going to find food up here?"

"Put the thought from your mind, Ponderos. There are far too many interesting things around to be bothered about food."

They had come to a stop where the corridor opened out. Calistrope nodded towards the hall. "Look! It is changing—look!" The dim lighting was brightening. The walls, which had seemed to be rough rock or the grey artificial stone they had seen before were now paneled with golden colored timber, tapestries and pictures were hung at intervals. The ceiling was loftier, made of planks of the same golden colored wood supported on wide laminated trusses, the illumination was coming from clusters of globes at the corners of each roof beam. A polished wooden floor lay underfoot and timber furniture of simple design with soft cushions was scattered at random.

"It's cold in here," Roli shivered and hugged himself.

"It is a little. Perhaps we became too used to the warmth in the lower levels."

They walked on. Everything looked new, gleaming, polished; as though it had been made only hours before and placed here for them. Ponderos wondered if it was all illusion and rested a hand on the surface of a low table. He felt a slight tingle in his fingertips but the table was solid, as was the glass candle sconce which it supported and the candle itself. The candle flame was hot but as Ponderos paused to watch it, he noticed that the wax was not consumed. He caught up with the others just as Calistrope halted.

"Have you noticed the furniture ahead of us is laid out as a mirror image of that behind us?" Calistrope asked.

"Perhaps it is a mirror," replied Roli in a reasonable tone of voice.

"It is an odd mirror, then, since it does not show us ourselves." Calistrope went forward to the dividing line and reached out a hand to the imaginary mirror. It was quite real, except that all their reflections were missing. "What do you say to that, Ponderos?"

Ponderos, on his knees, was conducting his own investigation. He was kneeling at the end of a low table, another table which bore a candle. Ponderos blew the candle out, an instant later it ignited again. He licked forefinger and thumb and pinched out the flame, a second after it was burning again. Ponderos flicked the dead ash from his finger and where it landed on the table top, it vanished with a tiny spark. In the mirror, the flame had disappeared and reappeared too. "I say that it is no ordinary mirror." And he scratched his gleaming pate.

"In that, you are exactly right," Calistrope sat down in a convenient chair and made himself comfortable, he closed his eyes. "Where do we go from here?" he asked, "We seem to have arrived—somewhere, at least. The location is right but apart from that crazed contraption we have just escaped from, no one is here."

"Did you expect someone to meet you?"

"Well, no. I expected to find some *place* with lots of levers and wheels and switches and things but so far, there has been nothing to suggest a control room."

"There's the corridor that was blocked off," suggested Roli. "That junction we came to before the exhibition..." the sound of Roli's voice petered out and then returned. "Er, Calistrope, Ponderos. Um, Morph..."

The two older men looked up and followed Roli's gesture. Morph, who was pacing around the walls examining the tapestries and paintings, looked on well. Reflected in the peculiar mirror, a person was visible. Disturbingly, it was seated in the same chair that, on this side of the mirror, Calistrope occupied; there was no basis in reality for the new reflection.

CHAPTER 21

The man in the mirror was tall; as tall as Calistrope and as spare, with dark hair and long, narrow bright green eyes. He appeared to be in the first flush of manhood, perhaps sixty or seventy years old.

"Greetings," said the man, who frowned slightly when he saw he had secured their attention. "How did you come here?" his image in the mirror seemed to pause for the briefest of moments before continuing, perplexity was added to his expression. "Every door seems to have been opened to you—the reason escapes me for the present. Somehow, our security is compromised."

Though his expression remained serious, the frown disappeared. "Well well, be that as it may. Now that you are here, I must say that I am pleased to meet you. My name is Gessen Fil Maroc, call me Gessen."

Calistrope heaved a huge sigh of relief. "And greetings to you," he said. "We were wondering what to do now that we had reached our goal. Finding someone here already is a relief, even though we were told to expect no less."

"Your goal?" Gessen leaned back in his chair. "What then is this goal of yours?"

"Why, to see if the engines which drove the world away from the sun could be restarted. The sun is shrinking, before too long the Earth will freeze."

"Aha." Gessen laughed briefly. "You have come to send us back."

"Just so."

"Well, well, you have come to the right place, if a little late. Will you not introduce yourselves?"

"Of course. This is the Sorcerer Ponderos, this is my apprentice Roli, and this is Morph—a being of uncertain provenance. Myself, I am Calistrope the Mage."

In the mirror, Gessen's image paused a moment. He stared hard at Calistrope before continuing, "Excuse me, your appearance startled me."

Calistrope looked down at himself. Since his renewal of magical energy, Calistrope thought he cut a figure of some excellence. "My appearance?"

"You bear a marked resemblance to a colleague of mine. Let me speak with him a moment." And Gessen froze in place, every movement stilled in mid-action. After several seconds, he moved again in the same, all-at-once fashion. "He will be here directly. The computer suggests a close family relationship, clearly an impossibility in these circumstances, it has been far too long for bloodlines to persist." Gessen half rose and then sat down again. "Please, our visitors are so few—in fact, there have been none—that I forget the niceties, please seat yourselves."

This they did and after a moment's awkward silence, Ponderos spoke. "We had some trouble with animals on the lowest level, did you encounter the lizards?" he raised his eyebrows in query. "Although you may have come by a different route."

"Lizards?" Gessen's eyes blinked slowly. "Ah, yes; the chameleons. There are a few but we tolerate them—they help to discourage the insects. Even so, some reach this far and make a nuisance of themselves; they seem to eat almost anything. However, it gives the janitor something to do."

"Ah. Now here is Calvin."

A swirl of dark colors became visible, the colors coalesced into the shape of a human being and became distinct. As with Gessen, the reflection had no original.

"Gessen," said the newcomer, nodding to his colleague. "And these are…" Calvin halted for several moments and his image became blurred; when it cleared, his face bore an expression of consternation.

For his part, Calistrope was no less astounded. Calistrope knew who Calvin was without a shadow of a doubt. Everyone has an image of themselves tucked away inside their brain. That image emphasizes those features which the possessor finds most attractive, and minimizes the characteristics which are least appealing. This picture of the self which only its owner sees ages slowly—it moves gracefully, its voice is harmonious, its speech compelling. Calistrope recognized all of these things in this tall, gentian-eyed man with features as sharp as an axe-blade. This, he knew beyond peradventure, was his own self-image made manifest. He could not fail to recognize his own idealized version of himself.

"You're…" said Calistrope, and then he stopped for the words he had been about to utter seemed meaningless.

Calvin, for his part, was experiencing a similar *déjà vu*—although from his point of view, the relationship between them was less easily identifiable.

"We are the same person," Calistrope stated at last. "Or you are my forgotten twin brother. Have you or I been cloned in the past?"

Ponderos queried, "*Cloned*? What is cloned?"

Calvin remained silent for the better part of a minute—a long time in terms of *his* existence within the computing machine. He looked up, having obviously reached a similar conclusion. "None of these is exactly the case," he said, showing Calistrope's habit of pedantry when unsure of himself. "My name," he told them, "is Calvin Steinbeck Roper. Shorten this to *Cal S. Roper* and you will see the similarity between my name and yours—Calistrope."

Calistrope nodded. "The name has some familiarity."

"A very long time ago, Calistrope, you elected to leave stasis and to journey out into the world. I am a copy of *that* Calistrope, the person you used to be. My—your—personality is maintained in the computer systems, so I can deal with certain matters here if the necessity arises. Do you see?"

Calistrope reviewed the one or two phrases he thought he understood, but they were not enough. He shook his head. "This copy of me? It's not a physical copy, such as the curator wished to make?"

"I don't follow your reference, but no, it was a data copy. It is used in the computer as a pattern for my electronic existence."

Calistrope struggled with the concept. "I infer that your existence is only within this *computer*? A machine?"

"Exactly so. We—that is, Gessen and I and the others—do not have physical bodies like yours. We are displayed here, at the interface, only so that we can communicate with corporeal creatures in a manner which they find acceptable."

Ponderos grunted. "You never leave this place?"

"That is an impossibility," Gessen answered him while the two versions of Calistrope sized each other up.

"Never to see the sun and the stars, never to feel the wind or the frost? I am sure I would lose my sanity," Ponderos replied.

"I can assure you that all these things and more are available to us, sir. We can simulate whatever environment you can imagine."

"Simulate and imagine," Ponderos shook his head. "This is *life*?"

Gessen smiled but did not reply.

"So who is the *real* Calistrope? You or me?"

"I knew that this would be one of your first questions. The answer is both of us. You are the original, of course, but now both of us are different people. Apparently you don't remember being here before, but you have lived a long life since then. Your experiences will have changed you as mine have changed me—however your friend may view the quality of my experiences."

"Excuse me," Gessen interrupted. "Did you mention a curator?"

"Yes. He—or it—had ambitions to make a more durable version of me and drain my memories into a facsimile."

Gessen frowned. "Where was this?"

Calistrope described his experiences and Gessen's frown deepened.

"I have a feeling that the caretaker has ideas above its station. One moment."

Gessen's image froze. It remained still for several tens of seconds, during which time it began to lose definition. Its colors lost their brilliance, its edges became fuzzy, and the image faded until it was almost transparent. Then it regained its clarity, grinning a trifle grimly. Calistrope entertained the notion that the personality which controlled this image had temporarily shifted its attention elsewhere and was now back, looking out at him.

"You have our apologies in this matter. Our janitor has decided its talents lie elsewhere and converted the old assembly hall into a museum. It has been a long time since any of us have taken the time to examine the more tangible world and meanwhile, our caretaker has added to itself and changed its programming." Gessen held out his hands. "The fault is ours. However, the fact that you were able to reach this interface without our being warned is now explained. All the automatic systems recognized Calistrope— he has as much right to be here as anyone," he grinned. "He's one of our own."

Roli spoke for the first time. "This... caretaker. Is it a machine or a person?"

"Oh, a machine," Calvin replied. "Not a very bright one at that—not originally, anyway. Just a few subroutines thrown together."

"Parts of it are human or animal. It has arms made from skin and muscle and blue eyes?"

"Well," Calvin's image paused in the now-familiar manner. "It must have sharper wits than we gave it credit for. It was built with two mechanical arms; in fact, it was purely mechanical, but now it seems to... blue eyes?"

Roli nodded.

"And oversized anthropoid arms and that hand?"

Again, Roli nodded."

Calvin shook his head. "I don't suppose we have looked at it for several hundred years, perhaps longer. So long as its duties were being performed, we wouldn't bother."

"How long is one of your years?" Calistrope asked, standing up and walking closer to the translucent interface.

"How long?" Calvin looked a little puzzled. "Ten thousand hours. Five hundred standard days."

"Hmm," Calistrope nodded. "A twenty hour standard day. Yes, about what we term an *old year*. Time scales have changed over the past epoch you see. A year no longer exists since the world stopped turning."

"Stopped?" There was a moment of inaction and then again, "No, I suppose not."

"Speaking of the world's turning," Calistrope continued, "It reminds me of our objective. Gessen told us, I believe, that we have arrived too late."

"What *was* your objective?" asked Calvin.

"The sun shrinks again—the engines which drove us into the colder parts of the solar system must be restarted to take us back again."

"Ah, I see. You really don't remember?"

"Remember what? I carry only the past, what—thousand old years? Before that, my memories were transferred to a vault for safekeeping."

"Really?" Calvin said with a smile. "So being part of a machine may have more compensations than Ponderos believes. *I* remember it all very clearly. The journey back to the inner system was begun a quarter of a million years ago—in old years. You and I were the engineers who came here to do just that."

Calistrope sat down heavily, for the shock of this news was considerable. "I am two hundred and fifty *thousand* years old?"

Calvin shrugged, his mouth twisted in a smile. "Give or take a millennium or two. But once the work had been done we—like most of our colleagues—went into stasis for several thousand years in case we were needed again. Awake and functioning, you will have experienced somewhere between five and ten thousand standard years."

The Mage absorbed this silently for a few minutes. "Did you say *engineer*?"

Calvin nodded.

"Hmm," Calistrope nodded ruminatively. "How many of us were there?"

"About four thousand at the start. The driving systems were several million years old. We needed a lot of old-fashioned work in the early days; the devices are spread throughout the world's mass, and all of them needed to be overhauled or replaced. Later on, only a hundred or so stayed on."

"And they're all copied as well, to live in *there*?"

Calvin shook his head. He raised his hand and appeared to tap the interface with a knuckle. "Twenty-five of us. Four are like me; our physical counterparts left to live out there, on the Earth. The others have also left, but to go to their home worlds or to other places. The system monitors the planet's course; it will call us if necessary."

"So we truly *are* too late? Our journey to this place was quite unnecessary?"

"Well, yes. But surely a journey can be sufficient in itself? Surely it has not been without interest? After all, that is why you left us originally—to find interesting things."

"Yes," Calistrope leaned back and thought. "Yes, it *has* been very interesting. Dangerous, too... You *are* right, however; the journey has been worth it, as has our arrival. It is an amazing place. And I really am—or was—an engineer?"

"Oh, yes. All who came here were among the best of our time—we came to save the mother world from extinction—as did those who moved it in the first place."

Ponderos, who had been listening to the conversations without taking part, rose and went to stand in front of Gessen's image. He tapped the glass with his finger. "Do you eat in there?" he asked. "Out here, we are hungry."

"Why yes," said Gessen. "We can eat in here if the fancy takes us. We can also provide victuals for you out there."

6⤢9

Later, the companions left on a tour of the place, with a disembodied voice giving them directions. Just before they left, Roli asked, "Where did Calistrope come from?"

"We came from Earth," Calvin replied. "Originally, we left and journeyed to other worlds. Eventually, we returned here, and as you see, we stayed."

Above them, the sky was almost black. Towards the west it changed degree by slow degree to a deep cobalt blue and at the horizon, to purple where the merest flicker of garnet sunlight might be seen between the mountain peaks. On the other side of the sky, the black became absolute with the hard, unwinking points of starlight punctuating it: a scatter of splintered gems across an inky backdrop.

"Voss once told me that I would enjoy this journey—that travel broadens the mind—indeed, that I would find myself."

"And now you *have* found yourself, Calistrope."

The remnants of the circle world shone redly, away to the east. The anchors which tethered them in place were rooted far into nightside, but at nearly eight thousand leagues above the surface, they still caught the sunlight.

The two companions fell silent again, and then they both spoke at once.

"You know, Calistrope—"

"Ponderos, I—"

Both had spoken together, both fell silent once more until eventually, Calistrope started again.

"Ponderos, I don't wish to return to Sachavesku, I can't say why. I don't know."

"I was about to say much the same," said Ponderos.

Calistrope sighed. "Looking back, I think I was bored at Sachavesku. I used to be very content there but at some point, satisfaction turned to boredom. And we're different people now, we have no real reason to return."

"The Mages wait for news that the world is returning to the sun," Ponderos sighed and turned to look towards the west. "Perhaps we could send the curator. I hear the creature has been rather morose since it was taken to task for sending messages to recipients who don't listen. It would, I'm sure, enjoy the journey."

Calistrope didn't answer the question directly. "Perhaps the Mages deserve to meet a machine with as much self-esteem as their own."

"Let us send the curator then," Ponderos smiled. "There are other things to do."

"Other places to see," Calistrope agreed. "That is, after we have recuperated sufficiently and I have taken time to examine these computers. The whole idea of computers opens up all sorts of possibilities."

The two slim segments of the circle world flickered. Earth's slow creep in pursuit of its sun was beginning to move the terminator.

In some future time, the world would turn again.

The low chime from the communicator drew Voss the Despondent's attention from the shining waters of the lake. That ramshackle collection of machine and creature parts that called itself "the curator" had already visited Sachavesku and returned to Shune. Nevertheless, here was a message from that creature, for he recognized the less than harmonious tones that followed, and wondered if he should indeed have gifted the mechanism with a communicator.

"I am told," the curator said in a rusty voice, "that Calistrope and his friends have now left the City of Shune." There followed what might have been an indrawn breath. "They travel in an easterly direction."

Voss nodded. The thinnest of thin smiles touched his lips. He was not amazed at the information. As it happened, Voss was guiltily absorbing the content of a memory vault—that which he had purloined from Calistrope's Manse—it had taken him until now to overcome the seal on the device. It was filled with the memories of those travels Calistrope had made and forgotten, but now, obviously, wished to retain.

The current segment bore the title *My Crossing of Lower Earth*. An image entered Voss' mind: a huge glass ovoid which held nothing but an energy-free vacuum and thus floated, bearing up a long punt-like undercarriage with a cabin and propulsion engine. A great wheel that was as wide as a man is tall governed the direction taken, as well as the speed of travel.

Voss' smile broadened fractionally; nostalgia came with the memories he observed. "I remember this myself," he murmured. And now, examining his own recollections, he saw the huge machine that Calistrope had assembled, how it had hung in the air, how the brass railings had gleamed and the vented steam had floated like fist-sized clouds in the thicker air of so long ago.

So long ago that there were still mornings, Voss recalled. Mornings were always the best time to begin a voyage. In his mind's eye, the sun edged above the dark horizon and Calistrope's craft and his tall, flamboyant figure became black silhouettes against the yellow sky. Calistrope's arm rose, his hand weaved briefly from side to side—his farewell.

THE END

ADELE ABBOT
graduated from Manchester
University, where she majored in law. Her interest in
Fantasy was first fired when she came across the Lyonesse
series by Jack Vance. Working backwards from there, Adele discovered
Vance's earlier works, including the Dying Earth series, and was immediately
fascinated by the way violence and evil could be hidden behind beautiful prose or
absurd situations.

After several false starts and plenty of encouragement from friends and family,
she began writing her first book, *Of Machines & Magics*. While shopping for a
publisher, Adele began work on another fantasy, *Postponing Armageddon*, which
she entered in the "Anywhere But Here, Anywhen But Now" contest for aspiring debut novelists, sponsored by Sir Terry Pratchett and Transworld Publishers.
Out of more than five hundred entries, *Postponing Armageddon* reached the prize
shortlist of just six novels.

In addition to pursuing a writing career, Ms. Abbot is a full-time law partner by
day. She currently resides in Yorkshire in the United Kingdom with her son. Find
out more at her website, www.adeleabbot.info.

ABOUT
BARKING RAIN
PRESS

D id you know that six media conglomerates publish eighty percent of the books in the United States? As the publishing industry continues to contract, opportunities for emerging and mid-career authors are drying up. Who will write the literature of the twenty-first century if just a handful of profit-focused corporations are left to decide who—and what—is worthy of publication?

Barking Rain Press is dedicated to the creation and promotion of thoughtful and imaginative contemporary literature, which we believe is essential to a vital and diverse culture. As a nonprofit organization, Barking Rain Press is an independent publisher that seeks to cultivate relationships with new and mid-career writers over time, to be thorough in the editorial process, and to make the publishing process an experience that will add to an author's development—and ultimately enhance our literary heritage.

In selecting new titles for publication, Barking Rain Press considers authors at all points in their careers. Our goal is to support the development of emerging and mid-career authors—not just single books—as we know from experience that a writer's audience is cultivated over the course of several books.

Support for these efforts comes primarily from the sale of our publications; we also hope to attract grant funding and private donations. Whether you are a reader or a writer, we invite you to take a stand for independent publishing and become more involved with Barking Rain Press. With your support, we can make sure that talented writers thrive, and that their books reach the hands of spirited, curious readers. Find out more at our website.

WWW.BARKINGRAINPRESS.ORG

Barking Rain Press

ALSO FROM BARKING RAIN PRESS

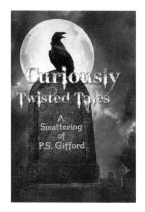

VIEW OUR COMPLETE CATALOG ONLINE:

WWW.BARKINGRAINPRESS.ORG

Made in the USA
Charleston, SC
05 February 2012